✦(A CRACK IN THE WORLD)✦

E-mail: jamesmordechai@gmail.com
Twitter: @JamesMordechai
Instagram: @jamesmordechai

First published in 2023.

Cover by Matt Barnes – www.mattseffbarnes.com

A Crack in the World

James Mordechai

To Omicron, whose high fever and forced isolation opened up the gates of inspiration and let my daimon loose.

Books are like food. Each plate is best with a specific wine, likewise each book calls for a specific soundtrack. This book is best experienced with "John Carpenter's Lost Themes" album. When the action starts to boil up any Black Metal album would do the job. For a full list of my 'blends' accompanying each chapter check the Discography in the Appendix at the end of the book. Enjoy the trip.

The haptic void

All they wanted was to climb out of that dark and gelid pit.

Flashing the beams of their electric torches upward revealed there was no way of seeing the ceiling. Was there any sort of cover or roof? It seemed so because no stars were blinking and no glow from other astronomical bodies was present. But every time they tried to point the beams up, the blades of light were simply swallowed by the darkness of the vast cave. Or was it a colossal chamber? The two minuscule figures standing in front of the centered stone pillar couldn't know. And how could they have known if even the powerful light beams could not reach the ceiling of that humungous structure?

A mist clung to the floor, unperturbed by their feet, hiding the uneven, rocky surface. The small creatures that used to scuttle the floor like cockroaches until a few hours ago were nowhere to be seen. They barely took notice of it, given that they had more dangerous entities chasing them. In fact, they were in a hurry. The hurry of the prey, the unmistakable and primeval urge to save your very skin from the beast that chases you.

Carter stopped his light beam from shifting from one side to the other. He focused his attention on the reel dangling next to the pillar they had left during their descent two hours ago. It was now floppy and several swirls were forming a heap. He pulled it down and felt it was still strong. A sign that the excavator to which they had attached it was still in place up there.

"You first," he said to a panting Gino behind him.

Carter waited for him to come to his side. He felt Gino's breath on his neck and, instead of finding it bothersome, he actually enjoyed that warmth. A truce from the chilling and damp cold of the cave they had been in for the last half an hour. Gino's breath stopped and shifted to his neck's right side now. They could see the vapour coming out of their mouths, the very sign of their life flying away from them. Each puff was a grain of the hourglass of their life gone forever.

A rumble reached them. Both threw their heads back to the opening of the corridor they came from, expecting something to jump out of the darkness.

Gino attached the carabiner of his harness to the reel and started to climb the rocky pillar. He was shorter than Carter and not as athletic but much lighter. Carter illuminated his way up suggesting every now and then where to place his hands. The rock was ancient, they couldn't tell how old, but given what they saw in the past few hours probably aeons old, full of cavities and protuberances. In fact, it was an easy climb if you had basic athletic skills and you were strong enough. Two minutes passed until Gino's hands reached the limit of Carter's torch beam. It was then that the rumbling growl reached them again. They felt it on their chests before their ears could even perceive it. The hairs on their backs stood on end, their senses heightened, their pupils expanded, the adrenaline rush pumped through their chest and limbs. They knew it was coming. An icy draught streamed out of the corridor and displaced the mist in one single sweep making Carter's feet suddenly visible.

Carter jumped up onto the pillar without even securing the carabiner to the reel. He climbed up as quickly as he could, his shoes sometimes slipping from the perilous crevices. It didn't help that Gino's dangling torch, still on, blinded him every time the beam hit his face. When not blinded he saw Gino's figure entering the darkness climb after climb. It was an ascent into the unknown, a vertical highway without headlights. They were mere flesh vessels of fear sandwiched between an approaching known threat from below and an upcoming unknown void above.

Heavy breath, sweaty brows and hands, dust from the rock that gave away flakes that got into the lungs, lactic acid in their limbs. It was all against them, but their will was stronger and the climb was almost over. They reached the summit of the pillar, the circular smooth slab that welcomed them when they descended into the Well in the first place. Right, where was the Well? Where was the green fluorescent rim that let them in initially?

Above them only darkness. Below the horror. Around only the void. Panic surfaced to their minds and if it hadn't been for the dangling reel, the only object that literally tethered them to their world, insanity would have ensued. The long vertical line of the metal reel disappeared a few metres above them, swallowed by the void.

Carter attempted the climb; however, the metal cable was too thin and sharp for his hands. They were trapped in the darkness that was pressing against them. They could feel it on their skin like a palpable object and their torches could not stop it. The void surrounded them like a blanket on a cold winter's night and tried to devour them.

Then, the rock under their feet trembled. It felt like an earthquake and they threw themselves, bellies down, on the rocky surface of the pillar. They held onto each other, legs spread as much as they could, hoping not to fall from the edge. It continued like this for a few seconds until they realised it was not an earthquake; it was the pillar rising. Suddenly the fluorescent green of the Well's rim appeared above their heads and it was getting larger and larger until it stopped a metre or so from it.

Carter decided to stand and poked his head inside the Well – or wouldn't it be more appropriate to say outside of the Well? – and his upper body disappeared in the darkness. Then he jumped up and even his legs were gone. Gino heard him saying something from the other side, like a faraway muffled voice, but he could not understand him. He stood up only when he saw Carter's hand appearing again from the darkness, waiting for his to grab, to help him cross to the other world again. And this time, perhaps because he was closer or because he was touching his hand, he heard very well what Carter was trying to say. And it stuck with him:

"This is not the England we left two hours ago."

PART I

The Vanishings

A beginning
12 hours earlier

Carter looked at the chalk lines on the blackboard once again. Mostly Roman numerals and Latin words, an array of Arabic and Coptic writings and runes of the most curious shapes. All written around a single symbol in the middle that would have taken everyone's attention. He couldn't decipher that orgy of a prolific mind himself whose origin he still had trouble to believe. He was told what the general meaning of them was, but he couldn't point out what each letter and symbol meant.

Ace of Base's *'Living in Danger'* was playing on the radio in the background. Before that Michael Jackson's *'Black and White'* made his foot follow the song's tempo. Quite a contrasting mood with the objects and themes that surrounded him in the office. An overflowing bookshelf towered to the right of the blackboard. Heavy tomes and ancient incunables with anonymous flaky brown spines shared their space with more modern books whose spines told of a collection of the most disparate weird and occult themes:

Nihilism and Affirmation
The Thessalian Witches
The Dead Mountaineer
Transylvanian Anger
Crepusculo Negro

Collapsing Cosmoses
Catenae Pneumae
The Bristolian Astralograph
Eschatologism for the masses
Cosmic Visitations
The Uncanny Manifestation
Astral Anomalies
L'Orrendo e lo spaventoso
The Blackened Malaise

On the left of the board a cabinet filled with hundreds of cassette tapes. Each shelf had a category label: *Psychic whispers, Séances, Postmortem elucubrations* and so on.

A Ouija board casually sitting on top of the low tea table in the middle of the room, a badly rubbed off pentagram half hidden by the sofa on the wooden floor, ritual knives with suspicious stains next to the kettle and the tea pot. He had been told that other offices on that floor, and possibly in the entire building, couldn't compete with the amount of occult paraphernalia in this one. And he had no difficulty in believing that.

He sipped from the teacup and let his sunglasses fog once again. When the white vapour dissipated from the lenses he grabbed the Polaroid and took another shot at the blackboard. Then, he placed the developing photo in the inner pocket of his blazer and let the miracle of chemistry happen. He waited more than he needed to, but he wanted the photo to be better than the other three he'd just taken. The photo had a characteristic sepia grain that gave the gibberish writing even more esoteric tints. It was all there - the Latin words, the Ge'ez letters from the Coptic alphabet, the swirls and soave inflections of the Arabic, the infantile lines of the runes - but the sigil. Once again, the light failed to impress the film of the Polaroid and the chemical did not allow any photons to develop but the darkness.

"It's useless that you continue to take photos of it. You will never succeed," Gino said dashing through the office.

Garibaldi, an emaciated constantly panting dog-wolf hybrid - or at least this is what the breeder told Gino when he saved it from certain euthanasia -, followed him wagging his tail. Gino patted the sofa inviting him to jump up and he removed the collar and leash.

Carter, taken by surprise, took his feet off the mahogany desk and almost knocked the teacup from its saucer.

"I would have excused the feet on my desk but not the tea spilled on the carpet."

Carter, embarrassed, managed only to cough and placed the photo on top of the others on the desk. He removed his sunglasses that – only now he realised – made him look so silly indoors. He reached for the teacup and sipped a bit while standing.

"Stay," Gino said sitting on the chair reserved for guests. He reached for the radio volume knob and turned it down. "I have some important news, my friend. Of Copernican consequences."

Copernican. What can he mean?, thought Carter, creasing his eyebrows and sitting down again.

He'd grown used to the eclectic vocabulary of his Italian friend but sometimes he had a hard time following him. After all it wasn't that common to be a colleague of a world-renowned occultist. One that was actually the son of the most famous occultist of the century.

He still remembered when they first met in the damp and mouldy underground corridor of the RPI, the Royal Paranormal Institute of London.

"You must be Carter, my bodyguard," said a minute man with dark eyes and curly hair that conflicted greatly with his perfect received pronunciation.

Carter Williams had never been very good at reading people's intentions, never mind distinguishing between a genuine conversation and a banter. And because he was aware of this, he generally avoided immediately engaging with anyone who sounded like they were teasing him. Who was this man? And why did he refer to him as his bodyguard?

The man stopped in the middle of the corridor where he was standing and offered a hand to shake. Carter looked at the hand, then at the face, then at the hand again and decided to shake it.

"So?" Gino asked again after receiving no response.

"So, what?" Carter asked.

"Are you the bodyguard I was assigned to?"

"Sir, and you are...?"

"What a brute I am. I'm sorry, I was so excited to have finally met you that... I'm Gino Marcotti. Nice to meet you."

"Marcotti, like the..."

"The Italian *occultista*. Yes, why, that's exactly the same family name. And the same profession."

Carter nodded and his eyebrows levitated for a second. He couldn't help but notice a certain self-deprecating tone in his voice.

"I've heard a lot about your father. My deepest condolences for his passing away. Such a tragedy."

"Oh, I'm sure he is enjoying his time now in another plane of existence, happier and fighting his favourite demons."

Carter was taken by surprise by that answer. *Fighting his favourite demons?*

"Shall we have a coffee?" Gino asked changing subject.

"Tea if possible. And I'm not your bodyguard." Carter said leading the way to the kitchen.

"You are not?" Gino said perplexed.

"I'm Carter Williams, the chief investigator."

"I'm sorry, I was told you would have protected me, so I presumed..."

"I will." Carter said patting his chest where, hidden by his blazer, a gun was holstered. "But we will be partners."

Gino stopped by the counter at the centre of the kitchen. He placed the palm of his hand on the faux marble and put all the weight of his body on it. His chin up to assert dominance in the conversation, his eyes fixed on his new partner. He looked very dandy in that pose. Carter took a while to notice what was happening behind his shoulders. He turned to ask if he wanted any sugar or milk but found a wall of silence.

"We will not be partners or start on equal footing, for that matter. Not until you solve a riddle. My riddle," Gino said with a smirk.

A riddle, my riddle, Carter thought with a smile now that Gino was sitting in front of him wearing the same old tweed suit of that day five years ago.

"Copernican consequences." Carter repeated his words taken aback by those memories.

Gino nodded stroking Garibaldi's ears and then taking his coat.

"A revolution in our field, Carter. Never will it be the same. Five years of research that led to nothing but today we will obtain many pieces of our puzzle."

Carter narrowed his eyes to a slit and leaned towards the desk; the slow vapouring of the tea warmed his chin for a while. He wanted to shout *Gino, tell me what happened. Stop with this theatrical play.*

And almost as if he'd heard him, Gino immediately replied:

"Hartesbridge has reappeared again."

From Kansas to Oz

One month earlier

"Hartesbridge. A small village in West Sussex. Population: 1472. One single school to serve a population of children equal to 25 pupils. Two parishes. One main street, the High Street, with a post office, a small café, a single supermarket, an Indian restaurant, a pub and several decrepit charities.

"Founded in 1637 to host the regional cattle market, gave birth to five martyrs victims of Bloody Mary and two Second World War heroes. Even the Queen paid homage to the quaint village once in 1964." Gino read the papers he'd just printed for the occasion.

"Over with the folklore. We are not a travel agency. Besides I would never pay to visit it."

"I was trying to give some context."

"Tell me what happened and when. Is it like the others?"

"Yes, it is. What a surprise, uh?"

"Twelve am, sharp."

"Yep, on the eve of Bonfire Night. I guess they're not going to light those fireworks from the Green anymore now."

"Any witnesses?"

"A lady coming back from a hen party in Brighton. Drove through the village, *literally*. She thought she

19

was still drunk, but she didn't realise her village, and with it her house, had vanished. She has survived to her fifty-two-year-old husband and a fifteen-year-old girl."

"Jesus."

"Scotland Yard has interviewed her already. They said we can have a go as well whenever she recovers from the shock. I thought we would give her twenty-four more hours to recover. Although, how can you recover from losing your family, house, drive and the entire village where you were born and bred?"

They left Greenwich at eleven, hoping to get there by two pm. They stopped at the services on the M25 for a sandwich and a Coke. The Royal Paranormal Institute didn't refund more than £12 of meals per day. "Outrageous!" Gino once said, letting a bit of his ancestral Italian accent loose.

Hartesbridge used to be on the flattest slope of a hill called Hartes Hill. There was an old manor on top, now part of the National Trust. They started their investigation from there. The car drove up the narrow single lane road flanked by enormous ivy-clad oaks that hid the sight of the village below. They arrived at the car park at the entrance of the mansion where they left the car. The house and gardens were closed that day. Whoever was supposed to tend the ticket office and the small shop probably disappeared with the village. They climbed the old mossy brick wall and jumped over. Then, went up the stone steps that climbed a hollow Victorian tower now in disuse. A sign said:

DANGER - DO NOT TRESPASS

From there they had a perfect view of the valley below. They could see the footprint of the village very clearly. A dark spot in the otherwise green landscape that surrounded it. No grass there, only ground dug out in place of the foundations. If they did not know what it was they would have guessed it was a scene from a World War Two bombing, except a bombing leaves much debris behind.

They could recognise the High Street going up the slope of the hill until the biggest building, the church with its graveyard. Lower grounds used to host the Green, where the fireworks were supposed to happen that night. The desolation of a bombarded town during the war, the silence of an old mine village, the curse of a poisoned-soil region. A road that arrives to nowhere and another one that starts from nowhere. That was Hartesbridge today.

Gino and Carter were not surprised at that sight. It was like watching the same film over and over again. Little Craiton, Stonebridge, Friar's Field, Hurstlivington, Stauntford, Mill on Grant. All gone. All at midnight, sharp as your old granpa's pocketwatch. The whole town uprooted from the earth, volatilised into the ether. No houses, no cars, no objects, not even the tarmac. No survivors, including the dead in the cemeteries. Not even the pets or the grazing cattle nearby.

"Another one that left Kansas and landed in Oz," Carter said wryly.

Gino nodded and without looking at him said: "Yep, we just need to find out where this Oz is."

As agents of the Royal Paranormal Institute, they were employed to find patterns. Patterns could not explain *why* these disappearances were happening, but they could give a clue to *when* they could happen next. However, five years of investigations had passed and they had no clue what was going on. Sure, they knew infinitely more than the average person in the street, but they were powerless to prevent them. Some of the citizens of the affected area, mostly Sussex, knew this and they accepted their fate with the same stoicism as the people from Naples had done for centuries of living next to the Vesuvio, the most active and destructive volcano in Europe. The ineluctability of a known cause of death put you at peace with yourself. If it happens, it happens. When it happens, it happens. This wasn't the view of the government though. It spent millions in research and policing to no avail. The whole of Sussex depopulated so much that only a few stubborn communities decided to stay put and live their normal lives. The exodus hit London quite badly with tens of thousands of refugees, some of which were now homeless.

They descended the hill on foot rather quickly having noticed the police cars and fire engines amassing around the perimeter of the defunct village. They saw another roadblock a mile away, where a bigger crowd of civilians and journalists was stopped. When they reached what was once the entrance to the village they immediately got stopped by the police.

"Who are you? This is an interdicted area. Please, move on."

"We are from Greenwich." Carter said showing his RPI badge.

"*That* Greenwich," a short but sturdy police constable said. "Let them pass."

Someone lifted the POLICE DO NOT CROSS blue tape up for them and indicated where the chief police van was. Inside, besides portable computers and men with headphones watching monitors and radar-like signals, they were welcomed by a sixty-year-old grey-moustached beefy man. He introduced himself as the Sussex Police coordinator for the communities' disappearances.

"I'm glad you boys are here so you can explain to me what the fuck you are experimenting on there in Greenwich."

Neither Carter nor Gino replied. The silence was deafening, interrupted only by occasional typing on the keyboards of the other agents.

"Because, if you didn't notice yet, *my* people are disappearing at an alarming rate. We are bloody tired of your esoboffins' experiments with those freaking satanic triangles."

"*Triangoli esoterici.*" Gino corrected him with a perfect Italian accent.

"I don't bloody care about your *tarangoli*. Make it stop. Right now."

Carter interjected and calmly said: "For your information, the Gateway was deactivated several months ago and we are currently experiencing a reduction of disappearances already."

James Abbot, his chest badge said, leaned towards Carter's face and almost spat on it while speaking, that's how close he was.

23

"The Soviets are not a threat any longer. The Wall, the Pravda, East Berlin. It's all gone. This weapon of yours should have stopped years..."

"It's not a weapon." Gino corrected him again. "It's a Gateway to other planes. This goes beyond the Cold War. It's of utter importance that we keep studying the paranormal phenomena."

Abbot looked at him like a bulldog would a burglar that had just jumped the garden fence.

"You are one of them techno-occultists, aren't you? The esoteric boffins that started all of this."

Carter placed himself between the two in order to defuse the situation. Carter looked back at Gino and asked him to get out of the van. Gino nodded and exited the vehicle. Outside all the policemen had heard the shouting and so knew who he was. Their eyes told of infinite hatred and disgust towards him. Gino was used to that treatment from the police. The RPI was administered directly from the Home Office, and its wide jurisdiction meant its agents did not answer to the local police.

He heard Abbot still shouting at Carter: "The Yankees got Von Brown and got to the Moon, we got this Sicilian prick that talks with the demons of the Overworld! What use we got from it?"

It was hard to hear common people talking like this about his own father. *Sicilian prick* wasn't even the worst he'd heard in the past few years. Anti-Italian sentiment was on the rise in Britain. And Gino couldn't blame the Brits. Amilcare Marcotti was supposed to bring Great Britain back to the glories of the lost Empire. He had promised Churchill he would take Great Britain to a future of unending energy independence, the biggest navy fleet in the world and the return of the Commonwealth colonies back to the Motherland.

True, the 1942 Messina experiment could not have been called a success story with the many islanders in the Aeolian archipelago disappearing into the thin air and Etna reactivating and almost erupting. So, why should replicating it here in Sussex have different results? But Winston Churchill believed in his father nevertheless. His father, who considered those disappearances and the island volcano's renewed activity just a small side effect, a trade-off for the most revolutionary discovery in the history of the humankind: the creation of a portal to another plane of existence. A plane where other powerful beings could be subjugated with the use of esoteric sigils. But could they? To date there was no way to know this. On the other hand, the anti-cosmic field created by aligning the three sigils in Greenwich, Chichester and Hastings had curious effects on the triangle thus created. Well, *curious* was probably not the best term to describe bizarre mutations occurring on newborns, sudden droughts that lasted months and the ever-increasing disappearances of the towns.

Seven towns and villages. A total of 36,000 people that had gone with them too. Gone no one knew where. Gino had some theories, but they were far from being certain and proven. A hecatomb of inane proportions.

A police officer on stilts distracted him from his train of thought. She walked past him in wide and precise gaits. Black suit, giant black goggles and the respirator. He'd seen these special agents before at the other disappearance sites. Two-metre-high metal stilts to avoid ruining the evidence and contact with the potentially contaminated soil. Special IR/UV goggles. Respirator and an oxygen tank on the back. They called them the *storks*.

Three of these storks were now roaming around in search of evidence. Barely any object had been left behind in any of the disappearance cases, but they were still hoping to find something. Their bird-like motions were somehow hypnotising. And entertaining given the crowd of other policemen and firemen watching them from behind the police tape. Some of them were hoping to see one of the storks fall for the laugh, but today they performed extremely well. Even jumping over ditches, standing for minutes seeking with their cumbersome goggles and changing spectra in the hope of finding any trace without trembling. These were professionists; however their talent was wasted. Gino knew why. The anti-cosmic field does not leave anything behind simply because it removes anthropogenic substances within its radius. There was no way they could find any man-made object in the field. The infrared and ultraviolet spectra were also foolishly useless. The other planes have other spectra, invisible to our eyes or technology. It would be like being colour-blind and trying to watch a film in technicolour.

But as he was just thinking that, one of the storks started to shout from far away from the fringes where he was now standing. It appeared to be the High Street area close to the church. The other two storks converged on the same spot and started to converse animatedly. There was quite a lot of excitement beyond the police tape line with many people guessing what was going on. An officer with binoculars started to describe what he could see from that distance.

"Jennifer found something close to the church's foundations. It might be the graveyard actually. Yes! It seems like it is. They are all three staring at something dark on the ground. James is using his prehensile stick to poke something. No, correct that. Not poking. Shoving in."

A lot of disbelief in the crowd commentaries. Gino got closer to them, pretending not to be bothered by their hatred. Everyone ignored him so that was good.

"The stick has been shoved almost all the way in."

"It's a two-metre stick!" someone shouted.

"So, it's a hole. They are investigating a hole?"

"Why? There are thousands of holes on the field."

"Not sure."

The man with the binoculars took the lead in the commentary again.

"James is dismounting from the stilts. Isn't it against the good practice manual? He shouldn't do that."

A wave of disapproving words and sounds came from the crowd. It was then that Abbot and Carter exited the van in a hurry and reached them.

"What is going on here?" Abbot asked with an imperative tone.

"Sir, the storks found something. A hole apparently. And James is getting off the stilts to inspect it."

"What? Tell him to get back on them immediately!"

27

Someone ran to the van and told the operators inside to communicate with the storks. A pause, then the same person who ran to the van shouted that their radio devices weren't working.

"Let me have a look with these," Abbot said snatching the binoculars from the officer.

Even without binoculars everyone could see that one of the storks was now off the stilts and kneeling on the ground. Abbot mumbled something while he kept watching. One of the other two storks still on stilts raised a hand and touched his helmet, signalling their communication signal was lost.

"Yep, their radio is off. Why isn't it working? Jon, make it work, damn it!"

"Sir, the signal is lost, there are interferences."

"It's the anti-cosmic field," whispered Gino to Carter, but loud enough for Abbot to hear him.

"It's your fucking Gateway, right?" asked Abbot turning his angry face to him.

"No, not necessarily. We turned the Gateway off months ago. And if it were, our devices also wouldn't work. This is something entirely different that we have never experienced. It's something local, something there in that hole which they are inspecting."

It seemed that Gino's explanation succeeded in calming Abbot's suspicions and he continued to watch the scene with the binoculars.

"What do we do sir?"

"Tell them to come back."

"But the radio doesn't work."

"Shout."

A pause. Then, almost everyone in the crowd started to shout and waved their hands in the air. The storks were far away, but they should have been able to hear them. However, none of them turned their faces to them, none seemed to have heard them. The shouting was loud enough to have reached them.

"If it's a field our radio waves, spectrum and even sounds won't be able to reach them. They are isolated," Gino said with a worried tone.

"Isolated?" Carter asked.

"Spatio-temporally isolated. They are not with us anymore."

"But we can see them."

"We see their footprint in our reality, but they are not on this plane anymore."

"I don't understand."

Then Gino grabbed Abbot's arm and spoke to him.

"Listen. You might not like me, but you must trust me now. I know what's going on there."

Abbot's face was in a state of shock. How dare he speak to him like that and touch him? Then, after interminable seconds he relaxed and let him talk. Gino's face was relieved, and he let his arm go.

"It's a local anti-cosmic field that is projecting from here, not from Greenwich. If it is I'm expecting they won't be with us for long."

"Are they going to disappear like the village?"

"Possibly. The field is already blocking radio, light and sound from reaching them. What you see is just a shadow of them now. It's like thinking you see a foot, but in reality it's just a footprint on the sand."

"What do we do, then?"

"Sigils are the only way to trespass on anti-cosmic fields. We need a sigil."

"Where the heck can I find a sigil here?"

"Sigils are not found, they are made. I can draw one."

And he ran to the van quickly followed by Carter. Inside he asked for a pen and sheets of paper. He received a black marker and several A4 sheets. He quickly drew two complex symbols on them, with convoluted arabesque-like lines. They were beyond Carter's comprehension. He then taped them onto his and Carter's chests and got out of the van.

"What are you thinking of doing?" Abbot asked.

"We are going to save them," Gino said trespassing in the prohibited area.

Puteus inferi

Carter followed Gino without thinking, despite Abbot and the others telling them not to go. The three storks were a mile away from them, so they had to hurry. Carter was in better shape than Gino and he quickly overtook him. Gino had to stop a couple of times to breathe and rest. It didn't help that the terrain was uneven and massive lumps of soil were disseminated everywhere. Ditches were omnipresent where the houses used to be, so they quickly understood that the best and smoothest way forward was to walk where the High Street used to be. It seemed like the storks were impossible to reach; the closer they got to them, the further they seemed to be. Gino couldn't get his head around it. That distortion wasn't predicted by his father's theories. The field should only affect the space within it, not outside of it. Nevertheless, he continued to run, following Carter, who had already distanced himself by a hundred metres. Then, Carter stopped at the fringes of the graveyard. When Gino reached him, he understood why. There was a physical wall made of distorted air, like the frozen glass in a toilet window. Gino held his arm firmly when he saw Carter trying to go across it.

"Wait," he said then he sat on the ground in a lotus position.

He started to emit strange sounds from his throat like the Mongolian throat singers used to do. He was chanting an incantation. Carter's frustration grew but deep inside he knew he had to trust Gino the occultist. He waited and breathed in and out to recover from the run. Meanwhile, the three storks were still unaware of what was happening behind them. Their movements were slower, almost like someone had pressed the slow speed button in a video. Then, although at a slower speed something happened. The man who was kneeling on the ground fell into the hole. No, he didn't fall. He was sucked in. Then, it was the turn of the female stork, Jennifer. For a short moment her stilts managed to save her from the fall, but the pull coming from the hole was so strong that it broke the stilts in half, and with them the poor Jennifer's legs. It was a gruesome sight that Carter had to watch without being able to intervene. A hand was holding his ankle. Gino still had to finish his incantation.

"Come on, Gino! They are all going to die!"

The third stork fell on the ground and he was trying to remove the stilts from his legs. In vain. The pull became stronger and stronger. His body was being sucked in little by little.

Carter had to sprint in when Gino let his leg loose. With the chanting finished the sigils on their chests glowed bright. Carter felt the heat burning his ribcage, then when he trespassed across the field an electric sensation pervaded his whole body. It was like thousands of sparks pierced his skin at the same time and yet it wasn't painful. Quite the opposite, it felt exhilarating. Once in he didn't waste his time and dashed towards the last survivor, grabbed his arm and pulled him out. The force that was pulling the poor man was very strong. It felt like a giant hand was playing tug-of-war with him. A giant hand that was inside that hole. He managed to have a glimpse of it above the man's shoulder and he didn't like what he saw. There was a glow, like a green fluorescent light, emanating from it. And spirals of vapour or smoke that were slowly expanding from it. Something was happening down there, and it wasn't good.

Gino's arrival helped him to focus on his task: saving the man. He pulled as much as he could and asked Gino to grab the other arm so they could pull together at the same time. The man was screaming so loud that Carter found it deafening and distracting. Several tugs, some of which must have been quite painful for the young man, managed to pull him over the rim of the hole. Then Gino slid towards his legs and detached the stilts, which in one single blow were sucked into the hole. The man continued to scream and cry like a baby while dragged out of the field. Carter kneeled next to him and turned him so he could see his face. He shook him and shouted to calm him down. It was all over, they were far away from the hole and it was safe now. The man stopped his whining almost instantly and Carter thought that was strange. He had expected the man to take longer to calm down. Why did he stop so abruptly and was staring at his chest with wide-open eyes?

Suddenly, he heard Gino screaming with the pain and running like mad into the fields, a cloud of thin black smoke coming from his chest. Then, Carter dropped to the ground and felt a devastating pain rooting inside his ribs.

***

"You were lucky we were so close to you." A high-pitched female voice pierced his ears.

Carter didn't recognise that voice. She introduced herself as Emma *Something* and she was affiliated with the police. Or at least, this is what he understood. His head was exploding and he really thought his hearing had been compromised, so intense was the buzzing in his ears, until her voice penetrated the wall of whitenoise he had been experiencing for hours.

He recognised the room as one that belonged to a hospital. He was alone but for her, sitting on a chair next to him. A long plastic tube with a liquid in it was leaving his arm and ended in a plastic bag hanging on top of his head. His chest was painful. It felt like a hot stone had been rubbed and then kept on it for hours. He had issues with breathing in, the pain was surging and ebbing in waves. He suspected what had happened but couldn't believe it. His hand slowly made its way to his hospital gown. He had a look.

"I didn't peek, I swear, but I suspect you've got the sigil's shape on your chest hairs," she said with a sneer. "Isn't it?"

He nodded without saying a word. The sight of his chest scarred forever by that symbol shocked him. He reached out for the glass of water next to his bed but couldn't manage. Emma helped with it.

"You might be asking yourself what happened."

Again, he nodded and said nothing while sipping from the glass.

"First of all, both your colleague Marcotti and one of the storks, Matt, are alive and well. They are in the other rooms next door. Yes, Marcotti had the same accident as you and he is as shocked as you. But in the end what matters is that you are all alive. On behalf of the whole Sussex police I thank you for your act of great courage or great stupidity, if you listen to Abbot."

Carter frowned on hearing that name. Did they really do something stupid? Sure, against all the regulations and orders, and completely unaware of whether it could have worked, but... it was the only thing that could have saved those poor people. Oh well, one at least.

"Jennifer and James are missing at the moment. Abbot instructed not to go close to the hole in the ground. They are using a helicopter to see what's happening."

"Any footage that you were able to see?"

"Nothing that you probably do not know already. A hole, some green glowing light. Not much else. The helicopter's images are blurred by the *anticosmic field* - is this what you call it? - or so I was told."

"I'm sorry for your colleagues."

Emma closed her eyes and pulled herself back in the chair breathing out all the air she had in her lungs.

"I guess Abbot would say that they knew about the risks."

"Sure, but it must be hard for the families."

35

"Yes. Look, I don't want to bother you more than necessary. I was told to keep an eye on you, but I..."

Carter tilted his head like a dog hearing a strange sound for the first time.

"No, no. Don't get me wrong. I wasn't told to watch over you in case you... whatever. I meant to look after you when you were going to wake up. It must have been a shock for you to go through that ordeal and wake up after being unconscious for so many hours."

"How many?"

"Six to be precise." Gino's voice resounded deep in the room.

Emma turned and smiled at him, then stood and left saying goodbye to them both. Gino was standing at the door with his ridiculous hospital gown and slippers. His uncombed hair, pale facial skin and the white tissue up one of his nostrils diminished his figure. Carter had never seen him so badly put, for he was always perfectly groomed. Apart from that tissue in the nose. He saw that many times and every single time it was linked to a nasty case. Last time? He remembered Gino standing in the middle of London Bridge during *a dark and stormy night*. Yeah, a cliché, however not *that* cliché if you think that he was the one who summoned that storm. And in order to do so a professional occultist must make incantations. The nosebleeding is just a consequence of the extreme stress that the body needs to withstand during these rituals. "One of the downsides of our wonderful job." Gino used to say. That incantation to activate the sigils on their chests must have been a difficult one for him, if his nose was still bleeding six hours later.

"You look ridiculous too, you know that Carter?"

And they both laughed. Gino closed the door and got closer to him sitting on the same chair that Emma had occupied a minute earlier.

"How did you know they would work?" Carter said putting a finger on his chest.

"I didn't."

Carter's face became paler than it was already.

"The *Omnibus Sigillorum* states that unless you carve it on the flesh it won't work."

"Carve it?"

"Yes, with a ritual knife."

"So, we could have died like those poor police officers!"

"I calculated the odds of that happening and I accepted the risk."

"Yes, but you also accepted it for me."

"We are partners, right? And you swore to protect me."

"Tsk, you are just a mad man."

"But it worked."

"It worked that now I'm scarred for life."

"Were you really hoping to go to the beach and relax with your family next summer?"

Carter didn't even reply.

"Besides, you can disguise it as a sort of tattoo. There are millions of people showing them off at the beach, you are not going to be less fashionable than them."

Gino paused. He understood that jokes weren't his forte and switched gear.

"Let's talk about what happened then, while our memories are still fresh."

"Fine."

"What did you see?"

"The hole, you mean?"

Gino nodded grabbing the same glass of water that Carter had sipped from. He drank it all.

"It was a strange sight. A glowing green like in a horror B-movie. It didn't feel real, but at the same time I felt hypnotised by it."

"Mesmerising, right?"

"Yeah."

"That explains why the storks were attracted by it, stood there for minutes gazing into it and didn't manage to pay attention to us."

"I guess so."

"And what do you think about the field we went into?"

"It was like an electric field, like millions of pins inside my skin, but it wasn't painful."

"I saw your hair going up like in an electric field. I assume mine did the same. So, I guess you saw and felt the same."

"Yes, did you expect a different set of answers?"

"Mmm, maybe."

"What? Why?"

"Our friend next door, the one we saved, has another story to tell."

"Oh, gosh."

"Incoherent stuff really, for the most part. However, there are things which are interesting. He spoke of another environment he was in."

"What do you mean? We saw him standing in front of the hole the whole time."

"He didn't see the hole, the one that we saw, or at least he doesn't remember it. He described a huge room, possibly a cave with one pillar so tall he could not see the tip. Dark, cold, clammy. He wasn't alone there. There were presences."

"Presences? Did he make contact?"

"I wish he was more precise with his description. At least I might have had more details to compare with what I have in my grimoires. Creatures, taller than him, not humans, possibly demons. He was scared to death by them. When you grabbed his arm, he thought it was one of them that was pulling him across the cave floor. That's why he was shouting so loudly."

"Crazy story."

"Yes, although it's not the craziest part of it."

"What do you mean?"

"Carter, even though I can't yet explain what he has told us so far, what he told me next is off the chart even for an experienced occultist like me."

Carter looked at his friend's face and saw a shadow covering his eyes. He had never seen him so shocked in all the years they had been partners together. They had been through thick and thin and Gino was by far the most experienced paranormal expert in the world, so he had probably seen unimaginable things. But this in particular seemed beyond anything he had faced before.

"He said that when you pulled his arm to save him from the sucking hole, it was the morning of the seventh anniversary of his imprisonment in that cave."

Seven years of pain

"Lizzy, I told you already: nothing serious. Just checking in with the doctor at the hospital."

Carter was trying to keep his voice low during the call with his wife. Other patients and doctors were passing by in the corridor while he was standing at the public phone hanging on the wall. An old lady sitting in a chair holding a dripping bag was eyeing him quite badly every time he replied to the worried voice of Elisabeth on the other side of the phone.

"Look, it's just a scar on my chest, nothing to worry about. Gino? Yeah, he was involved in the incident too. Same scar. What? Coincidence? No, look, it's not a coincidence but I cannot explain it here."

The lady's eyes transformed into accusing slits. Judging tight lips and neck leaning forward.

"The doctor said they will discharge me today, so I should be able to be home by ten. No, don't wait for me for dinner. I'll grab something here in the cafeteria. Yeah, food is rubbish I know, but I can't wait until ten. Kiss Jamie for me. Love you, bye."

Since he had been assigned to the RPI Lizzy had been extremely worried. He couldn't blame her: occultism, demons, summonings, portals to other planes. That was not a normal nine-to-five job. He had a family to look after. Jamie was turning six now and needed a paternal figure more than ever. However, how could he have turned down such an offer? One day, the chief officer of the local police station where he had worked for the past four years had called him into his office.

"Williams, please sit down," the chief said closing the door behind them.

"You might have heard of the Royal Paranormal Institute in Greenwich, right?" he asked.

"Yes, sir. It's in all the newspapers now."

"Right. They are expanding. And when a new police unit expands it needs new blood. They are recruiting and they've asked me if I have anyone who could be a potential candidate."

Carter's eyes bulged. How could he possibly be a good candidate for such a unit?

"You might be wondering why I'm thinking you could be a good candidate. Well, I don't."

"What? I'm confused."

"There was an officer working with you guys for the past six months, Smith. He is actually an examiner for the RPI. He was monitoring you people. I let him do it. Not that I had a choice, given that the order came from the Home Office, but I didn't see any harm in checking attitudes, skills, etc. of my men and women."

"Ah."

Carter had wondered why Smith was always present during the training and why he was also standing in the main room while they were doing an attitudinal test. Which Carter had thought was a routine test to assess them psychologically.

"It appears that you passed all the marks and ticked all their boxes."

"But I... but I do not know anything about the paranormal and occultism. I don't even believe in such things!"

"It seems that, for them, it doesn't really matter."

"What do you suggest I do?"

"Take it. Salary is better, good London allowance, probably less risky than working with the heroin addicted and criminals in dark alleys."

That night he spoke to Lizzy and as they used to do when there was a big decision in their lives they wrote down a list with pros and cons. Needless to say the pros won, and two months later he became a junior investigator at the Royal Paranormal Institute. He had never learned why they chose him (and in a way, he probably didn't even want to know) until one day his boss asked him what had made him choose this career. He thought it was strange that she didn't know. Johnson was a very intelligent and meticulous woman, she must have seen his file prior to taking him on her team.

She then followed with more questions, until he realised he was assigned to her unknowingly, rather than because she chose him. Why was that?

He went on to explain how he came to the RPI.

"The tests," she just said.

"You know about the tests?"

"Yes, very few can pass them."

"So, was there anything in those tests that could tell that I was born for the occultist career?"

"Occultist?" and she laughed like he had never seen her. Bending backward and all that repertoire of theatrical moves.

"I don't get it."

"You don't get it because the tests were designed to find someone as far away from an occultist as possible. Do you think they'd like to give a well-versed scholar in esoterism and occultism as an investigator to an *esoboffin*?"

And then he understood that they simply needed a bodyguard (as Gino had called him the very first time they met) with a big gun to protect the occultist that they were going to assign to him very soon. And that bodyguard needed to be as ignorant as possible in esoteric matters. This was by design, to avoid any disturbance during the rituals or during the investigations. In a way, that was a relief, although he took it as an offence at the time. That theatrical laugh from his boss didn't help with his self-esteem, for sure.

Now it felt different. Lizzy made him change his mind by pointing out to him that the dangers for an occultist were of a higher factor compared to a police constable. Or at least her perception of the danger given that not a single RPI had died in the line of duty since it was created. There had been accidents here and there, especially of a psychiatric nature, but spirits, poltergeists and demons never posed a deadly threat to the magicians who tried to control them. Until now of course. Carter did not mention that on that day two police constables disappeared into the Well. Everyone knew that they'd died, but the message to the families would be "currently missing".

He then stepped in Matt's room to find Gino, Emma, a doctor and a psychologist standing around a bed.

The policeman was still lying down, sheets pulled up to his neck. No scars for him, at least on his body.

"They had to sedate him. He was delirious," Gino whispered to him.

After a few words with Emma and Gino, the doctor left the room and the psychologist, an extremely lean – bordering bulimic - middle-aged woman, took the lead of the conversation.

"It was the second attack in one hour. He was shouting, in some cases howling, and was very aggressive towards the nurses."

"Any diagnosis you can share with us?" Carter asked.

"I've monitored his behaviour for the past few hours and what I can tell you is that these are symptoms correlated to people that have been kidnapped for long periods of time and developed a bond with the room/place where they were kept imprisoned and possibly with the captors too. They develop a child-like attachment to their prison, so when they get freed they experience a true shock. It will take weeks or months for him to recover."

"But he was there standing for barely five minutes?" Emma interjected, her mouth agape.

"I'm not sure what to say. All I've seen is consistent with this type of trauma."

Gino chimed into the conversation and thanked the psychologist, who left the room almost immediately after.

"Emma, right? What's your role here?" Gino asked after closing the door.

"I'm a Sussex Police constable."

"That I know. Why did Abbot ask you to be here?"

"To assist you."

Gino did not react to her answer.

"What are you trying to insinuate?" she asked with a frow. "You were found unconscious in the field. We saved you and took you to the hospital."

Gino put his hands forward, a way to defuse the already hot conversation.

Carter stepped in and said: "I'm sure my colleague here was not trying to insinuate anything. We are just curious to know what your role is here. That's all."

"I'm here to help, as I said."

Carter looked at her and saw a huge conflict in her facial expressions and tone of voice.

"Right, then we would like to interrogate your colleague here once he is back from the land of the dreams."

"I don't think that can be done."

"You said you were here to help us."

"Yes, to recover from the shock, give you back your belongings and take you back to your car."

"The knowledge that this man has is extremely valuable to us."

"Abbot said…"

"Tell Abbot I will ask Greenwich to issue a change of jurisdiction request."

Emma didn't reply.

"You know that once that is issued it will be the RPI's responsibility to continue the investigation," he said.

"Fine. I'll report it immediately."

And she left them alone in the room.

"Do you think I scared her too much?" Carter asked.

"You did what you are paid to do in these situations: threaten people."

Carter raised his eyebrows and wanted to argue with that, but then Gino raised a finger.

"Now, let's talk about this guy here."

Carter gave up and sat on one of the plastic chairs. Gino followed and sat in front of the bed.

Matt Barker was a mid-sized man in his thirties. Dark hair, receding line, well-shaved. Nothing out of the ordinary. In fact, he looked exactly like your average Joe. One of those faces that you see countless of times in the street, shops, the Tube, and despite this you are unable to recollect or describe. However, looking closer, like Gino was doing right now, his skin seemed older. Wrinkles of an older skin that weren't supposed to be there. Lines like trenches that drew canals in his forehead and cheeks, even though he was supposed to be relaxed due to the sedation.

"These are not age lines."

"What do you mean?" Carter asked, leaning closer to Gino and the man's face.

"These are from someone that suffered for a long time. Years maybe."

"Seven years," Carter suggested in a whisper.

Then, he put the hands on his face and pulled his head back breathing out. He never got used to these types of fucked up eureka moments. He stood up and walked back and forth in the room.

"It can simply be an effect of the shock. He is in a state of shock, right? Both the doctor and the

47

psychologist said this. You know when they say that if you get a scare big enough your hair becomes white? Might be something like that."

Gino didn't say anything. Still staring at the man's face. He was used to Carter's initial refusal to admit the paranormal. And he knew he would gradually accept it like he had done countless times before.

"There are two options Carter: he either invented everything out of the shocking experience he had, or he told the truth. There is only one way to find out if he told the truth."

Carter stopped walking and stood in the middle of the room.

"Gino. There is a limit to our curiosity. And there is a limit to what I can do to help you. I'm not going to follow you in..."

Emma stormed into the room without notice.

"You are going to interrogate him but with me in the same room. Is this acceptable?"

***

Hours later Carter was back home. Jamie was in bed next to his mother. A copy of The Wizard of Oz was on his bedside. Carter used to read it to him constantly. The boy loved it, and Carter found it more fascinating now as an adult than when he was a child. A house that vanishes and travels into another world, wizards and witches; all of it fit incredibly well with what was recently happening to his life. The fact that book was sitting next to his son's bed was a daily reminder of what Gino used to call "an acausal synchronicity". Gino would have seen that as a meaningful correlation with the recent chain of events, rather than pure coincidence. Carter could only accept his interpretation and go with the flow. It was very easy to attribute these ideas and explanations to plain insanity, but he knew that Gino was of sane and sound mind.

Carter didn't wake Lizzy up and headed towards their bedroom. He didn't even undress, and went to sleep straight away. After what he thought were minutes but in fact were hours – the clock's hour hand showed two a.m. – he felt a pressure on his chest. Lizzy's hand was touching his cauterised scar, her face shocked.

"I can explain," he said.

"You'd better do."

"It's part of Gino's repertoire."

She laughed, but she didn't mean it really. It was her way of dealing with something she could not control.

"It saved – *he* saved – our lives. Without the sigil we could have been gone today."

And he immediately regretted what he had just said. He saw Lizzy's mouth opening in a clear display of shock. He could see all her teeth and the two fillings she had done recently. Tears followed and he didn't know what to do. He had to justify the accident, but in order to do so he had to explain why it was necessary.

"Liz, I'm sorry. It had to be done. There are people disappearing, entire villages gone."

"I don't want my husband gone," she said through uncontrollable sobbing.

"Look, I've already told him that I'm not going to that well anymore."

"Well?"

"Yeah, it's in the middle of a Sussex village that disappeared last night. That's where I got this scar."

As he said that, it reminded him of his late father, the penultimate in a long line of police officers in the Williams family, who one night tried to explain to his mother why he had a knife wound on his shoulder. It was his turn now to do the same with his wife. He was nine, and he was listening to what they were saying, and his mother's sobbing from his room still haunted his memories. It clicked in his mind that even Jamie could have been listening to them. He did not want him to repeat what he had to go through when he was his age. He stood, signalling to Lizzy that he was going to check Jamie's room. The boy was there, fully covered except for his sweaty head, hugging a teddy bear. *The Wizard of Oz* was opened on the page where Dorothy's house kills the Wicked Witch of the East, and only her silver shoes are visible.

When he went back to their bedroom he wanted to whisper to Lizzy "I promise I'll be more careful and will not put myself in danger again," but she had gone downstairs, a quick weeping shadow taken away by the darkness of the staircase.

Venerable Mother

Chief Magus Hoffmann was the Director of the RPI and one of its eldest occultists. Older than Gino's father and one of the revered founders of the Institute. Framed by pointy skeletal shoulders, craning bird-like neck, brown-tinted maculae on strong always-clenching hands, a chest that heaved deep when ready to exhale the air necessary to speak, a head surmounted by the ever-present triple-ringed ritual tiara. Curly grey hair draped the contours of a drooping face, kept together by a very few tendons often cursed by sudden explosive twitches. Tiny eyes were sitting on the side of a potato-shaped nose. Both nose and eyes lived on that face rather uncomfortably, almost like they did not belong there, almost like they wanted to jump out of it. The lips were the worst of that conglomerate of parts crammed together almost randomly. The age dried them of all life so much so that now they were barely visible as darker lines on an otherwise yellowish malarial skin.

Gino, sitting uncomfortably on the guest chair, saw all of these features illuminated only by the smouldering candles dripping onto the mahogany desk, but he actually knew that this was just one of her many disguises. She could look much younger and even more eldritch than she was now. It was not about spells or pacts with a demon, it was all about perception. The Venerable Mother was, before anything else, the most able trickster the RPI had ever had. And this incredible feat was even more extraordinary if you knew that she actually had no way of seeing the person to trick in front of her, at all. For her little needle-head eyes were simply an ornament to her face. A blind that could see farther than any sighted person.

They were now in the centre of a vast room – probably the biggest of the Institute after the canteen – both perched on chairs each facing one side of a grand desk. One of those that presidents or popes have and use just to greet their foreign peers or officials. The two candles that partially bathed their faces in yellowish ever-changing light were placed on their left and right, in such a way that Gino thought of them as columns at the entrance of a temple, framing an unpassable line between him and the woman. And it was indeed a temple where they were facing each other now. The Temple of the Royal Institute of Paranormal with a scrawled pentagram at its central dais. Surrounding it, three rows of seats at the same level and three more on the mezzanine, now filled with darkness.

To the disappointment of many outsiders, it had never been used for altar-summoning rituals with virgin girls being sacrificed and all of that. It was simply the meeting hall for the most important quarterly congregations, where the High Council would discuss rather dull matters such as the RPI end of the year financial situation and the headcount.

When not used as a meeting room it was the Venerable Mother's office. It was said that she had decided to use that room, and especially the centre of the pentagram on the dais to make sure she had enough control over what was resting underneath. Just rumours – but don't rumours, like myths and legends, have always some truth? – avouched of a nameless entity being kept in charmed chains under the hall. An entity that she managed to tame using Enochian magic, which she was a master in.

Gino could not be certain of that, but he always thought of it as a very likely story. She was one of the few occultists able to master Enochian magic and she had constrained many entities in the past. Having one chained in the basement would not be such an odd choice given that the RPI was the safest place in which to keep demons constrained. The RPI was the perfect jail, built on top of one of the most powerful sigils ever created, populated by the most able occultists in the world. Reassuring but at the same time a chilling prospect.

Gino wasn't at ease knowing that a nameless eldritch something was lurking under his feet. What if the Venerable Mother got distracted? Who would hold the chains? And, most importantly, who would hold the chains when she was gone? There was no worthy successor among the inner circle. Or at least their name wasn't made public yet.

"I have heard of your report," she started saying breaking the silence.

Her lips were so dry that their movement made a scraping sound like sandpaper on wood. Her voice made an impact on the candlelight too, the first time in minutes that the air of the room had moved around. Gino felt it on his face's skin and he unconsciously breathed it in. It reeked of that musk and brine that only the elders' skin could produce.

"It is a great development. Something remarkable and unexpected. What do you make of it?"

Gino did not expect to be asked about his thoughts. Last time he'd met with her he almost did not have the opportunity to speak other than when answering with a monosyllabic yes and no.

"I believe we are on the cusp of knowing what is happening with these disappearances. I've seen a place that does not belong to our plane where a man's astral body has been tortured for seven years."

"That well that you described must be the gateway we were looking for. The one that your late father tried to open without much success."

"Yes. It might truly be."

"It is rather strange that this well opened just a few months after we destroyed the Chichester and Hasting's sigils. Don't you think?"

"Yes. I thought the same. It might be a rebound effect. Shutting a gateway might reverberate through the planes it was connecting."

"Mmm. Maybe. However, I think there are bigger forces at play here."

Gino did not say anything; however, his facial expression said *what?* louder than words could have done.

"Things are happening around the world that are connected in ways I still do not understand. We are looking at the wrong places."

"The disappearances and the weird events are happening in Sussex, the centre of the esoteric triangle."

"Yes, but occult forces do not follow straight lines and Euclidean laws. The clues might be elsewhere."

"This could possibly be, but the Well is in that place. That's our portal to enter."

"Perhaps that's not a portal but simply a conduit. Conduits do not require keys. Only gates need the key. Do you have the key?"

"I managed to save my colleague's and my lives thanks to an anti-cosmic sigil. The Well did not have any effect on us, so I'm confident we can traverse the conduit."

"Your confidence might kill you in the same way that it killed your father."

Gino felt a knife in his heart, not only metaphorically. The Venerable Mother had a way of using words that could pierce through the skin. Was it a spell she used, or was she simply able to access the others' inner fears? There was no doubt she knew of the complex relationship he had with his father, and how his legacy had left a mark on him. Was she testing him now? To check if the thought of his father's death could affect his capacities? He decided to stay calm and move that dark cloud away from his mind.

He reached out to the little red horn pendant that his mother had given him to ward off the *malocchio*, the evil eye. He used to do that when he wanted to concentrate, a talisman that helped to channel his strengths and remove the weaknesses. It was then that he realised the old woman had not blinked a single time since they'd started talking. *Blind people should blink regardless*, he thought. She was staring at him right in the eyes and he knew that she would have followed his gaze even if he had moved sideways, like sometimes happens with those weird Renaissance portraits. Their eyes follow you no matter where you look at them from. And yet, no blinking. It was very unsettling, and the coming of a chilly draught did not help either. A change in the light in the room followed. But it wasn't a trick of the flickering light. There was a shadow behind the Mother's shoulders. Something that could have been confused with her shawl floating on her back, but he knew it wasn't.

What is happening? he asked himself, thinking of standing up.

The moment that thought crossed his mind, the shadow was not there any longer, the feeling of the draught on his feet disappeared and the small eyes of the Mother blinked.

"Gino Marcotti. Watch the world around you. Look for connections. That's my advice."

He repeated her words inside his mind: *bigger forces are at play*. He thought of that entity chained under their feet and his imagination went wild. He shook his head in disbelief and pushed that thought away. He imagined shadows and chilling wind. Now there was no time for monsters. He just wanted to leave. This conversation was draining his energies.

She read his mind and waved her hand.

He stood, bowed to a blind woman, and said his goodbyes and thanks. When he touched the door handle, he hesitated for longer than needed, almost like he was waiting for her to say something. And she did.

"Our world is truly paper-thin."

The Dead Mountaineer

The rhythmic punching on the bags, the clanking of chains, the heavy breathing of the men, the smell of sweat and leather. Gino had to go through that ordeal again.

A long corridor led the way to the main room where the ring was. But before that he had to pass by the changing rooms, the steamy showers where his pace was always faster for the fear of seeing those swinging cocks again that shocked him last time. None this time, luckily.

The boxing ring towered over him as he entered the main room. The ropes were still vibrating from the massive body of a boxer that fell backwards. The coach was shouting something incomprehensible to the two fighters. One of them stopped and spat into a small bucket. A woman from the high balcony was cheering for him. He had to quickly dash to the side as a huge bloke with his shirt off bulldozed his way through the corridor's door to reach the showers. Gino had to be careful where he was putting his feet, as so many gloves, shoes, punching bags and dowel bags littered the floor around the ring. Several boxers were training, punching imaginary opponents or hanging bags. All ignored him, so he had to be careful to avoid punches or being walked over.

He finally reached the other side of the ring, where he found him. He was about to punch the bag again after resting and fitting his gloves in.

"I knew I would have found you here."

Carter didn't turn and started to punch. "How did it go with that poor guy?" he said between punches.

Gino found a stool and crossed his legs.

"It took him several hours before he woke up. You did well to go back home. How's Lizzy?"

"She didn't take it well."

"I bet."

"So?"

"Delusional. Still in shock. He repeated the same things as before. He *really* thinks he has been there for seven years. We explained what happened from our point of view, showed him the calendar, put him in touch with his wife but it wasn't enough. *It was real*, he shouted at one point."

"Did you get any more details of the place and the creatures he saw?"

"It's a big cave. Pitch dark – that's why he asked us to switch off the light in the room when we interviewed him – and extremely wet and cold. He survived on scraps and bugs that were scuttling around the stalagmites and stalactites. Gross. He said there was an abundance of them and they weren't that bad."

Carter paused and looked at Gino with a disgusted face.

"Do you believe him?"

"Oh, yes. I do."

"How can you be certain?"

"I have my ways."

Carter closed his eyes and rested his forehead on the punching bag while holding it.

"I know you want to punch me right now, but this is the most important breakthrough we've come up with in years. This is what my father always hoped to find!"

"To eat roaches for seven years?"

"Forget about that. I shouldn't have said it. My knowledge will protect us. Do I need to prove it to you again?"

"No, I know that your black magic works, although I know fuck-all about it. We haven't been so close to dying since that day on the Isle of Wight."

Gino's memories travelled back to a year ago, when they had faced a demonic manifestation that escaped from a recently opened portal, possessed a nun and then flew to a lighthouse on the Isle of Wight. Gino had to admit that that had been pretty scary. Several people died, the lighthouse collapsed on them and the demon managed to open another portal – which if he still thinks about it, seems impossible – that almost sucked them in. Luckily he had several tools at his disposal and with the help of several other occultists – an eighty-year-old Japanese former Shinto priestess and a Ukrainian young promise of the occultist world – he'd killed it and closed the portal. The next day the news talked of a particularly heavy storm that pull down the old lighthouse. A commentator blamed it on climate change, while a politician deprecated the lack of government money for the preservation of historical buildings. The nun never recovered from the coma she got herself into after de-possession. Crazy story everyone was still talking about in Greenwich.

"I think I know what happened and how to prevent these temporal anomalies."

Carter removed his gloves, reached out to his dowel bag, and gave him a tissue. At first Gino did not understand what was happening. What was that tissue for? He wasn't sweaty or with a cold.

"I suspect the 'I have my ways' and 'I think I know what happened' can be explained by this?" Carter asked, pointing at Gino's face.

Gino touched his nose, looked at his finger stained with blood, then at the floor where several drops blackened the laminated surface. He stepped back to avoid staining his shoes and took the tissue from Carter's hand.

"I'll wait for you in my office. I've got something to show you," he said walking away and avoiding a punching bag that swung straight at him.

When Garibaldi's tail started to bang the wooden floor, Gino knew that Carter was going to open his office door.

"Come in!" he shouted before Carter could knock.

"Hello, big boy!" Carter said to an overexcited Garibaldi.

"Sit, please," Gino commanded the way he usually did in his office.

He put the book he was reading away. Carter saw the title, *The Dead Mountaineer*. He'd seen Gino reading that book many times before and it had always been during difficult times.

It was Carter who started: "I promised Lizzy I wasn't going with you next time."

"Sure," Gino said dismissing him.

"What?"

"You will be coming."

"I said, I don't want to come."

"I said, 'You will be coming,' I didn't say that you don't want to come."

"Are you going to force me? Because if it's like this I can call HR and–"

"Just stop. You sound like an old woman. Let me explain."

He took another tissue from the desk and inserted an inch in his left nostril. He was still bleeding. Carter hasn't seen so much blood from incantation rituals since that accident on the Isle of Wight. And he had lost close to a pint there.

"I auscultated Matt's head when the nurse and that Emma from the police department left. He was sleeping again and I *saw* inside his head."

Carter shivered. He knew that he could talk to demons, dead people, open portals to other dimensions, but the creepiest thing for him was when he could get into someone else's head by *auscultating*. It was a type of astral projection that ensured him access to the memories of other people. It must have taken a tonne of energy, hence the amount of bleeding. That was some crazy shit.

"It was real. I saw it with my own eyes. Seven years of memories. Not one day more nor one day less."

Carter became suddenly rigid. He felt the urge to move his fingers in a cross section like his Irish heritage transmitted to him since childhood.

"It was dark, I couldn't see much apart from some fluorescence coming from some rocks. Crystals, maybe? I don't know. The dim light suggested there was a tall pillar made of stone in the middle of the vast room."

"How big?"

"I couldn't tell. As I said, it was very dark, so dark I could barely see my own hands and Matt's body. He was on the rocky floor most of the time, rhythmically banging his head back and forth. He howled for the rest of the time, especially after the demonic presences tortured him with endless shrieking and chill touches."

"You saw them?"

"Barely. A dozen at most. Class B, a minor demon in the Yuruniev scale. It was terrifying. That man must have gone through the most horrific experience a man can go through. I can't imagine anything more terrifying than living alone for seven years in total darkness, surrounded by demons that are torturing you."

He sat with his head held in his hands. The moment he did that it seemed like the office lights dimmed a bit. Carter thought of a bad wire. Garibaldi moaned next to them. There was a long pause, until Carter stood up and asked if he was okay.

"It's nothing, Carter. Anyway, the reason I came to search for you at the gym was because I wanted to show you something."

He stood up and reached the bookshelves, where he picked up a small mahogany coffer. He brought it to the desk with great care. Opened it with intentional theatrical movements and presented the contents to Carter. Inside, set upon red velvet fabric, there was a minuscule golden pin.

"What am I looking at?" Carter asked.

"You are looking at an exo-artefact. I saw it on the ground just after we saved that man from the sucking well, and I immediately knew what it was."

"You said nothing can be found after an anti-cosmic field has wiped out a village."

"Correct. Nothing man-made. But this, this is an artefact that doesn't belong to our plane, our Earthly plane."

He took a book from the shelf. Black leather embossed with runes. Carter managed to sneakily see the title from the spine: Colliding cosmoses. Gino opened it without much care, which was very unusual for him, given his reverence for his precious books. He searched for a specific page that he must have read thousands of times since he knew exactly where it was. There were some nineteenth-century prints. In one there was a representation of two planets colliding and not many details. But in the second one, opposite to that, he saw the drawing of the same golden pin inside the coffer.

"Science will tell you that these are the byproducts of meteorites crashing into our atmosphere. They are not Carter. These are the by-products of two worlds colliding."

"When you say worlds, what do you really mean?"

"I mean like two different dimensions, two different universes, cosmoses. Call them as you like. This is the proof that we didn't open a portal. The esoteric triangle that my father conjured did not in fact open a conduit to another world. It attracted it to us, it made it collide with ours. That's why we are unable to see the portal, we have crashed into the portal and are overlapping the two universes. Think of something like two galaxies, two discs that are colliding at different angles. We are seeing manifestations of this other world that intersected with ours. It's not a gate, it's a crash."

Carter looked at him extremely worriedly. He almost couldn't find the words.

"Is this bad?" he finally asked.

Gino paused for a few seconds, closed the book, and looked at him with a grave expression. Then, chinning up and sniffing the last drops of blood up his nose, he said:

"It is very bad indeed. Catastrophically bad."

Carter looked at him in shock.

"So, this is the part where I say, 'How does this reassure me and convince me to go with you into the Well?' and you reply…"

"I reply that I have the tools to keep us safe."

"That doesn't convince me. I still have the scars of your tools."

"That was improvised. You know that. And that sigil saved our lives. Or would you have preferred to have lived for seven years in that cave?"

Gino saw Carter's unconvinced face and decided to take it from a different angle.

"You care about your family, right?"

Carter did not even reply to that rhetorical question.

"Well, what about their safety? What about everyone's else safety in this country, perhaps the whole world?"

"You are changing your pitch to make me feel like a hero."

"We are on a mission, Carter. When you said your oath five years ago you thought this was just a joke? There are supernatural forces at play in this world that are threatening our existence. Now we have the proof that another plane is colliding with ours and we can't simply wait and watch."

He grabbed *The Dead Mountaineer* in his hands and showed its cover to Carter.

"Do you know what this is?"

"A book about someone who died climbing a mountain? From Crowley?"

"Crowley – yes, that Aleister Crowley, the occultist – was an accomplished mountaineer. He climbed K2 in the very first expedition in 1902. It was there that Crowley had a revelation that would change his life, but that was never transcribed in his or anyone else's book. But this one. I'm holding the only copy of a transcript of a recorded hypnosis session he gave to a friend in 1947, just before he died. In it, he says that at some point a heated debate raged at the base camp regarding which side of K2 to attack. He wanted to reach the summit through the south-east ridge because of a vision he'd had the night before, but the others did not agree. He took a revolver and made his point clear. Either they would attack by the south-east ridge, or someone would need to die. I think what convinced them was more his charisma than the revolver. The gun was just a tool to make his point clear: he had to go that way to fulfil his destiny. He had to follow what the vision told him to do. That night, just before the ascent, he had a restless night filled with nightmares and images of rocks and snow in the shape of crosses. All bad omens for him. The morning after, everyone was surprised to see him still at the camp, given that a rumour had spread that he had left in the middle of the night in full gear to the west ridge, opposite to where he threatened everyone to go. He thought they were all crazy. He didn't move out of his tent all night and his gear was all there for everyone to see. They decided to climb and they finally reached 7,000 metres. A great accomplishment!

"But now, the weird part starts. During the final leg of the descent they were reached by someone from base camp saying they had found a body in a deep crevice in the west ridge. No one knew who he was. They were all counted, no one was missing. Perhaps from another expedition, but it was clear that the body was fresh and the little snow that covered him left no doubt that that death was from the night before. Impossible to reach it and identify it, so, as was often the case during those early centuries expeditions, they left the body without any proper burial. The mountain is the best tombstone a mountaineer could ask for, really. Anyway, on the way back Crowley doesn't say anything, but he had recognised that gear, those clothes and that bald head. It was him. A doppelganger that took the other path, the one that his vision told him not to take. But, Crowley says at the end of the hypnosis session, what if he was the doppelganger and the real Crowley was still there covered by the snow?"

"Wow, crazy stuff," Carter said not understanding the point Gino wanted to make.

"Sometimes we have to make a choice Carter, like Crowley did on K2. There are forks in our lives. Our doppelganger will go in one direction and we can go in the other direction."

"But how do we know which of the two is the one to take in order to avoid ending up like the Crowley's doppelganger?"

"About that..., I know a person who will tell us exactly that."

Tarocchi

The lift arrived with its usual metallic *ding*. The old doors slid open and let Gino see the inside. A faux 1920s art deco car like the rest of the building interior. Wooden panels carved with geometric patterns that only the initiated knew contained esoteric symbolism. Beautiful to the layman, full of significance for the occultist. And empty as Gino liked. He had no intention of meeting his colleagues today. Especially the ones from the other departments. Once in, he took the key from his pocket and stuck it in the dashboard. He selected -4, six floors below his department. It was the last floor, the bottom of the building, the one closer to the huge golden sigil the Royal Paranormal Institute was originally built on. It was a damp and mouldy part of the building, quite fitting for its dwellers. The lowest class of the hierarchy in paranormal studies, the pariah of the institute. The likes of which used to sit on cold steps in the streets, amusement parks, circuses and brothels. The lift's door opened to an empty foyer. No decorations here, no wooden panels with fine art deco lines. No columns or lamps. Just concrete, poured in haste so the sigil down below wouldn't escape. The foyer led to a single door with a plaque: Clairvoyance Studies.

Gino opened the door and dashed into a long dark corridor. Illumination was intermittent, yellow cones of light coming from ceiling bulbs separated by five metres of darkness each. The corridor was lined with wooden doors mostly shut and leading to empty rooms, nowadays forgotten by everyone. He had to cross the long corridor for all its length to find the first occupied rooms. He skipped the first ones whose plaques read Professor Kowalski-Telesthetics; Professor Zapata – Applied Noetics; Dr Galli – Remote Viewing and Mass Parapsychology; Dr. Neumann – Precognition and Retrocognition Studies.

He skipped all of them and went straight to the small door at the very end, the one that looked like a janitor's cabinet door. A badly battered tin plaque hanging by a wire read: *Josepha–Fortune teller.*

He knocked. No one answered. He reached for the handle until he heard her voice shouting.

"Wait!! Give me a minute."

He waited for more than a minute and was about to lose his patience when she said, "Gino, it's you, right?"

The door opened and an old lady with long silver hair smiled at him. She was so short that Gino – not famous for being tall – had to bend his head to look at her eyes. She had a traditional Roma dress, one that she told him she liked to use so she looked more stereotypically gypsy. In fact, she loved looking at modern politically correct people getting mad at her being so stereotypical, including the term 'gypsy', which she proudly adopted even in her PhD dissertation.

"Gino, lo sapevo che eri tu. Benvenuto!" she said with a perfect Italian accent.

"Josepha, is there anyone else that comes to visit you on a Friday evening without any notice?"

"No," she said bitterly, turning her whole body in a single swirl that made her dress spin like a ballerina musical box.

Her office, if we can call it that, was a perfect replica of a traditional gypsy caravan. Cedar red and pastel green wooden panels covered it all. Even the ceiling, curved to resemble the shape of the caravan's roof. Flowery patterns were dotting each panel, furniture or object inside. A desk, two chairs, several bookshelves and a few other smaller furniture pieces. No windows as they were deep underground. Only two light sources: one from an old lamp on the desk and one from a candelabra on the low coffee table. The Tarots was spread on the coffee table.

Gino looked around in search of something. She saw that and turned her face to a bookshelf where she suspected what he wanted to find was. There, next to several Tarot decks and divination books he saw that framed black-and-white photo. Josepha next to Amilcare Marcotti, his father. Behind them the floppy banner of the *Convegno Internazionale della Società Teosofica – Roma 1927*". It was there at the international meeting of the Theosophical Society in Rome that they'd met for the first time. She looked so young and beautiful. Gino never knew whether they had a crush or not, but she had certainly kept fond memories of him.

"He was so awesome, wasn't he? You look like him, by the way."

Gino blushed and shook his head.

70

"Same curly black hair, same eyes, deep as wells. Same strong character. Same introspective third eye."

All true. Everyone said that, although he had some doubts about the last part. His father was way stronger than him in occult practices. The Messina Experiment was the tangible proof of that. The gigantic esoteric triangle with Messina in Sicily, Cagliari in Sardinia and Rome on the mainland as sigil points was an extraordinary endeavour. Much bigger than the Greenwich, Chichester and Hastings' one. And if it weren't for the Allies landing in Sicily, his father could have had more time to refine – or retune, as he loved to say – the anti-cosmic field to the Axis' advantage.

"If I'd only had three more months we could have won the war. Just three more months to summon Them and make Them side with us."

He heard these words several times during his childhood, both in Italy and in the UK where they had been forcibly moved after the war. He heard him saying them at home, after a few glasses of Malvasia, for he wasn't allowed to talk about these things at work or in the presence of the British. He had mixed feelings about those memories. There was a lot of nostalgia linked to those first years in England, buried in that old apartment inside the prisoners' camp. They were treated well in terms of accommodation, food and access to books needed for his father's work, but they were still the enemy. How could you trust your enemy, even after the war is over, especially if the enemy has occult faculties beyond your comprehension?

One summer evening, he remembered he was in his bedroom playing with the only toy he'd managed to bring from Italy: a wooden horse. He'd heard a knocking at the door, which was very unusual at that time of day. It was after dinner and his parents used to read all the newspapers of the past week. These were secretly brought to the Marcotti family by a camp janitor who happened to be Italian as well, but of second generation, so not suspected of fascist sympathies. Sometimes she had managed to get a copy of *Il Corriere,* which was usually very old, weeks old, but at least it gave a sense of what was happening in Italy without the filters of the British post-war propaganda.

His father opened the door and listened to two men, army officials. He had a very basic understanding of English at that time but by looking at his face after they were gone, Gino understood that something special was going to happen.

"Churchill wants to see me in person," he heard him saying to his mum.

It happened the morning after, when Winston Churchill came to inspect the prisoners' camp. Amilcare Marcotti was escorted to the main lobby of the reception building. There, several officials from the Home Office were chatting with the camp's army officers. In the middle of the crowd, a figure that could not be mistaken from anyone else. Churchill reached out to him, shook his hand, and said, "Buongiorno." Marcotti didn't reply in Italian, unsure whether Churchill had said that out of courtesy, or if he really knew Italian.

After several minutes of pleasantries and small talk they all moved to the meeting room. There was a big oval table. Churchill sat with three other officials, plus an army general with tens of multicoloured medal ribbons on his chest. Marcotti sat on the other side, together with an interpreter, the captain who managed his compound and a civilian who he had no clue who he was. They started by talking about the great results Von Brown and the other Nazi German scientists had achieved since they have been moved to the US. The V2 rocket technology could now be used by the Americans for ballistic transcontinental missile attacks, and possibly future space exploration.

When asked if he was aware of it, Marcotti said no, and he asked what the reason was for mentioning this in his presence. They told him they would like to replicate the same with him, to which he replied he was not a rocket scientist but a simple séance. The civilian who was sitting two chairs from him started to speak in Italian. Perfect Italian, with no regional accent. He said they knew what Marcotti was trying to accomplish in Messina, and that they would like to replicate the same there in England. The aim was to reacquire the now lost military superiority of Great Britain and overcome the other nuclear powers with a different weapon. There was an arms race brewing at the moment, and London wanted to try a different weapon but equally destructive. He was told that two years earlier the Royal Paranormal Institute was founded in London. This institute was hiring all the most famous occultists of the time to advance research in the occult arts. They were about to move to another new building, yet to be built in Greenwich, but they were waiting for his help. They wanted the *Aksum sigil* to be embedded in the foundations so they could recreate the esoteric triangle in England.

All of this was told to a young Gino that same night after dinner. That night, Gino understood that things were going to change for the better pretty soon for his father and them. Two months later, after his father signed the contract, they were naturalised as British nationals. They had to forego their Italian ones, though. And that was the most difficult part for his father. He had become the official séance of the Fascist Regime, acquired eldritch knowledge for the Italian Empire, and now he had to betray his country in favour of the enemy that took him and his family prisoners for years. Gino knew that although he accepted the offer, he would live in shame for the rest of his life. The few Italians he met in the following years were never told about his betrayal. He lived anonymously for all his life and never returned to Italy. His family thought he was killed during the Allies' invasion and a tombstone was erected in his hometown in Romagna. Although Gino had been very young when all of this happened, he never felt hundred per cent British and he inherited the same guilt from his father.

Josepha knew what was happening in his mind now. She had the same "mnemonic storms", as her colleague Zapata next door used to say, when she was looking at photos depicting her previous life in Romania and then in Italy. The emigrant's mind was always in limbo, in between two – or as in her case, three – worlds. Especially the one of who lost the war and now lived in the enemy's capital. It was a miracle they could still wake up every morning without suffering a mental breakdown.

She decided to take him away from those memories.

"So, tell me. Why are you here?"

"You should know what happened."

"I see the future, not the past. That's retrocognition, as Karl Neumann next door likes to say. If you need anything about the past, talk to him, the best retrocognitor in town."

"I had a vision."

"Alright. Are we talking about *you* or…"

"Astral projection."

"Oh, in that case," she took the Tarot cards away and started to rummage inside a chest. After a while she finally found another Tarot deck that she triumphantly lifted over her head.

"These are the ones I was looking for. As you can imagine, I rarely use them. Not many, even in the RPI, ask me to read cards involved with astral projection."

"How do they differ from the traditional ones?"

"There are minor details only I can see. And the spread is smaller, you will see. My interpretation will then be different."

Gino nodded trusting her judgement and professionalism.

"Okay, I need to know a bit more about what is troubling you," she said before even starting to ask him to shuffle them.

"I'm in a huge cave. It's dark and chill. There is one stone pillar. I can't see the end, so high is the ceiling.

There is a man, a worm of a man, on the rocky floor. I can barely see him, but he is shivering, his skin is pale and clammy, he is desperate and scared. They can see us."

"What? Who are *they*? And you said that they can see *you*?"

"Yes. And that's why I'm troubled. Entities. *Demoni*. They saw me as well."

"That's not possible. It's chapter 1 of the Basics in Astral Projection in year 2."

"Yeah, I guess that exam we took was about astral projection on Earth, in this cosmos."

"W-what?"

"Yes, Josepha. I did it. I used a man's mind as a conduit to another plane where he has been before."

"You astral-projected in a memory?"

Gino nodded wetting his dry lips with his tongue.

"I-I wasn't even aware it was possible. You projected in space *and* time."

"Yes, and it required a lot of energy. You should have seen the buckets of blood I –"

"Spare me the details. This is very dangerous, Gino. You could have get lost in there."

"It was the only way to know the truth. This man has experienced a space-temporal anomaly that lasted seven years in his mind, but only five minutes in our world. He is the key to understanding the failures we are seeing with the esoteric triangle."

"Okay, let me summarise for my own sanity check. This man lived for seven years during our five earthly minutes. That's already something that makes your head spins, doesn't it?"

"Yes, I give you that."

"Then, you auscultated him to search within his memory and astral projected in his memory. But, and here comes the wackiest part, you projected in time and you manifested yourself to these entities."

"Yes, you could definitely tell that *I* was the ghost to them."

"Alright. What do you need my abilities for, then?"

"I need to get inside that head and project my astral form again."

"You are crazy. Batshit crazy! I cannot allow you to do this again!"

"Josepha, I'll do it with or without you. But if you can give me the gift of your precognition abilities it will be easier. Much easier to prepare myself. If they see me a second time, they might attack me."

"I can't, Gino. For the love of your father, don't ask me this."

"It is exactly for the love of my father."

"What do you mean?"

"That man, slithering on the floor and eating bugs for seven years, howling like a hydrophobic dog in the darkness, surrounded by demonic presences. That man, that poor man, wasn't alone. At first, I thought it was a spitting image of my projection or an image cast on an obsidian mirror, but then I realised it wasn't me. Similar age to mine, similar curly hair and deep eyes. Like you said."

Josepha's hand reached her open mouth to cover the shock.

"He looked at me in the eyes, reached out to my projection with his trembling hand and said 'Figlio mio'."

L'Appeso, il Mago, la Torre e l'Eremita

My son. Those words resounded in Josepha's mind for minutes. *My Amilcare.* She couldn't believe it. Amilcare was supposed to have died thirty years ago. He died during the sigil's activation of the Greenwich point, the first sigil of the esoteric triangle soon to be activated. She saw his body still and cold. That accident, how terrible it was. The foundations for the RPI had been laid down and the construction of the building was going to start very soon. It only needed the initial touch. The sigil embedded in its foundations. Amilcare's main project was going to start right there in that very moment. All the most important occultists of the RPI were present. The representatives from the Home Office were there too. It wasn't a public event, as the government considered the esoteric triangle project top secret, but a considerable crowd of government officials and occultists was invited. The sigil's design had already been carved in the cement but it needed the pouring of liquid gold into it and most importantly an activation. Something that only Amilcare Marcotti could do.

The pouring of gold into the grooves worked well and it took only a few minutes for the hot metal to cool down completely. Once that was done, Amilcare recited an incantation, something he had already done in Messina and Cagliari before. But this time something went wrong, very wrong. As his humming grew in intensity, the sky became darker and darker until a thick mantle of low clouds loomed over them. Some people took out their umbrellas, someone else stayed put thinking that Amilcare's incantation was going to finish sometime soon. But no rain poured from those black clouds. Instead, a myriad of sparks and lightning started to dance in them. None of them reached the ground until a single powerful bolt dashed down and struck Amilcare just in the moment he had activated the sigil by touching it. The bolt entered his head, transmitted along his body and exploded out of his finger, burning the sigil until it became a magmatic red.

Amilcare's body was catapulted back several metres, his clothes in flames. Heart stopped a few seconds later. Josepha was there and she saw it all. She heard the loud snap, she felt the lightning's thunder on her chest, she smelled the burned skin. A moment that haunted her for decades. And most importantly a moment that she failed to foresee. How could that have happened?

"If we know his body has been dead for over thirty years now, that means that what you saw can be contacted through séance. You have to talk to a psychic medium."

"The people on the second floor won't be able to help me, Josepha. He is a trapped astral projection in a different cosmos, not a ghost trapped on Earth."

Josepha's eyes dropped down to her colourful skirt. She was trying to process all of it.

79

"Right. You are absolutely right. How can we help him, then?"

"We? I thought you said it was too dangerous."

"Forget about what I said. True, it is dangerous, but if there is a chance to help your father I'd be more than happy to help you."

"I understand. Thanks."

"But tell me: what's your goal?"

"What do you mean?"

"If Amilc... your father's body is no more, how can we save him?"

"I don't know, yet."

"I guess, and this is just brainstorming, if we save him from that extra-earthly plane his projection might either go back to his earthly remains or continue to wander forever, but at least in our cosmos."

"Not sure what's worse."

"Right. Let's see what the cards have to say, then."

He shuffled the deck several times and she asked him to split it in half. Then she started the spread. One by one the cards landed on the coffee table revealing a mix of different suits and minor and major arcana.

Many at the RPI have always been sceptical about divination, because they considered it a minor and less tangible occult art compared to others. The main issue was that it was based on interpretation, and so it was biased by the tarotphant. However, Gino trusted Josepha as much as himself and knew she would help him find out what was ahead of him.

Her spread was indeed different from the classic ones. She landed six cards only and she turned them up all at once. Four on the cardinal points like a templar cross and two in the centre of the cross, one on top of the other and perpendicular to each other so they made a smaller cross. You would think Gino's mind would be focused on the cards, trying to interpret that suit, that number, that figure, but in reality, it faded away from the cross made of cards in front of him.

"Four out of six cards are major arcana. I don't have to remind you that this is a good omen," she said breaking the spell of his inner thoughts.

On the left was the Hanged Man, the upside-down man hanged by a foot.

"L'Appeso," she said in Italian. "This is the past. I have no doubts this represents your father. Mussolini was hanged upside down and your father had links to the Fascist Party."

"*He* was a fascist," Gino quickly added.

His mood sank as it always did when the words "your father" and "fascism" were brought together in a conversation.

"Sure. It's linked with wisdom but also trial and sacrifice. He sacrificed himself to build this building. And he is enduring a trial due to his astral wandering."

Once she had finished talking, Gino's vision was suddenly sucked into a black hole. The room was filled with darkness. Josepha disappeared, her voice was gone, replaced by total silence. Actually, listening carefully, he heard voices. Distant voices of a mob, eventually shouting and cheering in a square, and now he could see two bodies hanging upside-down, magmatic faces, everchanging blobs made of bruises and blood, broken bones and teeth. It was the public execution of Mussolini and his mistress in Piazzale Loreto in Milan. How was it possible? Was this a dream? But it felt so real. He ran through the crowd, making his way with elbows high and pushes and crouches and sudden thrusts. He reached the first row of people, their fists filled with rage and vengeance. Some were throwing cobblestones at the corpses and these took the hits and swung and turned them. One swirl revealed their faces to Gino. No more blobs of broken bones and blooded skin but the clean faces of his parents.

"No!" Gino shouted trying to stop the next stone from being thrown at them. "Leave them alone!"

He moved forward and in a superhuman jump reached out to his father's body, grabbing it and bringing it down. When he tried to do the same with his mother, the stones had already started their trajectory to his face.

"The present, the crux of the matter, is The Magician." Josepha's voice penetrated his head like a needle.

"Gino, are you okay?" she asked with a concerned voice.

The room had reappeared. The deck of cards spread on the table. Josepha's reassuring presence in front of him, which, like a fisherwoman fished him out of that vision.

"Yes, yes. I just dozed off for a while. It must have been all the blood I lost during my projection."

"Would you like to lie down on the sofa? Water?"

"No, I'm fine. Please continue."

Josepha took the Magician card. A man wearing a white robe mantled by a long red cloak. One hand that pointed upwards holding a rod and another pointing down.

"I'm not sure who this could be. As above, so below. This means someone well versed with communicating between two worlds. A conduit between two planes of existence. My guess is that this is you, Gino."

The room turned black again and Gino experienced the same feeling of emptiness and complete isolation as before. This time no voices, no cheering crowds, no hanging bodies. This time a bolt of lightning appeared from nowhere and struck the rod held by the man with his arm pointing at the sky. The lightning passed through his arm, his serene head and then transmitted all its energy to the other arm pointing at the ground. He could not recognise the man but there was no doubt about his malignant nature.

"Gino, are you alright? I lost you again."

She interrupted his reverie again.

"Uh, yes. Please ignore me and continue."

Gino understood something was happening. It wasn't just a reverie due to his tiredness or stress. The cards were trying to tell him something. He was shocked but knew that he had to continue to see more of these visions.

"The King of Pentacles. Reversed. This is the challenge. Your challenge," Josepha said stopping for a long time.

Gino looked at the card. A man, fully dressed in a robe embroidered with red grapes, an armour-clad leg exposed, sitting on a black throne. He was holding a sceptre in one hand and the pentacle in the other.

"Ruthless and corrupt, this old man will try to destroy everything in his path," the King said with Josepha's voice.

Yes, Gino had to squint to believe it. The king replaced Josepha in front of him. Instead of a chair, a black throne. Instead of her dress, a robe and a crown. A pentacle was held in his hand. His face was calm and solemn. He was the master of the land, he was the owner of the high castle behind him. He/she continued to talk and said: "I am the King that wields magic. Do not trespass my realm and you will live."

Josepha's lips repossessed her voice. Her familiar face came back to reassure him that it had just been a vision. It wasn't real. Or was it? What was happening?

"It happened again, right?" she asked in a whisper.

Gino nodded in silence.

"I understand," she said. "Anyway, although the King of Pentacles is the challenge that you have to face, be careful. He is sly, deceitful. Don't fight him in his home.

"I continue. The Hermit card is in the obstacle position. It represents withdrawal from the mundane life, introspection, but also treason, dissimulation, corruption, disguise."

Gino waited for the room to get dark again but this time there was light, a lot of light. An old man was holding a lantern that emitted a blinding light. He couldn't see his face because of the light, but even if it wasn't pointed at him, his head was hooded by a robe. It was impossible to recognise him. Gino stepped forward, a hand raised to protect his eyes from the lantern's light. But the more he moved towards the man, the more the man seemed far away.

Josepha brought a glass of water to Gino who was recovering his colour and sat in front of him again. She looked concerned.

"I continue. I understand you are onto something and I won't stop it."

Gino nodded and waited for the next card.

"We are now in the Future position. Here we got the Tower, an unsettling card that brings trouble, and it's reversed! I'm sorry. I don't make the rules."

A dark card was revealed. A yellow tower was standing on top of a rocky island. Lightning hit the top and knocked a giant crown. Flames were erupting out of the windows. Two men were falling from it, horror in their faces.

Gino did not want to see this one. He resisted being sucked into another vision. He tried to focus on Josepha and he grabbed her hand. She smiled at him, and Gino thought that as long as he made eye contact with her and held her hand, nothing would happen. He exhaled all the air he had in his lungs and with it all the tension. He felt empty and light. Very light, like he was floating in the air. And that was happening to Josepha's hair, too. Did she jump into the air and now her hair was rotating, kidnapped by the wind? Was the wind playing with her dress and now showing him her stout legs and a glimpse of her pants? A whirlwind captured them both. They were going down in free fall, the many windows of a tall tower passing by their eyes. Gino looked down but he was unsurprised to see it was the opposite, for it was up. The world was upside down and they were falling *up* the tower.

The slap stang, even several minutes after his awakening.

"I'm sorry but I had to. You were shouting and falling from your chair," Josepha said, holding his face between her calloused hands.

"That's it. The reading finishes here," she said.

"But there is one more card and –"

"Look at you. You can barely stand. Something happened to you while I was reading the cards. What was it?"

Gino breathed out, and with that action he released not only the air from his lungs but all tensions he had accumulated during that tarot session.

"I think... I think I've been visited again," he finally said without looking her in the eyes.

"Do you mean like in Edinburgh?" Josepha asked with a worried tone.

Edinburgh, March 1981. Gino had just started at the RPI. A gateway was opened by accident by a famous Scottish alchemist. Spirits ran havoc. The alchemist's lab was invaded and he managed to seal the door, but not before one single powerful spirit escaped. RPI was alerted and a team of occultists was dispatched to deal with it. Given how young and inexperienced Gino was at the time, he was assigned to a team of more seasoned occultists with the grade of Level 2 apprentice. And yet when he arrived, he was the only one that managed to constrain the fugitive spirit, cast all the spirits back into the gateway and seal it, while the veteran occultists were confined in an anti-cosmic field created by the presence. How that happened was explained two days later during a hearing of a RPI committee. Gino was given a tip the night before by a presence during his sleep. Technically it is called "sleep paralysis". Gino preferred to call it "my night visitation".

Since then, that episode had marked his future career more than his blood links to his father. And that was both reassuring and scary for Gino. He did not want to be considered privileged because he was the son of one of the founders of the RPI. And at the same time, he was worried that a presence of unknown origin had marked him as a conduit. Being an esoteric conduit could be an honour and a curse. You can get access to knowledge forbidden to others, but you are at the mercy of an entity whose goals are unknown.

"I think this reading will finish now. I cannot interpret this spread with the querent in this condition. If there is a chance an entity had visited you while I was reading the cards, that makes this reading void. You weren't yourself and you were very impressionable. Your judgement and my interpretation are corrupt. Don't even think about its inner meanings. I'm sure we will find another time for a new reading. Now, go home."

Gino looked at the cards spread on the table, then he crossed Josepha's fierce eyes and he gave in.

"Right. I need to rest. It has been a very difficult and tiring few days."

"Good," she said with a smile and a pat on his shoulder while she accompanied him at the door.

"Thanks anyway. Good evening Josepha."

"Take care of yourself Gino."

Josepha closed the door behind her back and listened to Gino's steps in the corridor fading away. She exhaled all the air she had in her lungs and closed her eyes in order to relax. Then she dashed to the liquor cabinet, grabbed the best scotch she had, and poured in as much as the glass could take for good measure. She drank it all in one single swallow and for a moment the world became foggy. The cards were still in their position. She couldn't believe that spread. One of the most difficult she had ever done. The interpretation had been difficult. She had the impression that Gino did not even listen to what she said about each card, so much was he caught in his reveries. Or were they visions cast by this entity he was worried about?

In all the negativity and chaos brought in by the cards, at least the last one, the final outcome, was a harbinger of good news. The Two of Cups, with the lovers, man and woman, joining their hands and golden cups in perfect harmony. What could possibly go wrong after that card?

Intermezzo I

Rome, Italy, 12 September 1942. Transcript of Amilcare Marcotti's plenary lecture at the University of Roma La Sapienza.

"If we were to define occultism today, we would be inclined to associate it with Satanism such is the ignorance on the subject among the common people. Satanism has been popularised and mixed up with occultism and esoterism, so the common person associates the two and thinks they are the same. But – and this has to be extremely clear, especially to you first year students – the gods have nothing to do with the occult practice. The laws of occultism do not operate under the guidance of transcendental beings, if any exist at all, by the way. Occultism can operate in both theistic and atheistic universes. So, forget about Yahweh and Satan and their eternal struggle. If you are interested in them, the Faculty of Theology is next door.

"Occultism predates religion, let alone organised religion, and it will exist even when all religions and their gods are gone.

"Occultism's opposite is not religion, then. Occultism's opposite is Science. And, in particular, Modern Science; I had to make this distinction to avoid offending the alchemists present in this room, that as we all know are the first true scientists.

Modern scientists need to measure a phenomenon in order to explain it. For a scientist, if you can't measure it, even by proxy, that phenomenon doesn't exist. For an occultist, the knowledge does not come from measurement, but from previously acquired hidden knowledge.

"Hidden. You will hear this word many times during your studies here. In fact, *occult* means hidden or latent. I rather prefer the latter though. Because any person that ever walked the Earth can access this occult knowledge. As a matter of fact, we contain two minds: one rational, very recent in the evolutionary process and which makes us stand out from the other animals, and one that I like to call post-cognitive. The rational mind helps you in making this desk or this pen. Nothing is wrong with it. We wouldn't be human without it. But what makes us truly special is the balance between these two minds. The last centuries have brought the calamity of Modern Science onto humanity, favouring one at the expense of the other. Cutting out whole areas of perception, narrowing you down to causality and suppressing our occult powers.

"So, all of us can access these powers, but we use them so seldom that we are hardly aware of their existence. That's why you are here. To be awakened. To be able to access these powers by an act of will, so then you will be able to master magic and see the difference between coincidences and synchronicities. Where scientists see probability of chance, we see meaningful connections. And when they fail to see these connections, they simply say 'it's inexplicable, therefore it doesn't exist/happen'.

"Events have meaning and meaning emerges from events. The cosmos, Nature, the gods, The God – call it whatever you like – is talking all the time. But our limited perception prevents us from sensing this communication. It's shouting at us and the scientists are simply playing the three monkeys – can't see, can't hear, can't speak.

"There is correspondence between events and object and living beings. Links that we occultists can see. We just need the right devices to act as a bridge between this correspondence and our perception.

"The inexplicable is pure horror for the scientist. For the occultist, it is their bread and butter. We don't aim at explaining because the cosmos cannot be explained. We can, however, understand how to use some of its powers. Through magic, way older than any theory, hypothesis, experimental process.

"We don't indulge ourselves in cosmology but in cosmography. We don't study the cosmos, we draw it on our inner blackboards. Scientists think they can harness its secrets, but how can you train a horse for riding when you only see its head?

"Both scientists and occultists are sceptics, they just question different things. Scientists question anything that cannot be proved or experimented with. Occultists question anything that can be proved. Why, you might ask yourself. Because the scientists can only prove what they can see, the finite world linked to their five senses, but they are blind to the other worlds and to the invisible threads that link them.

"But, young students, the subject of our study is just a part of the equation, for the observer and summoner has an equal importance in the study itself. It doesn't matter how moody or morally degenerate a scientist is when they point their telescope at the stars. It does make a difference for the occultist, though, for they affect the subject of their study.

"'But this is Heisenberg's uncertainty principle,' you would say. Well, if a scientist shines a light on a particle, yes, that particle might change spin or momentum, but it will never, under any circumstances, try to devour the scientist.

"Yes, yes. You are all laughing now, but look: if an occultist makes a mistake during an incantation, the consequences can be dire. Portal creation is especially susceptible to the summoner's intonation, choice of words and even character. As Éliphas Lévi said in his History of Magic: *'The operations of magic science are not devoid of danger. Their result may be madness for those who are not established on the base of the supreme, absolute, and infallible reason. They may over-excite the nervous system, producing terrible and incurable diseases. Let those, therefore, who seek in magic the means to satisfy their passions, pause in that deadly path, where they will find nothing but death or madness. This is the significance of the vulgar tradition that the devil finished sooner or later by strangling the sorcerers.'*

"What I'm trying to say here is that you will not only be awakened and trained on how to access these hidden powers, you will also be trained on how to have total control of your temperament, character, and ultimately of your most hidden motives. Then, the final test in year five will reveal your real motives. Will you be ready to control the darkness you are harbouring inside?"

Cosmic visitations

"Darkness," Carter said, two days after their first meeting five years earlier.

He said this when leaning on a desk in the institute's library. Both palms down, holding all his weight on them, he was towering over a surprised Gino who was sitting on a chair consulting an ancient dusty tome. Gino tilted his head like his dog used to do when he heard a new sound. Dog that now was lying next to him on the cool floor. Gino said it was a dog-wolf hybrid; however, Carter barely saw any resemblance to a wolf. More to a jackal, perhaps; an old and gaunt jackal. Ribs were carving his heaving chest, eyes cloudy from cataracts, grey fur giving in to bald patches. There was a chance it looked more like a wolf in his younger years, but today it had lost all of its ferocity and pride.

"Darkness. It's the answer to the riddle, your riddle. 'When you have me more, you can see only less. Who am I?'"

Gino's smile appeared on an otherwise serious and severe face. He slapped his thigh and Garibaldi jumped in surprise. Someone two desks to the left jerked his body to that loud clap.

"Carter, you don't fail to amaze me. It took you only a few days to unlock my riddle. Well done! This is a clear sign that we are meant to be together as partners. Have you ever heard of acausal synchronicity?"

Now, five years since that day, Gino reminded him again of that moment. Same library, same dog next to him – albeit much older – same expression, same hand holding his little red horn pendant against the evil eye. And same talk about synchronicity.

"It happened again, Carter. Synchronicity is all over me again."

Carter sat down, predicting a long explanation from his colleague.

"Josepha read the cards to me and the spread was almost entirely made of major arcana. Each card she lifted gave me a hallucination," Gino said still shocked.

"Hallucination?"

Gino went on to explain what he saw during the cards' reading in great detail, probably more for his own benefit, so he could remember them than for Carter's.

"I've been visited. Again," he finished saying.

Carter's eyebrows rose to *this-man-is-crazy* level. Earlier he'd called them hallucinations, using a medical term that had an unequivocal scientific explanation. But then he claimed they were due to something of a metaphysical nature that visited him. It wasn't the first time Carter had heard that story. Gino's twenty-year career at the RPI was dotted with such visitations. Very highly concentrated, apparently random events, that led to him solving all the most difficult cases. Synchronicities increased to such levels that in Gino's mind it was like the eureka moments in some crime stories, when the investigator looking at the hanging map dotted with photos, pins and text evidence solves the case at last. He never gave credit to himself and his magic skills, but to some external force of vague origin.

He could not talk for the other employees – and how could he, given that he was one of the few non-occultists? – but he had the suspicion that Gino tried to justify his powers through the use of an idealised entity just to hide what he had inherited from his father. All of this was clearly unconscious, and Gino would never admit that his father was a heavy presence on his life, more now that he was gone than before, when he was alive. Some burdens stay with us forever.

"So, what now?"

"More things will happen, I have to be more receptive and observant and perhaps we will find the crux of the matter."

"Can I ask you something?"

"Sure, shoot."

"Five years ago, we were here in the same place, same desk, same positions relative to each other, and I revealed the answer to your riddle."

"Yes, true!" Gino suddenly replied with a bubbly expression, pretty rare in his face. "I can't believe five years have already passed."

"I didn't ask you at the time, but why did you come up with that riddle for me, and why was it so important for you? And most importantly, if that was a test, what would have happened if I had failed?"

Carter did not realise it immediately, given that he was distracted by some colleagues who entered the main hall of the library chatting aloud, but after he landed his final question Gino's face became a mask of grimness and austerity. He saw that only when the lights flickered for a millisecond and Garibaldi whined underneath the desk. Carter's heart pumped up immediately and he felt a sudden fear. Something dark had appeared on Gino's face, and dark shapes peopled the air around him.

He thought of stepping back and get out of the library, but instead his feet seemed to be glued to the floor. There was a battle happening between his will and Gino's will, or whatever had taken control of him. Their minds wrestled for seconds that felt like hours. Carter could not explain what was happening and he asked himself many times *why*.

"Darkness is not simply the absence of light. Some shadows are not cast by anything."

Carter heard those words in his chest more than in his ears.

"An occultist ought to master the darkness within, otherwise they will be consumed."

What does all of it have to do with me and with that stupid riddle? Carter asked himself, feeling the leash he had been bound to loosen.

"And yes, it was a test. I wouldn't have taken you under my wing otherwise."

Carter managed to get free and all he did was walk backwards like a scared prawn does in front of a predator. He was free from the Gino's gaze, he was liberated by the bond of that spell and his eyes naturally dropped to Garibaldi, who was now well in sight under the desk. He looked different. He looked like a wolf, a real wolf. Forget the foggy eyes; now he had obsidian dots so profound that they seemed like the churning surface of inkwells.

He had doubted for so many years, so many times, but now he knew it. And he felt the urge to say 'sorry, I didn't believe' to a non-descriptive entity he has never seen or heard, whether it was a god, the universe, or the darkness itself. All he wanted was to go back home and sleep inside Lizzy's arms and sob it all out. Because now he believed what Gino had said so many times: that he had been visited. That he was possessed by an entity.

Kosher food

There had been a time when the institute canteen was one of the most interesting and vibrant environments of the RPI, perhaps even more than the library, given that there were no librarians shushing you for your loud voice.

Mondays were particularly chaotic. It usually contained twice as many people than during the rest of the week and no one knew exactly why this was the case.

Gino was queueing up, followed by Carter, holding his tray mid-air, waiting for the three other colleagues before him to finish being served. Food wasn't great but today they didn't want to go to the cafeteria across the road. The fact that it was pouring outside didn't help, too. And so, he had to wait there, every second more likely to be approached by a colleague who he did not want to meet or talk to. During those dull waiting moments, he liked to focus his attention on the details of the environment. There wasn't much to look at in the canteen apart from the three black-and-white photos hanging on the wall behind the serving benches. The middle, bigger one depicted the founders and the first adepts of the Hermetic Order of the Golden Dawn, the Victorian secret society that flourished in Great Britain for so many years. It showed the poet W. B. Yeats, meaning that it was taken after 1890 for sure.

He recognised the founders Woodman, Westcott and Mathers. There were others dressed in Victorian clothes, whom he did not recognise.

The smaller photo on the right showed Madame Blavatsky at the inauguration of the London Lodge of the British Section of the Theosophical Society, circa 1870. She was wearing her renowned shawl between two men wearing dark clothes typical of the Victorian age.

The smaller photo on the left showed a more recent image from the 1910s, with Aleisteir Crowley in the middle of a small group of magicians. His intense eyes piercing the viewer no matter from where they were watching the photo. Below it read, *BRITISH O. T. O.*: the British section of the Ordo Templi Orienti.

The idea behind hanging these particular photos in this public space was that they all represented the roots of the RPI. The Royal Paranormal Institute came from the experience of these three occult societies and so it could claim a continuity with more ancient societies and practices that went back to Ancient Egypt, and probably beyond.

Gino knew this, and yet he thought there was something else that linked the three photos, not only to the RPI but to each other. He could not understand what, though. It wasn't the black and white filigrane, neither the almost possessed looks of their depicted people. Similar to other older portraits he saw hanging in the main lobby, his intuition told him there was something more than mere photons hitting the exposed chemically coated sheet.

His thoughts were stopped when he received his plate full of food from the server. He then moved mechanically along the bench, reached the till, and paid and waited for Carter at the table. It took a while for Carter to find him, given the crowd of people. Gino hated the canteen on Mondays for that reason. Too crammed, too noisy, too many people that he did not want to meet and talk to. Like Sadir, the necromancer, who was now approaching the table where Carter and Gino were sitting.

"Good morning, all," Sadir said sitting just in front of Gino and placing his tray on the table very carefully, to avoid its contents from falling over.

Sadir Hussein was a tall and lean man who towered over them all. Probably the tallest of the institute. His height, together with his lean figure, made him look like a lamppost. He was the first and only necromancer in the institute. Probably close to being the last one, too, given the new laws the British Government recently enacted against necromancy. One thing is to talk to the dead like a medium does, another is to bind the dead and command them to do what you like. There had been some controversy when some necromancers – and Sadir was among them – were tasked by a group of anarchists to contact dead artists, actors and musicians in order to seed chaos. He had a reputation for being very blunt and provocative, like he was going to be in a few seconds.

"How many villages have disappeared today, uh?" Sadir asked with a sneering smile.

"None," Carter said quickly, trying to dismiss that type of conversation.

Lately there had been many critiques against Gino's department, and Gino himself, after all the accidents and the towns' disappearances due to the esoteric triangle that his father built. Everyone – from the séances to the alchemists, from the kabbalists to the astral travellers – thought that all those accidents were bringing unwanted and negative attention towards the RPI and their professions. The esoteric triangle had been officially turned off a few years earlier under pressure from the government. All the RPI employees had given a sigh of relief when the sigils in Chichester and Hastings were broken. However, excitement turned down when the towns continued disappearing without a trace, even after the triangle was shut off. Gino and others thought it was due to the remaining effects of the anti-cosmic field. According to their calculations, the field would eventually disappear, but no one knew when. More towns would vanish at an alarming rate, so quickly that many doubted the RPI's strategy, which consisted of breaking only two of the three sigils. The third one, however, was underneath their feet, and breaking it meant destroying the whole RPI building.

Many of his colleagues had mixed feelings regarding his and his father's work. And yet, it was because of the esoteric triangle and his father's legacy that the RPI existed. Gino was torn inside between keeping a low profile and crying aloud how unfair it was that everyone despised his father; after all, his father's legacy was the very reason they all had a public job.

Sadir seemed one of the most vocal ones, always making jokes in public and openly leaving suggestions on how to fix the Gateway that had been opened by the triangle. It seemed that Carter's reply and his tone worked nicely, and Sadir started eating his lunch in silence. Gino and Carter felt relieved. They couldn't cope with a conversation of that type again during a Monday lunch. Meanwhile, more people joined their table, but Sadir didn't pay attention to them and continued eating with his head bowed to the plate. However, after a few minutes he craned up his head, his face dark, his eyes lost in a remote time and space, and addressed Gino with a grave voice.

"All those churches being burned in Norway. The assassinations. The spread of Satanic rituals among young Heavy Metal musicians. You know what I'm talking about."

Gino closed his eyes and kept his gaze on his plate.

"I heard the news today. A Norwegian MP floated the idea that there is a connection with us. He is accusing Britain of having triggered some sort of infernal portal because of the esoteric triangle."

Gino knew about all the things that were happening in Norway among the Black Metal music community. A new subgenre of Heavy Metal that had exploded in the last few years and seemed to have its roots between Bergen and Oslo. Some people thought it was no coincidence that kids as young as sixteen years old could gather occultist knowledge and use it in order to perform occultist rituals. Bands such as Mayhem, Burzum, Immortal, Darkthrone, Emperor and Satyricon started to appear between

1990 and 1991. The arson attacks on churches –
more than fifty had been burned down so far – and
homicides started in 1992.

"He said this a few days after this young man who
goes under the name of Count Grishnackh (can you
believe it?) was sentenced to twenty-one years in
prison for the arson of several churches. I spoke to
one of them. They are not crazy kids playing with the
dark side of magic because they are bored of their
lives. They have the Knowledge. Where did they get
it from?"

"Correlation is not causation, Sadir," Gino said.

"Now you speak like a scientist? *We* thrive in
correlations," Sadir said, spreading his arms wide to
indicate the whole institute. "It's our bread and
butter."

"Listen, the RPI has no responsibility for what is
happening in Norway at the moment."

"Marcotti, I don't care about those churches. They
can burn the Vatican for all I care. But they are
attracting unwanted attention to us. Some of these
bands are even flirting with National Socialism
symbolism."

"There is no proof these kids got the Knowledge
from someone inside our circle. They are all
probably influenced by films and D&D..."

Sadir dropped his fork and knife, making a loud
clang that made caused Gino to jump a little. He
looked more intensely than before into Gino's eyes.
Then, he leaned his long neck towards him in a
manner that could only be interpreted as a way of
keeping what was going to come out of his mouth
confidential.

"The kiddo I spoke to mentioned there is a leader who has taught them all they needed to know, and that in turn he has learned from an old man wearing a black hat. They call him the Man with the Hat."

"Are you suggesting there are lone wolf occultists who operate outside of the RPI jurisdiction?"

"It appears so. Or one of us inside this building is breaking the rules. I intend to report this to the Chief Magus. I'm sure she will start an internal investigation soon."

"Talking of the devil, here she is." A frail voice stopped their tense chatting.

It was Rabbi Chai Levy, the chief Kabbalist of the third floor. He was a short, round man with unruly hair. He still kept using the kippah, eating kosher and everyone referred to him as the Rabbi, but everyone knew that he was an atheist now, which put him at odds with the whole concept of the Kabbalah. He knew Gino's father very well. He was one of the few who had helped Amilcare Marcotti in setting the sigil that was incorporated in the foundation of that very building.

Everyone turned their head towards where the Rabbi had pointed. They saw Chief Magus Hoffmann walking into the middle of the room. She was wearing her ritual clothes and the triple tiara assigned only to the highest rank of the RPI. She wasn't there to eat – no one ever saw her eating among the lower ranks – but to talk to someone. She looked very different from the last time Gino had met her. Less ancient and less emaciated. She probably wanted to project a different image in front of the public.

Gino looked at the Rabbi and their eyes met for a millisecond. Gino hoped he saw in his eyes how thankful he was for having interrupted Sadir.

"That's the finance secretary. I heard the Home Office wants to grant extra funds for the RPI this year. Isn't it wonderful?" the Rabbi said, claiming all the table's attention to him. "Perhaps they will invest more money in this canteen. The kosher food is fucking rubbish!"

Mulder & Scully

"Do you believe what Sadir said?" Carter asked while turning the car's engine on.

Gino had just come back from the café bringing coffee and biscuits.

"About the Black Metal scene being an unwanted consequence of the Gateway that we tried to open?"

Gino sipped his coffee very slowly and said nothing for almost a minute, his mind focused on what Carter had just asked. There was no doubt there had been an acceleration in the events connected with the occult over the last few years. Since the esoteric triangle was activated the world had witnessed the disappearance of many Sussex villages; the rise of an obscure but now very popular subgenre of Heavy Metal from nowhere called Black Metal, that openly used occultism and Satanism, linked to the burning of churches in Norway and brutal homicides; the rise in popularity of TV shows classified as supernatural fiction or occult detective fiction, such as *The X-Files* and *Twin Peaks*; the killing of the actor Brandon Lee on the set of *The Crow*, a film about a man seeking revenge for his girlfriend after his death. And the list could go on and on.

"Why are you asking?"

"Oh, it just made me think. Quite a lot, actually. I joined the RPI five years ago and I barely knew what occultism was. Now, it's so popular I can talk with my wife about it and she might come up with a reference to *The X-Files* or Satanists burning churches in Norway. I mean, it's everywhere. Even if there wasn't a connection, it's definitely giving us unwanted attention."

"It's difficult to say. I wouldn't read too much into it."

Then Carter, instead of driving off after that dismissing sentence, pressed on. He reached onto the back seat and produced a copy of the *Daily Mail*. On the front page there was news of a man who had killed himself back in April.

"Have you seen this?" Carter asked, pointing at the photo of a blond man who looked like Jesus.

"No, what is it?"

"This is Kurt Cobain. He killed himself with a shotgun to the head."

Gino didn't react to that news. Carter understood he did not know who he was.

"Ah, he's... he was the singer of Nirvana, the most popular rock band on the planet. They are on the radio and on MTV constantly. You must have heard their songs from time to time."

"Maybe. But what does this have to do with our conversation?"

"Well, I was overhearing someone at the institute saying that he might have killed himself during a Satanic ritual; some of these Black Metal musicians killed themselves in the same way. He also left a note saying, 'It's better to burn than to fade away', which I found enigmatic enough, so I thought it could be connected to what is happening around the world as of late."

"These kids make constant use of drugs. Their behaviour might resemble the rituals and goals of occultism, but they are not the same things. I wouldn't worry too much. Let's move on."

Gino's last words were a command. Carter put it into gear and started to drive without saying a word. Gino thought of that particular case as just a coincidence – although he knew he shouldn't disregard these facts as coincidences – and yet Sadir's words resonated with him for days to come. Was there a connection? Something that he'd failed to see so far? How could this revival in all things occult have happened so quickly, in so many places in the world, and yet without any connection to what the RPI had been doing for the past few decades?

The words of the Chief Magus started to play in his head: "Things are happening around the world that are connected in ways I still do not understand. We are looking at the wrong places."

Even at the RPI everyone felt this revival. Although many considered this pop culture approach to occultism infantile and superficial, some of his colleagues used to divide themselves between *The X-Files* and *Twin Peaks* fans. *Twin Peaks* had become a Friday favourite of the afterwork cineclub. Below the veneer of weird fiction there was no doubt there were true occult themes. The Black and the White Lodges, spiritism, the esoteric symbolism, etc. *Fire Walk With Me* was acclaimed as the best film in the history of the cineclub. *The X-Files* had caused a sensation in the US a year ago and the cineclub managed to get some pirated VHS copies from the States before it was due to be aired in the UK this year. According to many it wasn't as good as *Twin Peaks*, more like a vulgarisation of many of the themes of the other show. Gino did watch some episodes of *The X-Files* and found it dull, although he had to admit that some parts of the plot were fascinating and resonated with his most occultist side. There were jokes running in the corridors that he was the new Agent Fox Mulder from *The X-Files*. He hoped Carter didn't hear them, because that would make him Agent Dana Scully.

He was so immersed in these thoughts that when the car stopped and Carter asked him if he had any change, he startled. They were already at the hospital car park.

***

There was no one guarding Matt's room. The corridors were mostly devoid of nurses and doctors, except for a nurse cleaning a room a few doors away. Gino gave a sigh of relief. It meant he didn't have to invent stupid stories for once. He left Carter at the door of the ward. He was the one who distracted the ward receptionist while Gino sneaked in undetected. He instructed him to stop anyone from entering. If disturbed, astral projection could have terrible consequences for the projector. He didn't want to get lost in between different planes of existence.

Matt was asleep in his bed. He was alone, the other bed still empty. Instead of a person there were a huge teddy bear – *Who would buy a teddy bear for an adult man?* Gino thought – and two bouquets of flowers with assorted Get Well Soon cards. He sat

110

next to him without making any noise and carefully hovered his hands over Matt's head without touching it. He did not know what he expected to find, really. The Tarot reading from Josepha had left him confused and he did not know if the visitations' visions were part of the reading or made it void.

First, he accessed the man's memories. The stygian cave, the stone pillar, his shaking body, the freezing cold. Exactly as he saw it last time. Then he used that memory as a conduit for his projection. Detaching himself from his body was always an exhilarating experience. It was like getting out of a dirty husk, cleaning oneself of mud. It usually involved him floating away for a certain distance but not too far. This time it was more like teleportation. His astral projection was catapulted inside Matt's memories in less than a millisecond. He was now floating in the dark cave. He went around the pillar trying to find the same spot where he saw his father last time. He remembered it was close to a specific rock with a good quantity of fluorescent crystals. He stayed there for a few minutes, listening to whatever and whoever was in the cave. He noticed an opening at the bottom of the pit that could lead to a tunnel. It was probably the main entrance to the cave. He decided to investigate that next.

Every now and then he could hear the moans and howling of Matt. He focused his listening away from those sounds. Then, he tried to cancel the whitenoise of the dripping water from high above. He waited and waited, and he found it very strange that this time no demonic presence nor his father approached him. Last time it had been a matter of seconds before the manifestations saw him and started to watch every single move he made. His father's projection appeared soon after, but this time things were different. The cave seemed empty. He floated to a lower level and had a peek at Matt's body, slithering on the jagged rocks. Poor man. He could barely see him save for the fluorescent dim light from the distant crystal. He lost sight of him after he went behind a higher rock. A rock that now was moving towards him.

What was going on?

Little by little, he realised that the 'rock' was of a human shape. The outline of a man that juxtaposed between him and Matt was walking on the obsidian pavement towards him. He froze, realising he was going to meet with his father again, or at least with his astral form. However, the more time passed and the closer his father was to him, the more he felt something was wrong. His frame didn't look like his father's, it didn't look like an astral projection at all, for that matter. He – because it was undoubtedly a man – wore a hat and what looked like a dark, thick overcoat. His steps didn't make any sound and used a walking stick. He was now less than a few metres away. Matt's howling increased in intensity and for a moment Gino saw a glimpse of his figure running behind the pillar. His instinct was telling him to fly away and go back to his body, but he could not bring himself to do it.

What is going on? Gino asked himself again.

The howling morphed into shrieking when the man with the hat showed his face and said:

"I was waiting for you. Why did it take you so long?"

***

Carter was surprised to see Emma alongside the two other police constables and the nurses that rammed into the room.

For the past ten minutes he had been holding a screaming and bleeding Gino, uninterruptedly. The nurses came in first. One tended to Matt while he was under a sort of a seizure attack; the other one helped Carter with Gino. He had lost a lot of blood from his nostrils and his eyes.

From his eyes!

He had never seen him losing blood from anywhere else other than the nose before.

Then, he heard the police behind him. One put a hand on his shoulder until one of the nurses told him off. The other one was standing, calling someone through the radio. Five minutes later Emma's voice took his attention away from Gino's screaming for the first time. He turned to look at her. She must have stayed in the building all this time, possibly waiting for them to get in undisturbed. Was it a setup?

"What happened?" she asked with a worried face.

Carter didn't want to reply. What should have he said? "Oh, yes, we just walked in without any permission and penetrated your colleague's memories so that my partner could see his father trapped in another plane of existence"?

That wouldn't have worked well, wouldn't it? And almost as if Emma understood it, she didn't ask again and focused her attention solely onto Matt, whose arms and legs were jerking uncontrollably. She helped the nurse in restraining him onto the bed. A doctor got in and the two policemen left the room. He brought syringes with him that he immediately gave to the nurses. One for Matt and one for Gino. They both relaxed after a minute. Gino was taken to another room using a stretcher.

"We are going to take care of him now," the nurse said to Carter.

Emma gave Carter the time to come up with an excuse while he was taking a coffee in the waiting area. But he had none, so he didn't know what to say. He looked at his hands, which still had some streaks of red. He realised his jeans had been stained, too.

"Oh, crap," he said, thinking more about what Lizzy would say than worrying about the stains per se.

"Cold water and *poof*, they are gone," she said.

Here we go. What do I say now? Carter thought.

Emma sat next to him holding a cup of coffee. The other two police constables were not to be seen, probably instructed to guard Matt and Gino's rooms for now.

"Look. Both you and I come from the same background. Neither of us will ever understand what these occult boffins, or whatever you want to call them, do. But I thought there was an understanding between us that from now on we would collaborate. This is not respectful. I mean, it's one thing to interrogate a colleague, another to sneak in in the middle of the night and cast some sort of spell..."

"It wasn't a spell."

"What was it, then?"

"Your colleague, Matt, has witnessed something that we have never encountered before and that could be the key to stopping the villages from disappearing."

"And the only way was to trigger a seizure in him?"

"Obviously, something went wrong. For both of them, as you saw. Gino probably had the worst."

"Well, we will see when they both wake up. If they wake up."

Carter stood and took a cup of water from the water dispenser.

"Just to let you know that Abbot has been informed."

"Of course."

"But we can still keep this conversation confidential, between you and me, you know. I don't care about the formalities, I just want to know what happened to my friend Matt. That's all."

Given the circumstances, Carter decided to open up.

"It appears that he has been kept inside another plane of existence for seven years. I know that it sounds crazy because we saw him standing there for a few minutes only, but... Look, I'm just the muscle here..."

He paused and pointed his finger to the corridor where Gino's room was supposed to be.

"...but he is the mind and he can give you more details about what's going on. It's about what we call astral projection. You can detach yourself from your body and float somewhere else, basically. And this is what happened to your friend and what happened to Gino tonight."

Emma stayed silent, listening.

"Believe it or not," he added.

"I'm trying to believe you. But... but it's difficult," she said.

"That well in Hartesbridge is a door to that plane. Gino wanted to go there again and study it."

"Study it?"

"I guess he meant he wanted to get in it."

"But he will end up in the same situation as Matt."

"No. He thinks he can trick the system with the use of sigils. The ones that saved us last time."

He lifted his shirt, although not enough to show the scar, but she knew what had happened.

"Abbot will never let you close to that well again."

"Tell Gino and see how he reacts."

***

Gino had been awake for the past two hours already. Carter was sitting next to him drinking the third coffee of that early morning. He needed the coffee to cope with all the things Gino had been saying since he woke up. He spoke of the cave, of Matt shivering on the floor, of a man with a hat and a walking stick who spoke to him and managed to hold on to him in a psychic way. Hence the screaming and the additional blood from his eyes? Maybe. Gino could not explain his reaction either. Neither he could explain why Matt started to have seizures.

"Did you see your father then?" Carter asked almost in a whisper.

"No."

"Sorry to hear this."

"I was hoping to, though. This time it was very different. I was expecting it to play the same. Being a memory, I thought it would simply repeat itself. Like in a film, right? It's like fast-forwarding a VHS. But it wasn't a real memory. It wasn't like a VHS. I was there, for real."

"What do you mean?"

"I travelled in space – well a mnemonic space at least – and in time."

Carter looked puzzled and sipped more coffee. It was going to become crazier, then?

"I was there when Matt was in the cave for real. It means that I witnessed the event, not a memory of the event in Matt's mind."

"What are the implications of this? In layman's terms, please."

"It means that that man with the hat was not a memory, a passive replaying of the VHS in Matt's head. He really saw me and he was expecting me."

"What do you want to do, then? I can already tell you that Abbot has been informed and Emma is furious. They are not going to get us close to that well again."

"No worries. I don't want to go to see the Well, at least not just yet. I need to talk to Sadir first."

PART II

Hideous Wolves

The necromancer

Sadir was sitting on his chair, smoking a pipe. With his oblong head, pointy black goatee under a generous chin, and his dark and penetrating eyes he did look like a villain character from an eighties fantasy film or a D&D manual cover. Sadir the Sorcerer.

Behind his tall and impressive figure two vintage anatomical posters were hanging: the one on the left had a full human skeleton standing and the left hand up; and the one on the right a full human body with all the muscles and tendons exposed like in a Leonardo da Vinci anatomical study. This had the right hand up instead. A grim reminder that necromancers used to dig out corpses in cemeteries to reanimate them. Gino knew of a Spanish one, also known as El Reanimador, who had been arrested during Franco's last years in government. He had managed to desecrate several tombs in the Balearic Islands until one day they escaped his house – or wherever he was keeping the bodies in – and ran amok on the beach of a resort. It didn't end up well for him. The authorities arrested him and passed a law that prohibited necromancy.

Sadir was different, though. Very discreet, and from what Gino knew he always asked for permission from relatives and authorities. Scotland Yard was particularly interested in his faculties given the staggering number of unresolved cases that could only be solved post-mortem. He was also sought for archaeological studies, given that he started his career in the Archaeological Museum in Cairo, communicating with ancient mummies. In that position he had managed to get so much information for occultists and black magic practitioners that the RPI contacted him eventually and offered him his current position. No more mummies in London, but every now and then the occasional murder where he helped the police trace who the killer was. These were services that paid extra, of course, outside of the RPI's time.

Sadir was now looking at Gino with suspicious eyes. Since the first day he saw him – a young and arrogant brat next to his father when he was still alive, but a few days before he passed away during an official ceremony – he took an instant dislike to him. And the feeling was mutual. Gino was not very fond of him. He even suspected him to be the King of Pentacles from Josepha's card reading. But he discarded that thought when he saw how arrogant he was. That King was regal and confident. Both of them were trying to keep their distance, even though they were forced to stay in the same room and had to interact.

"What can I do for you, Marcotti?" he asked briskly.

"The other day at the canteen you casually mentioned that one of your clients linked to the Black Metal scene had a man with a hat and walking stick as a mentor. Can you tell me a bit more about this?"

Sadir leaned back in his chair, relaxing his muscles. He passed his finger down his well-curated beard, his typical body language when he was trying to focus his attention on something unexpected. Like that question. *That* was truly unexpected. Why was Gino Marcotti, the person who was the most against the connection between the esoteric triangle and the Black Metal scene, now so interested in it? He had guts, Sadir had to admit, to show up in his office.

"This kid, my client, wanted to add a bit of spice, so to speak, to his lyrics and music, and asked me to get in touch with Aleister Crowley. These kids. Can you believe it? They always want to speak with him. I mean, we have much better occultists here at the RPI than Crowley.

"Anyway, I prepared the ritual, and while I did this he pointed at various tools and rites. He knew quite a lot about our practices. I asked him how come and he said the Magus taught him all he knew about occultism."

"The man with the hat?"

"Not exactly. He went on to describe a man who acted as a mentor for the Black Metal community. You know, he goes around and teaches these kids all about what is needed to summon demons or practise black magic. Or at least, this is what he told him. I doubt they can summon a single familiar or make contact with other planes' entities. Anyway, he talks and talks and brags about his capabilities and those of his Magus. Then, I asked him which occult society or school he belongs to. And he said none. I replied this is impossible, there are no solitaire occultists, we all claim our lineage from a society or school. He insisted he didn't belong to any, and then he told me 'in all confidentiality' that the Magus got all his occult knowledge from a mysterious man with a hat and a walking stick that taught him everything in his cave for a hundred years or more."

"A cave, huh?"

"Yes, but this is not the weirdest part. The most bizarre bit was what he said next. He said that a hundred years in this cave were like hours in our world. He was sitting on a rocking chair in his grandma's house, his spirit flew away from the world, and he was welcomed by this man who taught him everything there was to know about occultism."

"Astral travelling to another plane."

Sadir nodded.

"This kid wasn't lying. No drugs or alcohol. Straight mind, no psychiatric issues. I think what he said is true. We have a new occultist on the loose who received knowledge straight from the source, bypassing any school or society here on Earth."

"That's interesting. Thanks for these details."

"But it's not over, Marcotti. There is more."

"Okay, go on."

"After my chat with Crowley – Aleister and I are becoming friends, you know, with all these monthly summonings – this kid was very excited. It was his first connection, at least through a necromancer, with the dead, and a famous one indeed. He went very hyper and was more talkative than ever. He said many things I did not pay attention to and others I could not remember, but one impressed me especially. He said that this mysterious man lives on the disappearances of the villages. *'Each village that*

124

disappears is feeding His powers so that He will return,' he said."

Gino's eyes popped out of their sockets and he didn't even try to hide it. Sadir noticed and understood how important this conversation and all these details were for him.

"Where can I find this kid?" Gino asked.

Sadir reached out into a drawer and handed over a flyer to him for a concert in London in a few days. It was an A4 sheet with some black-and-white homemade graphics. The name of the band was an intricate jungle of vertical lines that made up the shape of a bat, or perhaps a raven. It was impossible to decipher, and it looked more like a ritual sigil than a band name. Sadir giggled, and after a pause said:

"Be my guest. If you can decipher the name of the band."

Trve Metal

"Gino, I think we are going to be out of place here. Extremely out of place," Carter shouted while paying at the ticket booth.

The overweight goth girl at the till smirked at them, then closed the plexiglass booth and laughed aloud with her colleague. Both had black lipstick, white paint on their faces, several piercings and metal band T-shirts with obscure logos.

The music was so loud now that he had difficulty hearing even his own voice, so he leaned down to Gino's ear.

"There is no way we are going to blend in here. We are like nuns at a striptease club. We stand out as wrong."

"Why are you so worried about being a nun at a striptease?"

"I have to think about our safety. It's my job."

"Then do it. It won't take long. The concert is almost over, we will stand in the back of the crowd, then we will talk to our friends."

The building was just a disused industrial compound on the east side of Camden. Medium-size exposed brickwork with occasional rusted wrought-iron pillars and concrete floor. They walked away from the ticket booth through a lobby where, next to a ridiculously small shop for merch and CDs, there was a huge black curtain. Every now and then, men and women dressed in black with leather studded jackets came out through there, either to go to the toilets or to smoke outside in the open. All, without a single exception, looked at them like they were looking at a nun in a striptease club.

Gino showed the ticket to the mountain of a bouncer who was standing in front of the curtain. He had a long look at the ticket and nodded before opening the curtain to let them in. Inside the gig was extremely small, a hundred people at most. All crowded at the centre, jumping, arms up with their hands making the horn sign. During the heaviest riffs many were headbanging, hair mills cutting the thick and rancid air filled with sweat and beer. The stage was short and looked improvised. The singer at the centre was shrieking and howling, his head pulled back like a wolf baying at the moon. The guitarist and bassist slightly back but already outside of the only cone of light, which was shining on top of the stage. You could barely see the drummer at the back, underneath the white name of the band printed on a black banner. An intricate forest of deformed letters impossible to decipher. It was all pitch black on the stage save for the white corpsepaint on the musicians' faces. An allegory of death, pain and evil.

The guitars were high-pitched and the drumming was... well, they had never heard drums so fast and loud in their life. It was a feast of cacophony and distortion of instrumental melody and of the human voice. Carter could not believe a man could shriek and scream to such a high pitch without destroying his vocal cords. The crowd was unaffected by the physical pain he heard in his ears. On the contrary they were relishing in it, captivated in a sort of trance. It was a single organism that moved in synch, like a school of fish swimming in random directions to avoid a predator. He felt out of place there, a heathen surrounded by a cult. He felt the physical urge to reject the cacophony that was massacring his ears. He had a quick look at Gino, who looked unaffected, before leaving the gig.

Fuck Gino, he thought, dashing through the black curtain in search of fresh air.

Gino didn't realise what had happened to Carter and continued watching the show. He found it all incredibly fascinating. He had listened to Heavy Metal before and someone had told him about Black Metal culture, but he had never deepened in his curiosity. He always dismissed it as a joke. A ridiculous joke. Yes, it was confusing and repulsive at first, and yet after a while he could see a pattern. Not in the music per se, although he managed to synch his inner ear a bit to the cacophony, but in what that whole culture was about. The music was barely a tool of communication. Something was going deeper here. Only later, after the concert was over and his ears were still ringing for hours on end, something would click in his mind: this is what occultism would look like to bored kids without any gnostic knowledge. This is primitive occultism, the one that European pagan ancestors would practise in the cold forests before civilization had even risen in Mesopotamia.

These are lost children without an occult guide or misguided by a mischievous occultist. Look at their search for a lost aesthetic and language. The logos of

128

the bands look like a sigil. This is a cult reserved for the initiated. They don't want us to understand, they don't want us to be here, they want the world out of their business. It's a mystical society like the Eleusian mysteries. They want to summon demonic creatures, but they use the Judeo-Christian pantheon and symbolism, thinking the summoning of the Christian Satan would really work. They are the by-product of a post-Christian society, so they behave like former Christians, thinking that being anti-Christian would be enough to master the occult.

It was during these thoughts that he felt the hand of Carter on his shoulder. He was telling him to wake from his daydreaming because the concert was over. The lights were on, the band was collecting their instruments. The crowd was exiting the venue like a dollop of black ink just spilled over a desk. Gino and Carter, the only ones not wearing black, metal studs or nails or corpse-paint, were still standing at the centre of this human blob in motion. They waited until most of the people had left. The floor was littered with beer cans, cigarette' butts, liquid and food stains. They had to cross that sea of rubbish to reach the stage with their ears still throbbing. Carter opened his mouth several times to apply pressure to his eardrums, and was amazed by the lack of complaining from Gino. Actually, it looked like he really enjoyed it.

"New fans?" said the singer while he was storing away the microphone boom.

He looked very different now that the lights were on. He didn't have the same evil aura, that demonic presence that made him so fearful on the stage. His band members were starting to remove the make up from their faces, exposing the real people they were underneath. Just normal kids who had an extravagant carnivalesque moment in which the real world was suspended.

"You could say that," Gino said with a smile.

The guy stopped, probably not expecting those words and that smile.

"Are you police?"

"No, but would it make any difference?"

"No, we are just making music and enjoying ourselves. If you want to buy our tapes and T-shirts there is a –"

"No, we are not interested in that. I would just like to exchange a few words between peers."

"Peers?" the singer laughed.

"Aren't you too old to appreciate Black Metal? Or are you one of those AC/DC fans, therefore you think you listen to the same music as us?"

The other members laughed. The bassist spat on the floor, nearly hitting the drummer's shoes, who expressed his dislike with a shout.

Gino didn't react to any of that. Silence followed, only broken by the people behind, collecting the rubbish; then his voice cut the silence: "Where did you learn the art of the occult?"

The singer's eyes pierced Gino. He dropped the microphone on its case and stood up, his chin well above his shoulder line.

"Satan taught me."

"Satan is just a symbol invented by the monotheistic religions to make sense of the occult reality. Just infantile diabolism."

"Don't you dare talking of His Infernal Majesty like that, grandpa."

And then, turning to his friends with a jump and laughing like a clown, he opened his mouth in surprise and came up with: "He is a fucking priest!"

He jumped off the stage and faced Gino, a few centimetres away from his nose.

"Get the fuck out," he said, grinning.

Carter had to intervene and pulled him by holding his shoulder. The singer tried to disengage, but Carter's grip didn't let go. Things got out of hand pretty quickly. The other three musicians jumped off the stage, and the singer swung his arm, trying to hit Carter's face.

Gino stepped back, realising the situation had degenerated and blows were going to fly in his direction soon. He saw the singer's reaction and he immediately understood what was going to happen. He saw something in Carter's face change. Something clicked and he morphed from a gentle giant to a deadly fighter. After the singer's punch missed his face, he immediately sprang forward with his left arm and his knuckles landed in the guy's face. He knocked him out, his whole body pulled down by gravity. The drummer, the bulkier of them, tried his luck while Carter was not looking, but Carter knew he was coming. Once the singer was knocked out, Carter immediately spun his upper trunk and faced the drummer. Gino saw the young boy hesitate for a moment when he saw Carter setting up his arms like a professional pugilist. A glimpse in his eyes told Gino what was passing through his mind: "I'm fucked."

The drummer went down as easily as the singer; the guitarist took a blow to his neck then slipped on the floor and saved his face from a certain disfiguring. The bassist stepped back until he touched the stage. Then his eyes shone with hope when he saw the bouncer joining the brawl. At that point Gino called Carter's name and Carter's body became rigid. It was like a commanding dog owner at the agility race. Carter knew he had to stop now. But the bouncer didn't have any reason to do it. He saw two strangers beating the shit out of the band members. He had to intervene and stop the brawl. He crossed the venue in a split second with his right arm ready to sink into Carter's face, when he suddenly stopped his charge. The bassist, who until a few seconds earlier had been smiling, thinking that Archie the Wardrobe, as they called him at the venue, was going to save him, now looked surprised. The scene was truly puzzling and he started to shout, "What the fuck are you doing, Archie? Kick his ass!"

But Archie had no intention of listening to that boy. The gun's barrel was halfway out of Carter's holster and was gleaming under the venue's powerful ceiling lights.

Gino stepped in, and with his hands up he showed the RPI badge and said, "We are not police, nor priests. We just wanted to talk but things went south for no reason. We all need to calm down."

Gino doubted they knew what the badge meant and whether they had true authority to ask questions inside a private property.

"As I said earlier, I just want to talk among peers."
And he looked at the bloody face of the singer on the
floor.

***

Abzu's nose was bleeding profusely and was ruining
all the carefully painted makeup on his face. He did,
however, look more wicked with all that caked blood
on his lips, chin and neck. So, Gino thought he should
thank Carter for improving his stage appearance.
Abzu wasn't his real name, obviously. He took his
stage name from a Sumerian god, the lover of Tiamat
who would give him many children, the young gods.
Gods that would in turn kill him. When asked by Gino
why he chose that name, he said, "Together with
Tiamat he represents the embodiment of the
primordial chaos."

They were now inside a small room, used as both
storage and changing room. Abzu was sitting on a
chair with some toilet paper up his nose, Gino next to
him sitting on a box of beers, and Carter standing at
the door. Behind the door was Archie the Wardrobe,
who had been instructed to guard it until they had
finished. The other members of the band were
probably already gone.

"I'm truly sorry for how the things progressed, but
I'm sure you can blame only yourself for the
overreaction," Gino said calmly.

Abzu did not reply and sniffed up the blood that
was still dripping from his nostrils.

"The reason I said we can talk as peers is because
I'm as much of an enthusiast of the occult as you are.

I'm a Gran Maestro at the Royal Paranormal Institute of Greenwich. I'm sure you have heard of it. However, I don't relish summoning demons or what you call Satan, as a revenge against society. I open portals, I interact with them, but I do have control over my powers. Do you understand?"

Abzu nodded.

"Now, I was told that you were in touch with a colleague of mine, a necromancer, and you told him – and I quote – 'each village that disappears is feeding His powers so that He will return'."

Abzu did not reply.

"How old are you? Nineteen? Twenty? Yesterday you were at school sucking your thumb and today you've got the knowledge, albeit partial, for summoning demons. How is this possible?"

"Everything I know is from other bands. Scandinavian bands, mostly Norwegians, where the true Black Metal comes from."

"Have you talked to them, any of them?"

"Not directly, just through newsletters on metal magazines, fanzines, most of us share music through cassettes too. We record on cassettes and send them to each other."

"I don't care about the music. I want to talk about the occultism part."

"I was taught a few things. Tricks, mostly. The lights go off during a ritual. The table rattles when we summon demons. Stuff like this, to scare the other kids. I don't know how it works, I don't even know if it's real. What I know is that it works, most of the time."

"Who taught you this?"

"The same man who said those words."

"Who is he, then?"

"If I told you, I might be in trouble, man. Don't do this to me."

"You might be in trouble if you don't collaborate. Think."

Abzu looked truly worried and he didn't know what to do. More blood came out of his nose and he had to tampon it.

"He calls himself the Magus," he said finally.

"This is what I wanted to hear, kid."

"He said he has visited a place for a hundred years while his body was here on Earth, sitting on a chair in his grandma's house. Nuts. Crazy shit, man."

"Astral projection," Gino said, raising his head to look at Carter in the eyes.

"What? Do you believe in this shit? There are a lot of nutcases in this scene. This isn't even the craziest I've heard. You can't believe this shit, man."

"Where can we find him?"

"These are people who would invent any story to boost their notoriety and appeal to the community and the girls."

"Like you, choosing a Sumerian god's name and using corpse-paint?"

"I'm a small fish in the scene, and although I believe some of the things I sing and preach, ninety per cent of them are just bullshit. It's made-up stuff!"

"Look at me. Do you think I make up stuff? I do know the way of the occult and the dark magic, so save these comments for your school teacher and parents," Gino said, grinding his teeth.

Abzu moved his head back like he hadn't expected that tone of voice from that man.

"Where can we find him?" he asked again.

"He is here in London. He owns a record shop, Inferno Records. Don't tell him it was me, though. I don't want to end up like Euronymous."

***

"Are you the owner?" Gino asked, browsing the LPs and cassettes.

He was the only customer in the shop at that moment, and the long-haired man at the till was all too focused on listening to the loud metal music to hear him. He decided to get closer and wave at him. The man saw him and nodded while chewing gum. Gino repeated the question, and the man's eyes squinted like he was trying to concentrate on the words he'd just heard. Gino saw the rolled weed in an ashtray next to the till.

"No, he's at the back. But how can I help you? We don't sell Ray Charles or The Beatles albums here, though."

Gino didn't react to the provocation and got closer to the counter.

"I'm quite interested in Black Metal, actually, so I think I'm in the right place. And I'd like to talk to the owner, please."

"Sure," the guy said, lifting the wooden counter that separated his little office from the rest of the shop. "Just one minute."

Gino saw him walking at a very fast pace through a back door, and heard a locking sound. He immediately understood what was happening and jumped forward, pushing the door. It was locked from the outside. There was a window that was facing the back of a small alley. The man was running away, and Gino could not chase him. The window was locked too, and it was too small for him to pass through it anyway.

"Carter!" Gino shouted, pointing at the window.

Carter jumped into the shop, his expression surprised. He had just finished his cigarette and hadn't expected this turn of events.

He heard Gino shouting, "He ran away!"

Carter understood what had happened and what was asked of him. He went outside through the main door of the shop and ran around the building, hoping to intercept the man. He scanned the road. There were several cars parked on the road, but none of them was occupied or with the engine on. He must have run all the way to the end of the road. He sprinted, hoping he could reach him in time before the upcoming fork. There was a man walking towards him, but he wasn't his target. He'd had a brief look inside the shop before Gino had gone in, and the man he was looking for was long-black-haired, in his thirties, with a black heavy metal T-shirt with some pentacle-and-goat drawing. He nevertheless had a very good look at the man, just in case his target had had a wig and time to change. The man passed and then it was silence, apart from Carter's rasping breath that filled the road with a sense of tension.

Then, he heard a screeching sound and saw a cheap red moped dashing away from a side alley and almost running over him. It was him, hair in the wind and a fake bullet belt at his waist. Carter didn't think twice and ran behind it until he managed to reach the back handle of the moped. The man must have felt the speed decrease by the jolt, because he immediately accelerated without much success. Then, he felt the moped being pulled to the side and then his head banged on the tarmac. It was only half an hour later that he woke up inside the shop.

"He must have been tipped by that guy, Abzu." he heard the man who had entered the shop saying.

The other man, the one who presumably stopped his moped and dragged him back into the shop, was a two-metre-tall, wide-framed bloke who was now standing in front of him with his arms folded across his chest. He felt his head spinning and something wet was pulling his hair to the scalp. But he couldn't quite understand what it was.

"Why did you run away?" Gino asked him for the tenth time. "I've just asked you a question."

The man wasn't collaborating. It looked pale from the shock and the head injury. Gino was a bit worried about that, actually. They weren't supposed to chase people or kidnap them in their shops. He was counting on this kid's fear of authority and hoped that he wouldn't press charges against them. Carter said it was just a scratch and that the kid was confused because of all the weed he smoked.

"We are not coppers. We just want to talk about demonic summoning and occultism with your boss. Do you understand?"

The man continued with his silent treatment and looked away until his gaze stopped at the opening door of the shop. The ding of the bell woke everyone up.

"I think that's enough." A tall woman dressed as a goth with high-heeled military boots and a leather jacket with hundreds of studs entered the shop. "I can take you to him."

The Mystagogue

The Magus was sitting on a wooden highchair, or what you could have called more appropriately a throne. All intricately carved with lions' heads on the arms' ends, floral motifs on the back crowning above his head, four claws and balls as feet at the end of the undulated thin legs. He was in his fifties, but the make-up and the long black dyed hair made him appear much younger. He wore a brocade vest with azure and golden tints, a white shirt with a high collar and huge cufflinks with a shape of a goat's head, black coat and trousers and elegant shoes. He looked more like a dandy from a vampire film than a Heavy Metal musician.

To crown all this, the wall behind him was a collage of album and concert posters with pentacles, inverted crosses, naked women, blood, images of Satan with a goat's head and raising three fingers in the air. They were all glued at different angles and overlaying, partially covering each other without any real care, like you would see in some periphery billboards. One single poster stood up at the centre. It was a promotional poster for his new album's band, Hideous Wolves. There he was standing with a brocade dress framed by a scarlet coat, holding a stick with a golden pome. His corpse-paint was minimal, just white background, purple lips and some black around his eyes, with reptilian yellow pupils. Behind him a gothic castle perched on a rocky hill, surrounded by a forest of dead trees. Blue and purple hues in the sky and the snow gave the only colours to the otherwise black and white landscape. He looked like a count, not even attempting to hide the resemblance to the most famous one, Dracula. To complement all this, Black Metal music was playing in the background with drumming blasts, guitar riffs and unintelligible barked vocals.

Two tall and pretty girls were smoking what clearly wasn't tobacco on a nearby vintage couch. They both wore gothic dresses with a splash of chains, nailed bracelets and bullet belts and the omnipresent black lipstick. They didn't even acknowledge their presence, and they were smiling at each other while producing smoke rings in the air. The Magus stood up, moved to their spot, and whispered something in their ears. Carter swore he heard him calling them "my whores". The girls left the room sinuously, one of them sending an air-kiss to Carter who, embarrassed, blushed immediately after. She was the one who had taken them down to the basement of the record shop. Once they'd left, the host turned off the music and showed them the two chairs in front of his desk before sitting on his throne.

"What can I do for you, gentlemen?"

Carter was the first to talk.

"First of all, we are not coppers, priests, or even school parents' association, etc. We are from the RPI."

"I'm glad you started with these words, because I was just wondering who the hell two *normal* people

141

like you were, and why you treated my friend with such bad manners." He said that and pointed at a small TV screen, where everyone could see a black-and-white live image of the inside of the shop.

"He ran before I could explain," Gino said.

"Yes, but you have to understand that we... uhm... our community has been rocked by some bad press lately. The burning of the churches in Norway, the homicides, Varg Vikernes from the Burzum band sentenced for arson. I guess you heard it, right? Housewives and nuns see us in the newspapers and think we are some sort of Satanists, who want to sacrifice virgins and eat babies. We are trying to keep a low profile here."

"I can see that," Gino said sarcastically.

"Oh, this? This is just theatre, my friends. Cosplay. Some people love to dress up as Elvis, I like to dress up as a seventeenth-century vampire."

"Let's go straight to the reason why we are here."

The Magus nodded silently, and by crossing his legs and leaning back, signalled he was ready to listen.

"We were told you are in communication with a man who wears a hat and a walking stick."

"Rumours," he replied immediately, without any change of expression.

"Rumours, huh? Are they also rumours that you are the source of most of the occult knowledge in the community?"

"I barely gave advice and guidance to the neighbourhood kids."

"Do Bergen and Oslo count as neighbourhoods too?"

"I entertain a relationship with the Black Metal community at large. Is this a crime? And you just said you are not coppers."

"We are not, but we can make them intervene if necessary."

"And why would this be necessary? As I said, there is no crime."

"Crimes abound at the moment, and we suspect there is one person who is the conduit for all of this. That man with the hat. You can either be a witness or a suspect in this story."

"As I said, I can't see any crime. This is just escapism, mere divertissement for bored kids."

Gino reached into his blazer' inner pocket and produced a parchment. The Magus leaned forward with a curious gaze. When the Magus saw the content, he threw his whole body back into the throne and sighed.

"How could I have known that you knew?"

"Well, the clue was that we are from the RPI."

"Yeah, boffins and occultists paid by the government. We are the real deal here."

"I know one or two things about demon summoning and the occult."

"Yes, I bet you do." Then, after a pause, "Catching spirits in haunted houses and saving little girls from possessions."

Carter did not know what had just happened. Gino showed him something and the man changed his attitude completely. From night to day. What was that? He also saw that Gino ignored that last part about haunted houses and exorcisms. They were both used to that mocking. It reminded him of that time in China Town, close to Leicester Square, when Carter was deployed for the first time with Gino.

"So, you are the new Ghostbusters in town, huh?" an old Chinese man had said to them.

That was not what Carter had expected when the emergency call arrived in Gino's office. Although their main project was the investigation into the towns' disappearances in Sussex, from time to time they were assigned to smaller projects such as demonic presences or other paranormal phenomena. That time a spirit had intruded onto our plane and manifested itself in a Chinese restaurant, China Jade. The cook had seen a fluorescent aura in the kitchen. It had the shape of a humanoid, although it proved a challenge to ask him about the details, given that he ran out of the kitchen yelling, "A ghost! A ghost!" triggering a mass escape of all the customers. Gino managed to restrain it and command it to leave the premises through a magic ritual. The Ghostbusters comparison didn't stop on that day. Pretty much every time the paranormal was mentioned, people would make jokes or references to the most memorable quotes from the films. And every time people were extremely disappointed to learn that there were no proton guns or trap boxes involved.

"What do you want to know?" the Magus asked at some point.

"Who is he and how did you meet him?"

"I was fourteen years old when it happened. There was an old man from the nearby village who used to collect ancient books, and let kids like me browse his collection. Next to the fantasy section, with hundreds of weird stories from pulp magazines, there was another almost untouched bookshelf on the paranormal. Many books on the occult, many more about magic. It was a marvellous collection. One day, he gave me a rare book written by one of the Golden Dawn's adepts. In it I learned of an ancient ritual that could take me to a place where I could be trained, so to speak, in the occult arts."

"And you performed such a ritual."

"Of course, otherwise I wouldn't be here," he said with a laugh, pointing at his poster on the wall.

"And that's it?"

"That's it. You, being of the trade, know better than me that I will not disclose more than this. I can't tell you where this place was and what I've learned. I'm sure you would have done the same with me."

"I'd like to talk to this man."

"Ah."

"What? Can't you disclose this information either?"

"No, I can, of course, but I can see that, albeit good with magic, you were not that good in maths as a kid."

No reply from both Carter and Gino.

"Gentlemen, I was fourteen and he was old."

"Of course," Gino said, quite embarrassed.

Gino didn't think about that. They were obviously too late to catch that old man in this world. However, he knew a trick or two on how to communicate with him in the other. He just needed more information about him. But he did not want to force his hand here and now. What if this man was the King of Pentacles, his challenge? What did Josepha say? *"He is sly, deceitful. Don't fight him in his home."*

He was sitting on a throne, he was the master of this realm, and he was corrupt. Better face him outside of his home.

"And now, if you'll excuse me, I have the rehearsals for my new album," the man said, standing up holding the chair's arms.

Carter followed but Gino kept sitting. He wanted to ask the last question.

"Why Hideous Wolves?" he asked pointing at the poster.

"The name of the band? Don't you know? The wolf is the preferred animal of the Beast," he started saying with a smirk. His tone and posture told them it was going to be a long explanation. "It's more than the wolves hunting Christ's sheep. That's a puerile symbolism. It's primordial, more ancient than your Christ." And when he said "Christ", he looked into Carter's eyes and his voice stressed the first syllable so much that the *r* sounded like when a Spanish or Italian would pronounce it.

Carter shivered. Why did he look at him in that way? Did he sense something on him? Carter wasn't that religious, although he wouldn't call himself an atheist, either; however, he grew up in a Catholic family and that name, Christ, had always been present in many domestic conversations and at the church. Hearing it with that strong accent felt like a knife in his chest. Maybe he was reading too much into it, but this man was giving him the chills, nevertheless.

"You can't domesticate a wolf, can ya? It hunts, it growls, it howls, it shreds its victims into pieces. It knows no regret, no shame, no sin. It's what we were before we were domesticated by civilisation. It's the return to the origin. It's a primordial force that cannot be tamed. It's the hunter in the forest at night against the farmer in the village at day. Did you get it?"

He stared at Gino and Carter one after the other, as if checking his story had impressed their minds.

Gino nodded, and he had a flash of a film he had seen the previous year in the cinema, Bram Stoker's Dracula. There was a scene that stuck with him where Dracula hears the howling of the wolves and says, "Listen to them, the children of the night, what sweet music they make." The wolf symbolism fit very well with what this music genre was about.

"When we sing," the man continued, "when we produce music, when we perform, we become wolves once again. Do you really think lycanthropy was just a myth? Before us many others tried to revert back to that state of sinless nature. Some succeeded, some failed. We will succeed."

***

"So?" Carter asked when they were both back in the car.

"I don't buy that. Just mere pomp. He was lying," Gino said with a pissed-off expression.

"Which part?"

"He is a mystagogue, that's for sure," Gino said, slumping low in his seat. Then, when he saw Carter's question-marked face, he added, "He is the one who prepares candidates for the initiation in a mystery cult, like a secret society. The part where he was

147

lying was the bit about his mentor. That mysterious man is still alive and behind the scenes. This Magus is a mere façade, a convenient scapegoat to impress the TV and bourgeois susceptibility."

"May I ask you what you showed him that made him change his mind so quickly?"

"That? Oh, that was just a sigil that only the initiated could know the meaning of. It was a way for me to test him and a way for him to understand who he had in front of him."

"Like the Masons. And what would have happened if he had not recognised it?"

"We would have walked away, because he would have just been a con. Not before extracting information about this man with the hat, of course," he said finally, smiling frostily.

Carter caught that sadistic smile and that morning in the library immediately came to his mind. Since that day he'd always had the suspicion that sometimes it wasn't his colleague who was talking, but the entity that possessed him.

"Can you call our Emma and ask her to trace the owner of this shop?" Gino asked, changing subject and with an urgency in his tone.

"Sure thing."

"What do we do meanwhile?"

"Let's go back to the office. I'd like to investigate this Black Metal community more and—"

"Have a rest perhaps? You lost a lot of blood."

"Yes, Carter. That's a good idea. We will need a lot of our energies in the days to come."

X-ray of a demon

Emma called the next morning. She told Carter that the owner's name was George Westerfield, born in Little Craiton, East Sussex in 1950. No criminal record apart from a brawl with another kid at school, but everyone failed to press charges. She even went the extra-mile and cross-checked his name with the flight records from Immigration for the last ten years, and found out he went to Norway fifteen times.

"Little Craiton was the first village to disappear in Sussex, just a few days after my father started the esoteric triangle," Gino said.

"Oh boy," Carter reacted.

"What are the chances that a kid from a small village who disappears after an occultist experiment then becomes the founder of a global movement connected to the occult?"

"But still, being born in a village that disappeared and being the inspiration for a branch of heavy metal is not a crime."

"No, it's not."

"What's our goal here, then?"

"We need to know more about his past and his relationship with the man with the hat."

"And how is this connected with your father? Pardon me, with the astral projection of your father?"

"There has to be a connection. Remember, in the cosmos there are no coincidences, but links and threads that need to be followed."

Carter was reminded of that episode in the library from a few days ago, when something of unspeakable dreadfulness had taken hold of Gino and bound Carter to him for a few interminable moments. Gino spoke of visitations, of a nameless entity that had visited him with visions. Visions that were needed in order to see these hidden connections he was speaking about so much. After that day they did not speak about it. Most probably, Gino did not even realise what had happened in the library, and Carter had decided to keep it that way. Carter hoped it would not happen again and was in a continuous search for clues that it was recurring.

Gino had changed significantly in the last few days; whether it was just a shift in his mood or those visitations he spoke about, that did not matter. For example, he was now obsessing over this Black Metal scene. After the tense chat with the Magus, he went to buy at least ten cassettes and vinyl at Inferno Records. The poor shopkeeper who they'd caught and wounded was in disbelief when he heard the doorbell ringing and saw Gino coming in again. He instinctively withdrew and shrunk his figure back to the wall. His eyes desperately searched for an exit.

Like now, Carter just watched Gino changing the cassettes over and over again in complete silence. He couldn't hide a certain disgust for the music he was playing. He couldn't believe, let alone understand, what Gino found so fascinating in that repulsive cacophony that they called music. There was no melody, no pleasurable notes or voice. It was just growls, screams, screeches, hate, evil. But Gino loved it.

Carter found some comfort in noticing that Garibaldi also didn't like the music, and was now sitting in between his feet in search of a hiding place. Gino wasn't paying attention to them at all, so focused was he on the booklets, artwork and lyrics while he was listening to the music. He got annoyed when he heard Carter trying to steal his attention from the subject of his study.

"Gino, can you please turn the volume down? We need to talk about the case. The investigation is not over, it has actually just started."

"Yes, and this is exactly what we are doing."

"What? You are listening to this rubbish."

"I'm listening to this *rubbish,* as you call it, and I'm studying it at the same time. It's part of the investigation."

"How can it be?" Carter asked in disbelief.

Gino pressed STOP on the stereo and the hissing of the tape stopped immediately. Both Carter and Garibaldi felt relieved.

"This, Carter, is one of the most important discoveries I've ever made in the field of occultism."

"How come?"

"These kids have rediscovered occultism fifty years after it has almost gone extinct. They had to reinvent it and they are using the same tools and symbols as the first occultists in human history, the shamans."

"I'm sorry, I don't follow you."

"During the fin-de-siècle and just before the Great War, there was a flourishing of secret and occult

151

societies: the Hermetic Order of the Golden Dawn, the Theosophical Society, of which my father was part, The Ordo Templi Orientis, the Astrum Argentum, the Stella Matutina, the Rosicrucian Order. Think about Aleisteir Crowley, Helena Blavatsky, Yeats, Bailey, etc. Occultism was mainstream and even many politicians were influenced by it. Churchill himself bestowed enormous powers and responsibilities on my father after the war. All these societies died out and their disciples disappeared from the public scene after World War Two. All these societies could vouch for an endless magical lineage that had its root back in at least Ancient Egypt. The Americans won and with them most of the occult sciences were replaced by the modern sciences, pop art and by consumerism. The part of man's brain that was receptive to the occult was shrunk and lobotomised by films, ads, products that need to be purchased for the sake of purchase. But these kids are different. They hate mainstream music, hate pop culture, hate consumerism. This hate managed to keep their part of the brain receptive to the occult open. They rediscovered the occult and they are using this music to channel it. They use the writing of their bands' logos as sigils. They use this whitenoise that they call music as a tool to get into a trance, to achieve the connection with the other planes of existence. The album we were listening to, *Hvis lyset tar oss* from Burzum, is a mystical litany. It could have been conceived by a shaman four thousand years ago in the forests of Norway, and it wouldn't have been out of place to the taste and ears of those primitive men.

Primitive men that used drums and drugs to achieve an ecstatic trance that would put them in communion with the other spheres of existence. They are the shamans of the modern age. They are like my ancestors."

"That's why you used the word *peers* with Abzu and the Magus. You really think they are doing the same things as you occultists of the RPI?"

"Yes, but in a very primitive way, and they are unaware of this. They think they've got this original new way of making music, something that they think is transgressive, but they don't realise they are just repeating history once again."

"How can this help us in our investigation, though?"

"They think they are geniuses and that it all started from within the Heavy Metal community. This is not possible. All this hermetic knowledge, the mysticism, the occult rituals, are not their inventions. They come from hundreds of generations of shamans, occult priests and priestesses, kabbalists, mages, etc. that span thousands of years, through many civilizations."

"Someone taught them."

"Yes, and I think I know who started all this."

"The man with the hat."

"Exactly!"

"And the man came about right after the esoteric triangle was opened."

"Perfect, Watson."

Carter stayed in silence for a while, trying to digest what Gino had just said. He always had a hard time grasping the occultism. Gino was a good teacher, granted, but many concepts went over his head. Gino used to say it was normal that he couldn't understand. It was believed that only five per cent of the population could channel these powers. Carter was carefully chosen through a probationary test as someone who did not belong to that five per cent. These types of attitudinal tests were quite accurate, and Carter didn't doubt their results. Sure, the manifestations and the phantasms he saw and fought against (without much success) in these years were real to his eyes and other senses, but Gino said that what Carter saw was just their earthly form. The tip of the iceberg, or as he used to say, 'you saw a shadow of something, but not *that* something'. It was like he and the occultists like him had a sixth sense.

Despite this, he was conscious of the truth behind those occult sciences. Although he was a sceptic by nature, he couldn't deny what he saw in those few years he had worked for the RPI. He saw tens of portals opening, visions of other planes of existence, the summoning of entities, kinesis, astral travelling, precognition, and the list could go on and on. It was actually more believable than the organised religions which had always failed to prove anything of what they were preaching. However, he was a child of the modern era and his subconscious was a by-product of the scepticism of the scientific method. It was still incredibly difficult to believe in these things. Even though they were there in plain sight for everyone to see.

"How do you want to proceed?"

"Let's call Emma. This time we'll do this through the legal ways."

***

George Westerfield was sitting in the interrogation room by himself. He was facing the closed door, arms up to the elbow on top of a cold metal table. Emma, Carter and Gino were standing behind a one-way mirror in an adjacent room.

Gino didn't expect this to be exactly like in the American movies. Carter wasn't impressed, given that he'd worked in a police station for many years, but for Gino that was an unexpected scene. Also, because it meant he could use the one-way mirror to his advantage while Emma was interrogating him.

Emma hadn't liked that call she'd received two days earlier. She thought she had been courteous enough in releasing all the information she could find about this Magus to the RPI people. Twenty-four hours later she'd received a call from Carter asking to get a search warrant from the court for Inferno Records and the basement, and a request for interrogation for Mr Westerfield. Abbot went ballistic and she had to use all her persuasiveness to calm him down. He then caved in and signed the request to the court, but it seemed that this collaboration with the RPI was going to become sourer and sourer.

Emma went inside the interrogation room and sat in front of Westerfield, who appeared to be stoically serene. When brought to the police station he didn't flinch or protested. It was almost like he knew it was going to happen. Gino suspected he had *second sight* powers. If that was true, what he was going to try to

155

do behind that mirror wouldn't be unexpected by Westerfield. So, he had to protect himself against Westerfield's mind. He asked Carter to lock the door of the watching room and guard it in case someone tried to enter. He then drew a circle in white chalk on the pavement, and inside it a pentacle. He stood inside the drawing, hoping that Westerfield wouldn't be able to penetrate that area with his ESP abilities, if he had any. Better safe than sorry.

Emma was instructed to ask simple and sometimes vague questions to him. "Where were you on X day?"; "Who did you do business with in Norway?"; "What do you think of Satanism?"

Westerfield replied to every single question in a calm voice with very vague answers, but none of them sounded misleading or like lies.

Gino started his incantation and closed his eyes. He was going to perform something very difficult, especially because of the distance and the physical barriers between him and the target, such as the mirror and the walls. He had performed that type of *telaesthesia*, or mind reading, only a handful of times and it didn't work that well on several occasions, but at that time he was much younger and less experienced. Once he had tried to penetrate the mind of a classmate in secondary school. It was one of his first attempts at magic and occultist practices. His father gave him some books to read and some tips on how to focus his mind. He used to teach him that all humans could access the inner forces that reside in parts of the mind that were usually chained by our consciousness. In order to unlock these powers, it was necessary to stop the rational part of the mind from getting a hold on the unconscious. That's why rituals and chants were so important. All humans could access this, but only a few gifted ones could control it and truly use it at their own advantage. This gift was hereditary and could run in some families for generations. The Marcottis' bloodline was one of these.

That day after school when he performed telaesthesia on his classmate was unforgettable. He went inside his mind relatively easily and was so thrilled that he could see all his inner-most thoughts and dreams. He felt so powerful, a real séance like his father. His excitement passed away quite quickly when he lost control of the tether that linked his mind with his body. He realised he'd got trapped in his classmate's mind. He could not return to his body. Without realising, he'd turned telaesthesia into astral travel. Now, the curious fact was that when his classmate was taken to the hospital because of the severe convulsions that followed, Gino's body did not sit soulless on the bench of the school's courtyard as you would expect. It went back home in a catatonic state and mechanically did all its daily actions, such as opening the door, saying hi to the parents and going to the bedroom. It was only when his classmate was given a sleeping drug at the hospital that he was able to return to his body. That day Gino learned two lessons: the occult arts are dangerous if not well mastered, and our consciousness is independent from our biological mind.

This time it was going to be more difficult because of the mirror, and the subject, who apparently had psychic powers. Gino focused his mind and opened his third eye. Figuratively, of course, but still he was able to see the environment around him with his eyes closed. It was like a dream, and unlike astral travelling he was able to explore someone's else mind without moving his spirit. He saw Westerfield's aura over the one-way mirror and focused his attention on it. He accessed it with ease and was surprised by the lack of complexity. Usually, he had to dig through several layers, or substrata, of the consciousness. It was like his mind had been cleared up of clutter. Gino wouldn't have expected this to be the mind of a fifty-year old person. It was more like that of a baby. And yet he could see many "adult" thoughts and processes in it. Like the answers he was giving to Emma right now. Very linear, rational thought without a single glimpse of emotion. Incredibly unusual, especially in an interrogation room. You would expect some tension, some sort of uneasiness. Even the most innocent person would stammer and their voice tremble before a police officer.

Gino was so concentrated on trying to find an answer to those abnormalities that he did not realise the clock was ticking. He heard Emma asking the penultimate question from her list. Perception of time is very different when performing telaesthesia, or astral travelling, for that matter. Minutes could be hours in the real world. He decided to focus his attention on the childhood memories rather than the present ones. He went back years and years until he found a wall. A wall of darkness. The little drawers, as he liked to call them, of his mind were devoid of memories. It was like this man had been born already adult. No school, no parents, no teenage years (the most complicated memories to navigate into), no first love. He decided to check the oldest memory he could find, and there it was from Westerfield's point of view. A dark moonless night, acres and acres of plantless landscape, soil dug up everywhere and a single source of light behind him. Westerfield turns and sees a dim green fluorescent light emanating from a ring on the ground. The internal rim of which was precipitating in a bottomless pitch-black hole. A well.

Westerfield turns his attention to the countryside again and walks away from it, and then the memory stops. Gino could not understand what had happened, but he was certain that the memory would have continued. Something or someone had cut him out of the memory and stopped the tethering. He felt his mind sucked back into his body. It was like being a spider in a filled bath when the plug has been lifted. A whirlpool uprooted him from Westerfield's mind and pulled him away. He could now see Westerfield still sitting in his chair, calmly answering the last question from Emma.

What happened? He cut me out. He severed the connection and pushed me away. Who is Westerfield really?

Gino was still recovering from the difficult task when he saw something in Westerfield's body changing. He was the only one seeing this, thanks to his third eye. Something cocooning was wriggling inside Westerfield's chest. Actually, it was bigger than the chest because long protuberances were filling his legs, arms and the head. It was like seeing an X-ray image, but instead of bones he could see a white cocoon with white filaments. A documentary that he'd seen on BBC came to his mind almost immediately. It was about a wasp that injects a caterpillar with an egg. The egg hatches and a larva starts to grow inside, at the expenses of the caterpillar. The perfect parasite.

When the interview was over, and Carter put a hand on his shoulder to tell him to wake up from his concentration state, he felt an unstoppable urge to tell him his discovery.

"He is not human," he almost shouted to Carter, without realising that Emma had already walked into the room.

Intermezzo II

From the Diary of Amilcare Marcotti
Eritrea, Africa Orientale Italiana, 23 March 1941

We left Asmara five days ago and according to my Ethiopian guide we should reach Aksum, the obelisk city, tomorrow. Tamiru Tesfaye has been a loyal and knowledgeable chaperon. He is the son of a Coptic priest from Lalibela, the city of the churches built in the rocks. He speaks Amharic, Tigrynia, Oromo, Italian, English – all fluently – and has a good understanding of French. He knows this route very well, having guided several Italian expeditions before this one. He knows the local Tigrayan gangs that roam these highlands and he told me he has a pass written in both Ge'ez and Tigrynia that gives immunity to him and the people in his company, like us now. He has never showed it to me, but I suspect it might have the Imperial coat of arms stamped on it: the crowned Lion of Judah holding the flag.

I mentioned people in his company because we have three Eritrean ascari that are escorting us too. We ride on five donkeys plus a mule, to carry all that's needed for the journey. These animals are independent but very hardy. They haven't drunk a single drop of water since we departed, and didn't protest a single time about the ragged and arid terrain we had to traverse. They are like machines, much more reliable than our horses. The mule in particular, at the back of the party, does not even require a rope. It just follows the last donkey and never deviates or stops. Tamiru told me that if something were to happen to us – sadly, a terrible reminder of how dangerous this area can be – these animals would know their way back to Asmara. To their exact owner's house.

The ascari are tall, battle-scarred soldiers that the Italian embassy personally recommended to me. They wear the khaki uniform of the Royal Corps, the typical red fez, and they use old muskets last seen at the Battle of Adwa. They are all very proud of their *gorade*, their curved swords that look like sickles, attached to their belts. Abdel, the *sciumbasci capo*, is the oldest and most experienced of the three. The others respect him more out of fear than true deference.

They fought in the Battle of Adwa and even after the defeat they stayed loyal to the Italians. No throat-cutting in the middle of the night, I was assured. The same cannot be said for my Ethiopian guide, who without me would probably have ended up killed – or worse, mutilated – and left on the side of the road. Easy prey to the hyenas that roam at night. Ethiopians and Eritreans are sworn enemies and they would happily be at each other's throats rather than collaborate. The ascari haven't talked to Tamiru since we departed. They've simply ignored him. However, at night, when we sit around the fire and Tamiru and I talk amicably about our mission, I can see their gazes pointed at him. Many of their comrades were killed or taken as prisoners, mutilated and tortured for days by the victorious Ethiopians in the Battle of Adwa. So, I wasn't surprised by their hate. Tamiru isn't either, but his loyalty to the Italian Empire is much greater than his fear of his ancestral enemies.

Eritrea, Africa Orientale Italiana, 24 March 1941

Tonight we set our camp at the foot of a rocky promontory. Tamiru tells us there is a spring somewhere. The ascari explore the area before we start the fire. They find a ravine and at the very end of it the spring he told us about. That is something that can be found so easily in this area. One of the perks of travelling during the rainy season, although something that is not advisable. They fill up their gourds that they use as water bottles. Both Tamiru and the ascari were not very happy to travel now, due to the torrential rains. But there was no other solution. The British have won in Somaliland and are now advancing in Ethiopia. Addis Ababa capitulated and they are now marching up north. Aksum is on the trajectory to Asmara, so this is our only chance to reach the Church of Our Lady Mary of Zion.

Tamiru is very interested in Italian culture. The only Italian city he has been to is Asmara, which is far from being your typical Italian city. However, Italian architecture, schools, cinemas and cafés have flourished in the past years, making it the most European-looking city in East Africa. He is fascinated by the language and by the Fascist ideology, which he refers to as "religion". He has this idea of Il Duce as a prophetic figure, similar in importance to the

Pope. I had to explain a lot of things to him during our journey; however, he clearly demonstrated that he didn't fully understand the difference between the secular ideologies such as Fascism or Communism, and religion.

On the other hand, I, too, asked him about his culture. I have a copy of the *Kebra Nagast* or *The Glory of the Kings*, the national Ethiopian epic, with me. Every night I ask him to translate a part for me. It is fascinating how this text has never been fully translated and appreciated in the West. The *Kebra Nagast* describes how the Ark of the Covenant arrived in Aksum and where it is kept. He thinks I'm interested in the Ark and that it is the reason for our mission. He is unaware that I'm actually interested in the church where the Ark is kept. It was erected on top of an Egyptian temple to Thoth, the Egyptian god of the moon. There lies the occult knowledge that I need for my mission bestowed on me by Il Duce himself.

Eritrea, Africa Orientale Italiana, 25 March 1941

We climb up a series of ragged hills that are going to take us to a higher altitude than yesterday. At the end of the day, we had ascended by 1,000 metres. Tamiru tells me we have now reached 2,500 metres. And I can tell that: I feel very tired and out of breath, I can barely stand in the evening. When we are sitting around the fire, one of the ascari comes close to me and opens a tiny package made of fabric kept closed by a string. Inside there are some dried brown leaves. He takes a couple and puts them in his mouth and chews them. It's *khat*. I've seen many Eritreans in Asmara chewing on its leaves. Yemenis cross the Red Sea in small boats and sell it at the local port. It is supposed to relax your senses, give you euphoria and increase your blood pressure.

"It will help you with the altitude sickness," Tamiru says to me while I'm already chewing it.

He doesn't need it, his body is so well adapted to these highlands, as opposed to us lowland and coastal people. Tonight the ascari are very merry and sing songs while Tamiru and I clap our hands to keep the rhythm. For one night the differences between all of us seem to have disappeared. This khat works miracles.

Eritrea, Africa Orientale Italiana, 26 March 1941

The day after, we feel dizzy, like after a night of revelry. The ascari make a quick breakfast and urge us to get on our donkeys before the sun goes down at six. They don't want to stay in this area anymore than necessary. Tamiru tells me that it's Tigrayans' territory now. There are gangs that will be very happy to rob us or worse. Some white people have been kidnapped in the past for ransom. And the whites are the lucky ones; for the others, it's either immediate death or mutilation. I tell him that he has his official pass.

"Yes, but not all of them can read or recognise the imperial coat of arms."

Better cross this area quickly, then.

We reach a bushy highland surrounded by high rocky peaks. The sciumbasci capo is worried. This is the perfect location for an ambush. He talks with his men and they start to discuss what to do. Tamiru wants to go through this route, having done it several times. It is safe, he assures us. But the ascari are not convinced. They want to take a longer route around these rocky peaks that will keep us far away from potential ambushes. Tamiru insists, and with his eyes is asking me to take a side, his side. I'm unable to make any decision. Of course, I trust Tamiru but the ascari's plan seems safer and more sensible. We will add twelve hours more to our journey but at least we will have our heads still attached to our shoulders. Luckily, that grave decision is taken away from me, for something suddenly happens on those rocks that distracts us all.

A sound echoes through the passage. Some small rocks start to roll down in between the massive grey boulders. They are stopped by the heavy and thorny bushes. On top of one of the biggest boulders a figure is standing, crowned by the noon sun. Long brown hair that form a mane around his face. A red triangle on his chest. And long sharp canines that can tear you to shreds. The figure rises on its feet, lips go up exposing the huge fangs and the pink gums, the arms beat its red chest repeatedly. We can hear the beating echoing through the rocks like drums.

"Gelada," says Tamiru pointing at the other monkeys jumping from boulder to boulder.

The bleeding-heart baboon, the highlands monkey, what a wonderful creature. The one we saw first is the male, the leader of the pack. All the others are females and juveniles. I'm so excited and I feel so blessed to be able to have this encounter. However, this excitement quickly changes when I hear the shot. One of the ascari has hit the magnificent creature right in the chest. The baboon rolls on the top of the boulders and then drops onto the thorny bushes below. The other monkeys scatter, shouting and grinning their teeth at us.

The ascari's smile lasts only a few seconds, just enough time to celebrate his incredible shot, because the sciumbasci capo slaps him on the back of the head. His fez falls on the ground and he almost drops the musket. He gets pelted by punches and kicks in the face and chest. The soldier drops to his knees and pleads, but the sciumbasci capo continues to kick him and shouts at him what I can only assume are insults.

Tamiru translates for me and says that what the soldier has done was very stupid. Now, the Tigrynian gangs know where we are. We have to move faster, and the only way is now through this highland surrounded by these high rocky peaks that could hide our future ambushers. When the public punishment is over, we all get on our donkeys and we push them at high speed. The beaten soldier is last, next to the mule, his head down. Tamiru tells me not to look at him and to forget what happened. These are army dynamics that I should not get involved with. I suspect these are things that happen in every single army, including the Italian one. Different methods but same goal: keeping the hierarchy.

The donkeys are at full speed, although it can't be called a gallop, more like a trot. Even if they could go faster, we have the mule transporting most of our food and tools that is dragging us. Two ascari position themselves on the flanks while the third (the beaten one) is riding on the back next to the mule. Tamiru and I ride with our heads low, in the vain hope that the ambushers, if there are any, will not see us.

We ride for several kilometres until we see a clearing in front of us and we get the rocky terrain past us. We enter a bushy landscape with occasional acacias that are blossoming thanks to the recent rains. Huge clusters of yellow dot the brown and partially green environment. According to the ascari it is the least likely place to get ambushed. But they are completely wrong, for our ambushers find us exactly there.

Ten men armed with rifles and *gorade* swords are standing on their donkeys, camels and horses. They wear no recognisable uniforms or insignia. Their clothes are ragged and inconsistent. I hear Tamiru saying the first swear word to come out of his mouth, and it is Italian: *merda*. We are at the mercy of thugs.

The ascari throw their guns and the swords on the dusty ground. Their hands go slowly up, as do Tamiru's. I follow.

One of the Tigrynians get off his horse, he feels so safe that he leaves his rifle on the saddle. He gets closer to us, and with an arrogant facial expression orders us to get off our donkeys. We obey with our hands up and well in sight. I think he is coming straight for me but he ignores me. I'm like a ghost for him. He goes straight to the ascari and starts to slap their faces, then kicks them in the stomach. The others of his men laugh and shout. Tamiru is next, but the words coming from his mouth are pronounced in Tigrynia. The thug stops and says something as a reply. Tamiru's hand slowly reaches to his pocket. One of the Tigrynians is aiming his rifle at him, pointing at his head. Tamiru knows and, trembling like a leaf, extracts a folded envelope. It's the pass with the imperial insignia. He hands it to the man and says something. The man snatches it from his hand, almost tearing it apart. He starts to read it, or at least his eyes suggest that, until I see that the pass is upside down. This man cannot read! We are in trouble. Deep trouble.

The man looks for interminable minutes at the paper, pretending to read and understand its contents, perhaps to impress his men. Then, he folds it and gives it back to Tamiru, who ignores the analphabetism of the man in front of him. He does not expect the butt of another man's rifle on his head. Shouts and laughs are erupting from the men. Tamiru collapses to the ground. The ascari are pleading, one is crying.

It is in that moment that I start my incantation. I close my eyes and I chant. I can hear the Tigrynians surrounding me, I can feel their perplexity and the utter confusion. *What is this Italian man doing?* they are asking themselves. Is he crazy?

I don't think I've ever summoned spiritual entities so fast in my life. It usually takes half an hour of continuous chanting and the right concentration, but this time it's just a matter of minutes. I can feel many dead in these highlands, both local and Italian. They are very upset, extremely revengeful towards this gang of thugs. That's why they were so quick to summon, and that's why they are so brutal in their execution. When I open my eyes, I can already see the men with fear on their faces, some in shock, some in panic mode. Different people react to supernatural horror in different ways. They scramble in all directions, while those in a state of shock are unsaddled by their donkeys and horses. Also, the animals can see them. Perhaps not as clearly as humans can but they can, for sure feel the chill in their bones, exactly like us. The chill coming from the sight of entities beyond our comprehension, the horror coming from the feeling that those creatures are not of this world. In less than two minutes they are all gone, either riding or running. Some leave their weapons and other objects. The last to flee is the boss of the gang, the one who beat the ascari and tried to read the pass. The one who, so bold and arrogant even left his weapon behind to face strangers. I can hear water, like a spring sprouting from the rocks. Some drops are splashing on my boots. Both him and I look down at the pond of urine that blackens the ground. He looks at me again for the last time, then he flees to the bushes.

I look around. The spirits are gone. Tamiru is still unconscious on the ground, the ascari are still on their knees and in disbelief. They mumble something in Arabic that only later, in our room in Aksum, Tamiru will translate as Shaitan.

"Il Diavolo!"

The devil. They think I'm the devil.

The trap

"I can't arrest him because you are claiming he is not a person. Even if he admits this, this is not even a crime," Emma said in a low voice hoping that no one could hear them from outside, although it was unlikely given that the watching room was acoustically isolated.

"We are not at the RPI, where you can claim things without any proof. Abbot is already on the fence and will not tolerate another foolish request like this one. He barely accepted the warrant request."

Gino shook his head when he heard "without any proof" coming out of her lips. It was the typical sceptical mantra. Proof, proof. Objective proof, even. There was no such a thing as objective proof. *He* was the proof, and each proof was *subjective*.

"He could be extremely dangerous."

"He has never been accused of a single crime. What makes you think he will now?"

"We are onto something here and he knows it now. What would you do if you were not from this plane of existence and someone found out?"

"I'm not sure what we are even talking about here. Is this like the Ghostbusters? Are you going to capture him, or capture it with your proton streams and the trap..."

"Ah, enough!" Gino said, standing up and making an attempt to leave the room, before Carter stopped him with a hand to his chest.

"Gino, explain yourself so we can understand," Carter whispered to him. "Maybe she can help if she only knows what you saw."

It seemed that Gino agreed on that, because he turned back, sat down, and began to describe what he saw.

"Mr Westerfield disappeared with the whole village of Little Craiton in 1959. No one is able to return but him. How? I reached out to his mind, to search through his memories. There is nothing in his memories about his life prior to the village disappearance. The only memory I experienced – or, should I say, *he* experienced – was when he got out of a well in the middle of the countryside, presumably where the village stood. The Well was incredibly similar to the one we barely managed to escape from days ago."

"Which is impossible, unless you got a sigil," Carter interjected.

"Exactly," Gino confirmed.

"Whoa," Emma said, thrusting her palms forward. "Hold on there. This is beyond anything I've ever heard of. Can you care explaining what these sigils... *things* are?"

"Sigils are like keys that we use to pass through planes. Without them your flesh and spirit can be ripped apart due to the differences in the space-time fabric. In lay terms: each plane has different physics and psychic laws. It's because of sigils like the one we taped to our chest that Carter and I managed to get out of the gravitational pull of the Well in Hartesbridge. And it's because of the sigils that esoteric triangles are possible."

"Okay, a bit better, although still crazy to my ears."

"Now, Westerfield either had a sigil before his village disappeared – and that would imply he was very knowledgeable in occultism; definitely a bright kid, but this is very unlikely – or he is a native."

"But he is clearly not a... demon. Look at him," Emma said, standing up and pointing at the one-way mirror.

"Appearances are misleading. In the nineteenth century people thought that they could see spirits through the use of photography. It was called spirit or ghost photography. Similarly, there are other psychic techniques such as thoughtography, where the psychic occultists claim they can burn images from someone's mind onto a photograph. Now, my theory is the following: an entity from the other plane took his body and 'printed' its astral body inside Westerfield's body."

"Possession," Emma said.

"No, nothing to do with the Christian possession. In Christian possession a demon gets inside the body of a person and commands them, but after the exorcist performs his ritual and the demon gets out, the person is back to normal. All superstitions, by the way. Westerfield's body is just a vessel, an empty husk. Westerfield is no more. If we remove the entity Westerfield will simply collapse, for he is only a collection of flesh and bones."

"Like a parasite," Carter suggested.

"That's creepy as fuck. You are telling me I was talking to a demon in there and that man is just its dress?" Emma asked.

"I probably wouldn't have used the dress metaphor, but I guess you described it quite well."

"Okay, still crazy, but how can I tell my boss all this? Or the judge, for that matter?"

"We have to frame him with something else."

Emma stood up again and assumed an imperative pose and tone.

"No way. I'm not into this..."

Carter chimed in and tried to be the appeaser.

"Gino, even if it were the demonic entity you are describing, and don't get me wrong, I have no doubt – 'cause that man has given me the creeps since day one – jail time won't make any difference to it. It won't solve our investigation, either."

Emma interrupted Carter's train of thought and asked: "What are you investigating anyway? I thought your investigation was about the disappearing villages? How is this... larva-man linked to them?"

Gino and Carter looked at each other, and their eyes told Emma the struggle they were in more than any words.

"Look, if you are not willing to open up to me, how can I help you with your investigation? You are my only chance to get on with Abbot. Don't forget, it was thanks to me that we got Westerfield here, against Abbot's wishes," Emma said, with a body language that reminded them of a spoiled child.

Gino sighed like he had found no other way of escaping a maze he had been trying to get away from.

"We think what's happening is bigger than just those villages disappearing," he admitted.

"What can be bigger than all those villages disappearing with thousands of people in them? It seems like a pretty big deal to me."

"There has been an acceleration in occult practices. There were almost none for fifty years, and now, all of the sudden, hundreds of metal bands are summoning demons and claiming they possess occultist faculties. Even Hollywood has sensed something with these *The X-Files* and *Twin Peaks* series."

"Yeah, but these are just music and shows. People love mystery and thrills. I like Twin Peaks and I don't see any occultist theme. It's just surrealistic. Right?"

Neither Gino nor Carter answered her.

"All of this, we think it is correlated with the opening of the Greenwich esoteric triangle. Then, from 1990 onwards to this day, we saw an explosion in these occultist practices and manifestations in popular culture. We think someone got out of the gateway and started to teach and mentor people, in most cases artists and musicians, around the globe."

"I see," Emma said with a sudden change in her expression, now more serious and focused. "You are chasing this *someone*, hoping they will lead to an explanation for the disappearances. But again, without a Laura Palmer's body, my hands are tied."

"Let's untie them, then," Gino said.

***

The trap was set up two days later. Nothing illegal, as Emma asked. Just a gentle nudge that would expose Westerfield for whoever or whatever he really was.

It involved the clever use of a bait. Emma did a thorough investigation, and found out that Abzu had sold some drugs in the past. Technically not enough to press charges against him, but enough to scare him. Abzu realised he was going to be the bait only after the visit from Gino and Carter, which he didn't expect. He also did not expect that they would have to meet inside a room that had been secured with a sigil to avoid Westerfield *seeing* what was going to happen through precognition.

Abzu didn't like it, but he had no choice and couldn't say no. The plan was that he was going to call Westerfield and ask him to meet with an excuse. The excuse was chosen by Abzu himself. It was related to music, and Westerfield could not say no to a disciple who cried for help with the next album's occult lyrics and artwork. The meeting had to be set up outdoors in a specific location in London, carefully chosen by Gino.

"Why did he choose this place out of the thousands he could choose in London?" Emma asked, crouching behind the oak tree and avoiding the big drops of rain that where falling on her hair and shoulders.

Carter was standing next to her, unperturbed by the rain. He was carefully scanning the whole perimeter they set up in the middle of Hyde Park. Three more constables were standing on the other side of the perimeter, a hundred metres or so away from them. They'd volunteered, just because Emma had asked them as a favour. None of them wore a uniform or carried a weapon such as a baton or pepper spray. Carter was the only one with a gun. It was quite ironic that the only person allowed to carry a gun among those ten million inhabitants of the city was not a police constable.

"He said the ritual requires a perimeter of at least hundred metres, and far away from buildings and people that could compromise it."

The perimeter, as they called it, was simply a series of ivory pegs (the same size as those you would use for your tent when camping) that defined a circle on the lawns. A pentacle was then drawn with black ash. At the centre, Abzu was waiting next to a wooden bench. All was carefully disguised using leaves and twigs.

Gino was nowhere to be seen. He asked to be ignored and he didn't reveal his location. He feared Westerfield could read their minds, and if they knew where he was, his location could be compromised.

He can't be too far away, Carter thought searching for his figure across the park. It was close to midnight and together with the miserable weather it meant there were no tourists or casual passers-by. Emma made a call to one of her Scotland Yard friends and asked them not to intervene between midnight and one a.m. if they received a call that involved that part of Hyde Park.

Carter gave up in looking for Gino and focused his attention on Abzu. With no tree cover or umbrella he was drenched, his black hair sticking to his face and neck. He didn't seem very happy and couldn't wait for all of this to be over. Westerfield was supposed to be there already, but the park was deserted. Was it possible that he understood it was a trap? Did his occult abilities surpass Gino's? Carter trusted Gino's occult skills but they couldn't deny they were facing a demon from another plane of existence. What powers did it have? Was it capable of precognition and telaesthesia? One way or another, Carter wasn't sure his gun would make any difference that night. If there was something he'd understood in his five years at the RPI, it was that many of their foes or clients (as sometimes it was the case with benevolent spirits) were unaffected by normal weapons. The chalk and the incantations could be more lethal than his bullets.

Emma's radio woke him from those thoughts. It seemed the others hadn't seen anyone coming either. The plan was that if Westerfield didn't show up within the twenty-minute limit, they would abort the operation. Emma was frantically looking at her watch and praying for the minute hand to go faster and reach the number twenty. It was past ten now and Abzu was starting to become nervous too. He was walking back and forth within the length of the bench to keep himself warm. The studs on his leather jacket were sparkling under the lamp light at every step. Then, the radio buzzed three times. It was the signal that the target was in sight. Westerfield appeared from nowhere and startled Abzu, so much that he gasped and jumped back.

"Hey mate. You scared the shit out of me."

Westerfield was much taller than him, wearing a long trenchcoat and high-heeled military boots that protected him from the rain and mud.

"How are you?" Abzu asked hesitantly.

"Cut it short, Abzu. What do you have for me?"

Abzu reached into his backpack and showed him several vinyl albums and cassettes which were supposedly very rare, and could be sold for a few hundred pounds per piece at the Inferno Records shop. Westerfield looked at the contents of the backpack without removing them, to avoid getting them wet in the rain. He did not look very interested though. Abzu talked and talked but he didn't listen to him. He closed the backpack and shoved it with an unexpected force against Abzu's chest, then he turned his head.

He knew something was wrong. He looked first to his left, then to his right, exactly where Carter and Emma and the other constables were, respectively. He now knew it was a trap. Carter had to prepare himself for the worst. Everyone, humans or animals, reacts violently when they sense danger, especially when they think they are trapped. How would a demon react? He didn't have to wait for too long, because Westerfield's body started to shake. Carter had never seen something like that. All the rain drops on his trenchcoat were displaced – was there a better word? – from its surface, and any additional drops that touched it suffered the same fate. It wasn't like convulsions or Parkinson's tremors. The only comparison Carter could make – and he knew it was very silly – was when one day he placed some kitchen cling film on top of a stereo speaker lying on its side with the drum up. When the music was cranked up to the highest volume, the drops started to jump up and shook in all directions until they left the top of the speaker.

From his mouth, a high-pitched scream erupted. So loud that both Emma and Carter had to cover their ears. At some point they thought their eardrums would collapse and Carter instinctively checked his fingers for blood. Luckily there was none, but the scream did have an effect on their senses because they felt disoriented and could barely stand. Carter dropped to his knees outside of the oak cover and checked the scene at the centre of the pentacle. Westerfield was still standing next to Abzu and the bench, but when he saw Carter he immediately jumped in his direction, arms and hands forward like a bird of prey moments before it grabs its victim. He was so fast that Carter thought he was going to die on the spot. But after his leap into the air, he fell on the ground, badly hurting his face and hands. It was like something had pulled him, like an invisible string was attached to his ankle and he had been tied to the ground. Carter took his gun out and pointed it at him, knowing it might not work. Westerfield grimaced like a caged beast and sent another ear-piercing scream into the air. Carter lost his balance and with it his aim. The scream screwed up with his ability to concentrate and command his muscles. Given the absence of Emma and the other constables around him, he thought he wasn't the only one experiencing this.

He saw Westerfield jumping up again and trying to leap, but again the invisible chain pulled him down.

It was Gino. The pentacle and the incantation worked, then.

Carter saw his colleague walking towards the pentacle, coming onto the scene from nowhere. Where had he been hiding until now? How did he sneak in so quickly? His lips were moving but Carter has been deafened by the demon's screams. Gino's palms were facing the demon's face now. Each of Gino's steps forward was one of Westerfield's steps backward. The demon was retreating using all four limbs, rain still being brushed away from his trenchcoat.

Then, finally, Carter started to hear again. First it was the rain pelting on his coat, then Emma trying to talk to him, then the words that Gino had been shouting all this time: "I command you, I constrain you."

The creature, because Carter could not consider that four-limbed crawler and shrieker a human anymore, had now retreated to the very centre of the pentacle, where Abzu was still standing. The kid was in shock, unable to move or react, mouth agape and eyes filled with terror. He hadn't expected to make contact with the very demons he always wanted to summon. And he hadn't expected it to be so terrifying. Behind him, the two constables that had dashed forward to take him away while the demon was attacking Carter were standing still as well. They didn't know what to do.

"Get away from there! Run!" Emma shouted at the top of her lungs.

The two men ran away and took refuge behind the oak trees outside of the pentacle's circle. But Abzu didn't move, standing as still as the lamppost that was illuminating his head.

Gino continued to advance, and now he entered the pentacle's circle. Carter followed him with his gun pointed at the creature, but Abzu was in his line of sight, so he had to move left, and that meant getting very close to some bushes and another oak tree. He jumped over them and used the oak tree as cover. But when he did that, the demon changed its behaviour and jumped back, grabbing Abzu by the chest. The poor kid awoke from his hypnotic slumber and started to scream, doing his best to escape its clutches, but it was all in vain. The situation had degenerated. Now there was a hostage. What would Emma do now? Would she call Scotland Yard? Carter looked at her, but she was as shocked as the kid a minute ago. He decided to make contact with Gino, although he knew he might have stopped his concentration. Gino might have read his thoughts (and in his case, that might not have been a figure of speech) because he turned his face towards him and nodded. It was the signal.

Gino changed the position of his arms from a defensive stance to a more summoning posture. His arms went up almost as if to invoke some inaccessible power from the heavens. Sparks started to exit from the tips of his fingers. Then, they started to envelop his hands, wrists and arms down to the elbows. It was a wonderful and yet terrifying image. Something that Carter have seen him performing only one other time, two years ago during a demonic *extraction* in York. Like that time, Carter knew what to do next. The sparks reached a momentum and a low buzz filled the scene with tension. Then, they shot forward and hit Westerfield without touching Abzu. Westerfield's body started to convulse and the real him, in like an X-ray, was revealed in its demonic form. The entity was exactly as Gino had described it at the police station. A wriggling larva encysted inside his torso with white filaments reaching the very ends of his limbs. During these convulsions, Abzu was freed. Carter moved forward, grabbed his wrist, and dragged him away from Westerfield. The kid was still in shock and had to be pulled with all Carter's might.

What followed might have come up from a horror B-movie. The man's chest lacerated, the ribs opened up like springs kept for too long under an enormous weight. No blood, no visible organs. It was like Gino said, just a husk, a dress that this entity used to walk around our plane. The creature slipped out of its *costume* in one single motion, leaving the body of the former-Westerfield to drop in the mud like a wet towel. It had no head, or at least it wasn't like it is usually supposed to be, and it tried to slither towards Gino, until the electrical discharge coming from Gino's hands was too much and it gave up and rested on the ground. A few seconds later it started to burn from the inside, fizzing in the rain, and it was gone. Gino stopped his ritual and, panting heavily, walked towards the spot where it was. He brushed the ground with his shoe and a sparkling silvery ash was displaced and flew away.

Listen to them, the children of the night

According to the unofficial autopsy recording that was deleted by Emma Westerfield had died several years earlier, decades possibly. That recording was also speaking of a total absence of internal organs, blood and fluids; presence of an abnormal peripheral nervous system that did not look like any other the coroners had ever seen. Something so explosive that it must not have reached Abbot's desk. Emma had no jurisdiction in London, but the three constables who were present during the Hyde Park demonic extraction swore they would cover everything up to their superiors. They were still shocked after what they saw that night, but were wise enough to shut their mouths. Who would have believed them anyway? And why did they agree to get involved in the first place? It was in their own interest to stay silent.

The two coroners were literally bribed with £1,000 each and asked to postdate Westerfield's death, given that the tissue examination confirmed a much earlier death, decades ago. It was a dirty doing and Emma had seriously thought of resigning before any of that could surface up. Carter and Gino felt somewhat guilty to have involved other people, but they knew that what they had done was necessary.

Now, it was time to investigate further into the Black Metal community to understand if there were other "Westerfields".

The poor Abzu – whose real name they learned was James Ingram – was referred to a psychologist who took great care of him in the following months. Emma took his health very personally as she felt responsible for what had happened to him. Apparently, a few weeks after the accident he left the band and shaved his head almost to zero.

The Inferno Records shop had a not dissimilar fate. It closed almost immediately, and the shop assistant claimed benefits for a few months before finding another job. No one knew who the girls in the basement were and where they were now. Emma asked Scotland Yard to do a background check on the shop but they failed to find anything suspicious. All legal, nothing out of the ordinary. The demon knew how to do business on Earth.

Another disturbing fact was purposely ignored in all the reports. Something that kept Gino awake during the nights that followed. The inner part of Westerfield's body had an imprint. Almost similar to the mark that gets burned on ranch cattle's skin. The thick, leathery hide that corresponded to the upper back of Westerfield had a blackened symbol drawn on it.

"Someone put a mark on the inside of his body," one of the coroners announced in disbelief before Emma and Gino.

Gino asked to see it immediately, because it could have given clues to what was going on. The coroner took him to the dissection table and showed him.

Gino could not believe his eyes. There, in front of him, was a sigil drawn by another plane's entity.

"Very clever. Very clever indeed," he whispered sitting down, trying to metabolise what he had just seen.

The demon could cross the gateway between the two planes, but the human body could not, so it marked it with a sigil. First time he'd seen something like that. Actually, it was the first time he'd seen a sigil drawn by a being that was not a human.

"What does it mean? How is it possible?" the coroner was asking with a hint of panic in his voice.

"Better you don't know. Trust me. Just forget about this night."

"But, I need to know if—"

"Your job is to perform autopsies on humans. This is outside of your competences and experiences. It is quite literally *out of this world*. Let the RPI deal with this."

The coroner didn't reply or protest.

"Now, hand over that Polaroid."

Gino grabbed the camera from the coroner's hands and took a series of photos at different angles. After the ten-minute wait, he had a look at the first developed photo and to his surprise the sigil wasn't there. He moved the photo next to the burned shape of the sigil: the leathery skin was there with all the recognisable minute details, but the sigil was not. Then, he checked the second one and the third one. None of them showed the sigil.

How is it possible?

He could not comprehend it. He grabbed a pencil and a piece of paper and copied the sigil by hand. He then walked out of the room. The coroner chased him.

"What do we do with him?"

Gino turned, and with a dark tone to his voice said: "You'd better burn it as soon as possible."

***

"You look like you were the one that was extracted between the two of you."

"Probably."

"What do you mean?"

"I lost in there, too. My plan was to capture it and let it speak. Instead, it all went wrong, that demon decided to harm Abzu and I had to use the full potential of my powers to save him, but I lost the chance to interrogate it... I mean, to interrogate Westerfield."

Carter realised he had touched a very sensitive string. Sure, officially Gino had been hired to investigate the disappearances of the towns, but this had become more personal. Not only did he feel the responsibility of the failures of his father. Now, he also believed he saw him in that cave. Still wandering the planes without rest. Carter was very worried by the current situation. Emotional bonds could jeopardise the investigation. He even thought of talking about this to his superiors, bypassing Gino. However, his respect for him was much greater than any following of internal regulations.

"Anyway, let's stop talking about me and let's focus on work. I want to show you something," Gino said, standing up and moving a wheeled table with a TV and a VHS player on it.

Carter had seen it earlier when he got into his office and had found it odd, given his colleague's allergy to anything technological, but thought it was fair for someone to watch a film every now and then. Gino also fetched a cardboard box from under his desk. It was full of VHS cassettes. All the covers seemed to be printed with a xerox at home. Black-and-white photos of Nordic forests, Gothic castles, skeletons, vampires and the omnipresent corpse-painted musicians.

"I watched all of these. They are live concert tapes and some official videos, but I'd be surprised if MTV decided to buy them. Not only because of their themes, but especially because of their quality: next to zero."

Gino laughed, finding what he was going to say very amusing.

"These people, these kids, produce lo-fi music and videos on purpose. I've never heard of an artist that decided to make his art so bad in terms of quality and accessibility. They don't want common people to listen to it. I find it amazing. This is pure hermeticism. Anyway, I spent hours and hours watching these concerts, pretty similar to the one we attended, and..." He stopped with a suspenseful pause.

He pressed play and the TV image flickered a little. Video and audio were awful, as Gino just described. It was difficult to make out what was happening. Carter could see stage lights illuminating what he presumed were the band members. A silent crowd was waiting below the stage. Then, high flames erupted from the back and highlighted the dark silhouettes of the musicians. A guitarist, a bassist, a drummer and the singer holding a guitar. That was like a trigger for the crowd which, as soon as the pyrotechnics started, broke its calm and silence. From a placid dark lake at night to a stormy ocean hitting the rocks with enormous violence. The drums were shockingly fast and the guitars were blasting at full power. More flames and stage lights illuminated the scene and Carter could finally see the corpse-paint on the singer's face, the long corvin hair of the guitarist rotating incessantly. At some point everyone, both on stage and among the audience, started headbanging. It was ridiculous to Carter and yet fascinating. It was like an orgiastic ritual. The video went on and on throughout several tracks, and Gino had to forward to where he wanted Carter to focus his attention. Once, he stopped the tape when the singer sprayed the crowd with beer coming out of his mouth. Another time a man went up on the stage headbanging and with his horned hands up, then the bassist kicked him off and the man fell on top of the crowd, who held him up on their hands. He was passed on from hand to hand until his body was thrown onto the ground somewhere at the edge of the concert. It was all crazy stuff like this, and Carter thought he had seen enough, but "the best is yet to come," said Gino.

The singer disappeared backstage and came back with what Carter at first thought was just a puppet, some sort of furry toy. However, it soon became evident that it was in fact a goat's head. A real, bleeding-from-the-severed-neck goat's head. He pulled it up on top of his head and during the most incredible blast of guitar riff and drumming he showered himself with the blood dripping out of it. It was so disgusting that Carter had to look away.

"Why are you making me watch this... this stuff?" he asked.

Gino stopped the video at an exact time he had previously wrote on a Post-it. He then turned back to Carter and with his legs crossed started to explain.

"Because what you saw was just a veneer of what is really happening here. You saw an act. As disgusting as it might look, it is just theatre. Perhaps, it's not even real blood. Who knows, maybe there is a lot of ketchup there. Good luck washing your hair afterwards, though!"

Carter didn't find the joke very funny.

"Look closely," he added, putting his index finger on the screen, just on top of the singer's head. "What do you see?"

"A light? A halo? But it might be due to the stage lights and the fire behind."

"True, I thought the same, but then I wanted to have a closer look, just to be sure. I gave the tape to the IT guys, who were very surprised to see me, given my refusal to use PCs in my work. I've asked them to analyse these images and they went through it frame by frame. They added filters and other things I can't understand or describe really. But in the end, this is what they got."

He ejected the tape and pushed another one in. This time the image was very different, like a negative image very similar to the diapositive slides that Carter's father used to play at Christmas. The spectrum of the colours went from white to some violets and metallic blues and greens, but the predominant hue was into the greys. The man's outline was clearly visible, and so was the goat's head, but there was another shape that crowned his head. The halo appeared to have a proper outline, a round shape the same size as the man's head, almost like a duplicate but few inches back and above. It was a head with eyes, mouth and ears, but it wasn't human.

"It's a demon!" Carter said, very startled.

An impressive number of teeth, fangs really, outlined its exaggeratedly open mouth. Eyes pierced their viewers with evil intensity, pointed ears and huge cavern-like nostrils reminiscent of a mythical beast. The most disconcerting thing was that it had been there the whole time, for the whole concert, and no one saw it. Perhaps even the singer was unaware of its presence. Or most likely, Carter thought, the singer was possessed by the demonic entity, so the "act" (as Gino called it) was simply the demon's concert all along.

"That, my dear friend, is a Class A entity in the Yuruniev scale. What you saw is just a projection of a physical demon inside that man's body. Like with Westerfield."

"Where is this from? And when? Who is the band?"

"Bergen, last year. The band's name is irrelevant, I can't even pronounce it myself, so... that's it. The most important issue here is that there are more Westerfields out there than we originally thought."

"You mean, every Black Metal musician is a demon?"

"No. I wouldn't say that. I went through all these tapes and, well, I cannot say this for certain but at least through these tapes I didn't notice anything suspicious."

"There might be more of them out there, then. We need to let the police know."

"I don't think this is the right way forward."

"Why not? People could be in danger. Kids especially."

"It seems like these demons have been in hiding for decades (or at least this is true for Westerfield). Meaning that they don't want to attract any attention."

"The homicides and the burned churches in Norway beg to differ."

"Well, we don't know if those crimes were committed by these demons or by brainwashed kids."

"Still a crime. It's called 'instigation' or 'premeditated intent'."

"Possibly, but we don't have any jurisdiction in Norway."

"Interpol has it."

"Look, I don't understand why—"

"Because I'm still a policeman and I want the bad guys behind bars. Why don't you?"

Gino felt attacked by that comment. How dare he accuse him of leaving criminals on the loose?

"But these are not criminals. These are demons. Jailing them could prove impossible, or even dangerous to people who aren't able to use the occult arts."

"But we have to do something!" Carter said, getting on his feet.

Gino looked at him leaving his office. Not a nod nor a hand gesture to say goodbye. He knew where he was going. To the gym, to relief his stress. He needed to punch the sack, or perhaps some other pugilist. He let him go. Although he could have reported him to HR – and he could have done this so many times on similar occasions – he didn't. The situation was very stressful for everyone including himself. But he had no ring in which to exercise, no family to borrow a shoulder to cry on like Carter had. He had thought about that fundamental difference between them so many times. Carter was young, happily married, with a kid. Instead, he was getting older, and he had been alone for all his life. He lived a quasi-monastic life dedicated to the occult sciences instead of a god. He followed in his father's footsteps, and what he had managed to achieve was just to fix his failures. A life dedicated to justifying his fascist father's choices, to minimising or even hiding his ancestry for the fear of being called out as a fascist too. He had lived in his father's shadow.

And now look at me, he thought. *He is going back to his wife and son, and I'm watching a psycho pouring goat's blood on his head. Wasn't he?*

Gino startled on his chair and had a quick look at the time on the player. The time didn't change, but why was the goat's head now much lower, the blood already all poured on the man's forehead and the halo gone? The more he looked at it, the more he realised the scene was going forward although the player had the PAUSE symbol on and the time wasn't changing at all. It was an excruciatingly slow-motion scene, but it *was* moving. He placed a finger on the screen, and that proved that the man's arms were indeed lowering the goat's head. His face was turning to the camera millimetre by millimetre, and in doing so a smile started to carve on his face. The black lipstick curving up and revealing the white of the teeth underneath. He started to look ghoulish.

Gino crept backward until his back touched the chair. What was happening? He couldn't understand it. Was the VHS possessed? How was that even possible? Suddenly he had an idea. He launched himself towards the power socket and pulled the cable. The player and the TV went off. As they should do. He sighed and closed his eyes. He wasn't a man who tried to find a scientific explanation for the realm of the weird, but this time he had to admit that it must have been a hallucination. Too much time devoted to this Black Metal, too many images of blood, evil, demons must have crept in his mind. He pulled himself up onto the chair with the help of his arms, when the furry head of Garibaldi touched him.

"Hey big boy. No worries, it was just a hallucination," he said ruffling his fur.

Garibaldi responded with a deep growl, showing off all his white teeth, jaws clenched dripping saliva, blood-shot eyes and ears down. His eyes had a flickering that did not belong to the animal world. Gino's hand flipped away from him. The old Garibaldi had become a real wolf, a few centimetres from his face. If he had attacked he would have taken half of

194

Gino's face off. Gino stayed still and moved himself backward slowly. The chair stopped his path again and he felt it didn't give in, a sign that it had reached the skirting board already. He was trapped by his own dog, which had never ever acted like this before. He decided to talk to him.

"Buddy, I know you are a good boy. Why are you doing this? This is not you."

Garibaldi flipped his tongue in and out between his canines several times, keeping all his teeth well visible. Dribbles of saliva dropped onto Gino's trousers, the growl increased in intensity, and Gino thought he was going to attack when the TV turned on and the blasting of the drums and guitar riffs exploded in the office and made both Garibaldi and Gino jump. Gino took advantage of the temporary disorientation of his dog to launch himself away from the desk towards the door. Garibaldi lost precious seconds, and when he attacked, launching himself, Gino was already gone.

Outside of the office, Gino could hear Garibaldi barking like a mad rabid dog, despite the loud music coming from the TV. He was trying to barge in through the door with his paws, to no avail. How was that possible if not through the lens of the supernatural? He closed his eyes and focused his inner eye towards the door. There was no doubt there was a demonic entity in his office and it had possessed Garibaldi. The only explanation he had was that the demon possessing the singer managed to pass over to his dog when he played the tape. More difficult to explain was how it had passed from the singer to the tape. That was a first even for an experienced Gran Maestro such as Gino. Trans-species transmigration had been documented several times in the past centuries. Black cats, bats and owls had certainly been the hosts of choice for many demonic entities in the past. But a demon or spirit getting "imprinted" on a tape and then jumping on another species... well, that was unheard of.

Now, how was he going to solve this? He could have cast an anti-cosmic field in the room but that could have been lethal to Garibaldi. He could have also called for help, but it was late at night, his floor almost emptied of colleagues, and it was a matter of pride. Could a Gran Maestro ask for help? He decided to inspect the scene through the astral plane.

When he projected his astral body into the office, things got confusing. The TV was still on but with a static signal, like when the antenna has been moved. This despite the power cable being unplugged and lying on the floor. An aura was emanating from the TV set and it increased when he got closer. It felt like a poltergeist case more than anything else. However, poltergeists did not possess beings.

Gino was so focused on the TV that he did not realise Garibaldi had stopped barking, and he was gazing at him with an intensity that he thought was only possible in humans. He could see his astral body. He'd heard that before. Animals, or at least some animal species, could see the other planes' manifestations. Gino hovered around the room with Garibaldi's gaze always fixed on him. The dog's eyes were following his every turn, every floating up or down, until something changed and they locked onto the blackboard. Something clicked in the dog's mind, almost like his attention was caught by something else, something more important than his master's astral body floating around the office.

And that is when things got weird. What followed belonged more to the realm of dreams than to the astral plane, or Earth. Garibaldi's barking was profound and cavernous, like it was coming from the depths of a bottomless abyss. His baying had an effect on reality. Each "syllable" warped the air, creating ripples that pushed their own ethereal weight towards the blackboard. White chalk-like lines started to carve on the black surface. It drew words all around the centre that, saved for last was filled with a giant sigil that Gino did not recognise. Then, Garibaldi's head turned to him and with the most serene face he spoke to him.

It was a dream-like experience, and like in a dream it ended abruptly. When he woke up to Rabbi Chai Levy's voice, he was still in shock. The Rabbi was holding his head up and was kneeling at his side. He had found him lying on the floor of the corridor after hearing the loud music and the barking dog. He immediately started wiping the blood that was dripping from his nose.

"Are you alright, Gino?" he asked.

"Yes," Gino lied.

In fact, how could he be alright after all that had just happened? After a demon possessed a VHS tape and took control of the TV set? After his dog, being possessed in turn, had tried to attack him? After his barking drew words and a sigil on the blackboard?

But little by little, a sense of achievement started to creep inside his mind. The state of shock transformed into a state of satisfaction. Because, although at first it sounded like an alien language to him, he now understood what that strange barking was all about. He understood that Garibaldi was in fact not barking at all, but speaking in tongues. And among Latin, Arabic, Ancient Egyptian and other forgotten languages all mixed up, he recognised two English words, the only English words: THE WELL.

Supersonic

He got off the Tube just in time for the rain to start. It was a strange evening. Dark clouds were crowding in small pockets and they were menacing the Londoners with spotted and intermittent pourings. Gino had to navigate through running umbrella-holding commuters at the entrance of Blackfriars. Luckily the Swan and the Shield was just a couple of streets from there. Once he got in, all drenched, he scanned the pub for any sign of Emma. He saw her in civilian clothes by herself at a table next to the window. He brushed through a thick assembly of young lads. Students from the uni, perhaps celebrating something, cheering with pints high up and already a bit tipsy. Past them, he ordered a pint at the bar and joined her at the table, apologising for the delay.

"Horrible weather," she said with a strong Mancunian accent, and cheering his arrival with her pint high up.

"I didn't know you were from Manchester," Gino said, amazed by her change in voice and attitude.

"Yep. Once I remove the uniform, Emma becomes the *dibble* from Manchester," she said with a loud laugh.

And just as she finished saying "Manchester", a music video on the TV started up. It was Oasis with 'Supersonic' on MTV.

"That's weird. I called it and now the quintessential Mancunian symbols show up," she said with a smirk.

"I wouldn't dismiss that as pure chance," Gino said, sipping his beer.

"What do you mean?"

"Well, we – and with *we,* I mean the occultists – do not believe in chance or probability. Technically, the term we use is *synchronicity.*"

"Ah. And how does that make it different from pure randomness, such as throwing a die?"

"*Occult* means hidden. What normal people see as the objective reality, we see just as a veiled world. Beyond the veil there are connections, patterns. If you look carefully into this hidden world, you can see small threads that link everything."

"Fascinating. But I'm still a sceptic for these things."

"I'm a sceptic too, but towards different things. So, even after what you've seen over the past few days?"

"What I saw... it's still difficult for me to comprehend. I need time to process it and find a rational explanation."

"You will not find a rational explanation for these sorts of things."

"How can I believe that demons from another world, or plane as you call it, passed through a portal and possessed a man?"

"It's not about believing. This is not about making a leap of faith or trusting a priest. It's about seeing beyond the veil of the faux reality our society has methodically built to keep our minds sane."

Emma did not reply and gave herself a long sip, froth on her upper lip.

"Look behind you. What do you see?" Gino said at some point.

"A group of young men celebrating something?"

"Look at what the man on the right is wearing."

There was a tall young man, probably the tallest of them all, who was cheering happily at the centre of the group. His red football shirt was standing out.

"Okay, there might be thousands of Manchester United shirts in London right now. How could —"

"Within five minutes of you mentioning your city we had two things that are linked to it. This is the synchronicity. The cosmos is trying to tell you something."

"Yes, that I should leave this madhouse called London and go back home."

She said that after the last sip and stood up. Gino grasped her arm but let it go immediately after, realising it could have been read as too aggressive. His eyes switched to the floor, signalling an apology.

"Wait. This is not why I invited you here. Sit down, please."

Emma kept standing for a while, then sat again. Gino relaxed, knowing that she was going to stay for a bit longer. He was growing fonder and fonder of this woman, and for a moment something that he thought he only had felt when he was younger – much younger – passed through his mind. Could it be that she was the one? The one from the Two of Cups in the card reading? The card that Josepha did not even finish interpreting? He remembered it in the Final Outcome position. A woman on the left and a man on the left, looking surprisingly similar to Emma and Gino – or was his memory being hijacked by this train of emotions? – holding two golden cups. A winged lion was floating between the two, symbolising wisdom. Love, the joining of two opposites, peace and harmony. Was it the end of his lonely life? The life he was recently dreaming about? He had become so jealous of Carter's domestic life that he wanted to replicate his happiness. He shook his head and got himself together. He wasn't thinking straight, he wasn't rational. He also should not make the mistake of giving so much meaning to a single card that was part of a spread. The spread needed to be read as a whole, and the rest of the cards were not that positive in his opinion.

He forced his mind to focus on what he wanted to say to Emma.

"What's happening is getting out of hand. I play the wise man here, but in reality I understand as much as you. These things..." he waved his hand at the window, as if there were gnats flying around his face, "...should not happen. They have never happened, for all I know. I need your help as much as you need mine."

"Okay."

"I got the key to the Well."

"What key?"

"It's a sigil that will allow us to get into the Well without our astral bodies being dislodged – let's use this word – from the space-time fabric of a different cosmos."

"How did you get it?"

"Well, let's say that it would be extremely confusing to explain this now. Let's say someone bestowed it onto me under particularly weird circumstances. Like you, I still have to process it, because I don't understand it yet."

"So, what would you like to do? What would you like me to do?"

"We want to descend into the Well, but we don't want any trouble. We don't want to attract attention from your superior."

"Abbot? I think you worry too much about him. I can sweettalk him if needed, but we would need a good excuse to give you permission to get into that site. Let me sleep on it and come back with an idea."

"Fine. Thanks. Another thing. Can we trust you to give us any inside information you might have about these metalheads and the village disappearances?"

"Yes. I told you before."

"But why?"

"Why what?"

"Why are you willing to give us all this help? Since the beginning, you have volunteered to help us. You lied to us about Abbot asking you to escort us and all that BS at the hospital. I might be a bookworm withdrawn from society, but I understand when someone is lying."

Emma turned her eyes down, staring at the foam the beer was leaving on the sides of the glass.

"Because I'm vested in it. I might be originally from Manchester, but my brother is from Sussex."

Gino's brows furrowed and his head shook like he was trying to say, "And so?"

Emma raised her chin like she had suddenly found the courage she had lost just a minute earlier.

"He disappeared together with a village a few months ago."

***

After Gino left the pub the sky cleared almost immediately. The group of young men took their fifth round of beers into the pub garden. Emma decided to follow them to finish her second pint. She lit a cigarette and tried to relax, although it had become harder and harder given all the events of the last few days. Her mind flew to the previous Christmas, the last time she saw Harry. Her family gave up on him and thought of organising a funeral. A mock funeral for sure, with an empty coffin. *Such a stupid idea*, she thought. And now that these occult-boffins, as Abbot used to call them, had found a way to enter that well, the chances of finding Harry went up considerably and that idea sounded even crazier. She really wanted to call her mother and tell her, but she also did not want to give false hope. She had to talk to Abbot first, calm him down and make him accept the collaboration with the RPI people. That was the only way.

The man with the red football shirt interrupted her train of thought to ask for the lighter. She gave it to him and waited for him to finish, but there was a draught that didn't allow him to light the cigarette.

"Move over there, there's a bit of cover from the wind," she suggested, pointing at a sort of alcove in the external wall of an old house next to the pub. A climbing wisteria in a pot gave extra-cover, and its twisted branches framed a metal plaque on the wall in front of which the man was lighting the cigarette.

It read:

George Arthurs (1875–1944), songwriter and composer from Manchester lived here.

It was only after the third time the man said "thank you" that she realised she had been staring at the plaque for more than a minute, her half-burned cigarette dangling from her fingers, the ash dripping on her trousers.

It was right then that an old man with a shiny bald head stepped in front of her.

Back from Oz

Gino looked at the trees passing by his window. A much better view than the M25's dull succession of grey cars flashing away like meteors that they had left half an hour earlier. Just two hours had passed since he was told by an overexcited Emma that Hartesbridge had reappeared. He couldn't believe his ears, and had asked to repeat what she'd said at least three times.

"You were right," she said. "About your synchronicity theory. It's all connected. Yesterday all those signs about Manchester and today the reappearance of Hartesbridge. Someone or something is trying to show me there are connections I have to follow and..."

Gino heard her almost starting to cry and decided to say something.

"Yes, why don't we talk about this in Hartesbridge, okay? Let's meet there."

"Yes. I'm on my way. I'll wait for you guys there."

"Emma, last thing. Did you talk to Abbot about the Well?"

"I didn't have time yesterday, but I will today. I'm sure he will understand, after all that happened. Trust me."

Carter was driving the Ford Escort, as usual. He hadn't spoken for almost the entire trip. Gino knew what was going in his mind and he knew it without making use of any of his mind-reading tricks. He couldn't make use of them anyway, even if he wanted to. He, like everyone else at the RPI, had made an oath that he would never use his powers on his colleagues.

Carter had made a promise to Lizzy that he was not going to get involved with magic and demonic entities again. A promise he could not keep. Gino had met Lizzy several times, but he could not forget the mixed expression of fear and loathing that her eyes directed at him the first time they met. She hated him because she thought that one day he would bring her husband back in a casket with a national flag and the emblem of the RPI on top. Gino could not blame her, really. The chances of losing your life during an RPI operation were low, but with all the things that had happened recently... well, if he were her, he would be worried too.

Lizzy was very religious. She was raised in a Catholic family and she considered occultism and spiritualism akin to Satanism. Like the majority of people, she had no clue about these matters. Once, at dinner at the Williams' house, the topic arose again and the evening became sour. He tried to explain to her that the position of almost every spiritualist, at least in the RPI, had always been the agnostic one. That is, the belief in other planes of existence and their entities' manipulation through magic did not imply the existence of gods or even of a First Cause. He, by the way, although raised in a Catholic community, could not take any position in the existence of gods, let alone the Christian God. For all he knew, he had no experience of their existence through spiritualism or black magic. Let alone the devil, Satan.

He finished his monologue with: "What both spiritualism and religion have in common is the belief that materialism cannot explain the complexity of the universe."

Gino never knew if Lizzy understood the meaning of his last sentence or the justification he gave to her as to why he wasn't a Satanist, because after that dinner, Carter's house became off-limits and Gino *persona non grata*.

"Copernican consequences," Gino said that morning in his office. Carter thought about those words for the whole trip to Hartesbridge. They had thought that the villages, once vanished, were lost forever somewhere, God knows where. The aim of their investigation several years back was to prevent other communities from disappearing, not to bring them back. The fact that a village came back from that *somewhere* was proof that all their premises were wrong. It meant you could come back from the Land of Oz after all. Now it was just a matter of knowing where the silver slippers were and how to use them. *Correction Carter*, he said to himself leaving a sarcastic smile on his face: Gino had just told him that his dog spoke to him two evenings ago and drew a sigil with his barks. A sigil that would take them to Oz, their silver slippers. Yes, because, why not? This is absolutely normal, right? A possessed dog that speaks to you in tongues and draws a symbol on a blackboard. And two days after, a village reappears.

208

"It's all connected!" Gino said, trying to convince him there were some logical reasons behind all of that.

All that talk about synchronicities, about patterns, about doppelgangers that die in the mountains. He was tired of that mumbo-jumbo. Lizzy was right. However, the reappearance of one of the villages changed everything. He had worked on this case for more than five years now, with a dull succession of disappearances marking his whole work experience at the RPI. This was the first time a town had reappeared. How could he say no to a visit? Even if that was a simple act of curiosity? Besides, resigning would require at least a month's notice. He had to take a decision quickly and he decided that this investigation to the reappeared village would be the last one.

They arrived in Hartesbridge at noon.

Several cars were lining up at the side of the road. Curious people, mostly, but also several journalists with their cameras and long mic booms. A cordon of policemen separated the crowd from the hollow village.

The sky was overcast, and the empty and silent streets gave off an eerie vibe. Once they'd parked the car on the side of the road, they waded their way through the crowd until they reached Emma. She was standing next to a police van, talking to a lady that they later found out to be Laura, the only village survivor they had read the report about the day after Hartesbridge disappeared. Once Emma saw them, she let them in by asking two police constables to open a gap between their ranks, and she lifted the POLICE DO NOT CROSS blue tape for them.

She didn't say anything, just chaperoned them to the beginning of the High Street, a long road leading up to the old church. Empty as only a postapocalyptic urban environment can be.

"It's like the town is back to Kansas after all," Carter said, breaking his self-imposed silence.

***

They strolled up the High Street, looking at every single shop, house door and window. A café first, then a small grocery shop, a church, several charities, a bookshop, a pub, a petrol station, the post office. All empty and in good order. Apart from the power and phone cables that were dangling everywhere, it was like the town had never been displaced. Gino was left speechless by the level of general cleanliness and order in the village. For the entire journey in the car, he'd thought he was going to witness a town in ruins, with hundreds of dead bodies lying on the streets.

"Where is everybody?" Emma asked like she'd read his mind.

It felt like a ghost town, one of those fake film sets built in the middle of a California desert not far from Hollywood. Gino expected the camera crew behind the facades, the caravans that hosted the actors and the director's chair somewhere.

"Is this real?" Gino asked Laura.

Once news of the village's reappearance had spread, Laura had immediately called Emma. Abbot gave permission for her to be among the first to enter the village, given she was the only one still alive that knew it well.

"What do you mean?" Laura asked, visibly confused by that question.

"Is this the Hartesbridge you have always lived in? Do you see any difference?"

"Of course it is. I don't understand why you are asking such a question. Well, obviously it is a bit different. It is empty of... people."

And on the last word her voice stopped in her throat. She suppressed tears. Gino regretted asking her that question, but it was important to check it with her. She was the only town's survivor, or at least the only one they know of and had interviewed at length.

Gino decided to peek through one of the shop windows, the barber's. Nothing was out of place, scissors, combs and hairdryers were kept in their resting places. No hair on the floor, no signs of people leaving the place in a hurry. Same with the bookshop next door. All the books were in orderly rows and piles on the bookshelves. You would expect some sort of disorder when people are displaced from one place to the other, together with their town. On the other hand, the vanishing happened at night, so the places they should look would probably be the houses. He looked at Carter and they both nodded. They got close to the nearest door of a two-storey townhouse. Carter was ready to knock down the door when Gino made a sign to stop. The door wasn't locked and it was ajar. A quick look at the other doors on the street, and it was exactly the same. Carter got in first, his hand resting on the holster under his coat. Gino signalled Emma and the others to wait outside.

Once in it was again all eerily normal. Nothing out of the ordinary. A short corridor, then a lounge with a fireplace, a kitchenette, stairs that led to the first floor where two bedrooms were kept pristine. If there was someone sleeping in this house when the vanishing happened, they'd had the time to make the bed, fold their pyjamas in the drawers and, while leaving, mop the kitchen floor. This was either a town model or someone had cleaned it up before sending it back to our world.

When they got out, it was clear to Gino that Laura was in distress. She said she feared what she was going to find in her house. If Gino's gut feeling was correct, they would find another empty and immaculate home. So, he led the group to Laura's home, knowing she would not see her husband and son's corpses. Or so he hoped. However, he also thought that the lack of their bodies could trigger another type of reaction in Laura. Don't we find ourselves at peace when we finally see the body of our loved ones and we can give them a proper burial? Isn't the sight of them in a way comforting rather than distressing, because it gives us a sense of closure? He hoped her reaction wouldn't be too difficult to manage. He wasn't very good at those things and hoped that Emma could support her better than he could. He spoke to the dead on a regular basis, and yet he had more difficulty in speaking to the living about these sorts of things.

Her home was around the corner, in a small lane that led to a cul-de-sac. It was a detached bungalow surrounded by a simple garden. There was a BEWARE THE DOG sign at the small metal gate, but no dog to be seen or heard. She was the one who led the group through the gate and up the short-pebbled path to the main door. Carter moved up in the queue and volunteered to open the door. Unlocked like all the others. And empty as all the others. They let Laura tour her home from one side to the other until she was sure no one was there anymore, dead or alive. Like Gino, she thought it was very odd that the house was so tidy and the beds were meticulously made, like no one had slept there for weeks. But she knew her husband and son were asleep the night the town vanished. Gino could not imagine what was going on in her head now.

Gino wasn't happy with the whole situation and decided to lead the group back to the High Street and the police vans. It was better to ask Laura to leave the place and let them investigate the town by themselves, using their own tools and skills. Especially the church on top of the hill, which was mastering the whole town with its tall steeple. Gino knew all the answers would be there and in the burial ground.

They had reached the middle of the road when they saw a commotion from the police crowd. Some constables were running towards them. They could not understand what was going on, the voices were too distant to differentiate each word from the other. Carter moved in front of the group and Emma to the back. They scanned the road but saw nothing, until Laura shouted, pointing at a side lane. There, walking towards them, was a kid, a boy in his early teens. A glance devoid of recognition. He wore a tattered red jacket and his shoes were unlaced. He was wandering aimlessly and with his gaze lost somewhere else. He didn't even acknowledge their presence, or that of the policemen who had just arrived, panting. He walked in between the two groups and now was heading up from where they had just come.

"It's James, Claire's son!" Laura said, stepping forward to touch him.

Gino grabbed her hand and did not let her get closer to the kid. She opened her mouth in surprise, and it was like her eyes said, "How dare you!"

Emma came close to Gino and asked, "What are you doing?"

"There is something odd about this kid. Let's not rush this."

"James," Carter shouted to test the kid.

No reaction. No answer.

Gino got closer to him but at a safe distance. He heard Laura and other constables talking. They were puzzled by Gino's reaction. Why was he suspicious about this kid? It was just a boy. The only survivor of Hartesbridge!

Gino knew he could count on Carter to stop anyone getting too close to the boy. Because Carter knew what the danger could have been. He heard him saying "Westerfield" to Emma, and she gasped.

Good, he thought, *now they know*.

He started his incantation, but it was too late. And this time there was no pentacle to restrain it. The kid shrieked and in less than a millisecond jumped at his throat, knocking him down onto the tarmac. Gino managed to stop its mouth from reaching his face, but he could not resist for long. Carter knew it and dashed forward to help him. He grabbed the kid, or whatever he/it had become, and tried to remove him/it from Gino's body, but it was all in vain. His/its strength was so much that even a giant bloke like Carter could not manage to dislodge it. Emma came to the rescue and pulled one of its legs, shouting at Carter to do the same with the other leg. They heaved with all their strength, but they just managed to pull both Gino and his attacker across the tarmac.

The demon turned its head and growled against them. Then a ghastly howl erupted from its wide-open mouth. Gino saw the opportunity to summon the sparks that killed Westerfield once again, but he knew it wasn't going to have the same magnitude of power as the last time. He placed his hand on the demon's forehead, risking being bitten at any time, and he shot. A thunder erupted from the contact of his hand and its head and the demon jumped into the air, followed by sparks and smoke. Carter and Emma fell to the ground and could not understand what had just happened. The beast landed a few metres away, its head cracked in two from the hairline to the nose. Gasps and shouts broke out from the crowd, more due to the sight of the kid still being alive and walking rather than because he was shot. How could he have survived such a wound? How could a small boy like that attack an adult man with such ferocity and strength? Everyone was left guessing until a whitish shape started to protrude out of the wound. And that left no doubt as to what had happened to the poor kid.

Gino stood up and focused more energy into his hands to finish it, but again it was too late. The demon stood up like nothing had happened to its head and attacked him. Gino thought that was going to be the end of him, even when the shots exploded and the kid's body collapsed to the ground. When he opened his eyes, he saw Emma next to him and heard Carter still unloading the whole gun's magazine into the lifeless body. Although not hurt by the bullets, the demon's body suffered immensely due to the destruction of its host. So, when it got out it took Gino only a fraction of his power to reduce it to ashes.

***

"Now, you must tell me in layman's terms what's happening here. Why did this village reappear? Where are all the people, and why did only that kid come back, possessed by... that thing?"

Gino was sitting on the pavement, his back leaning against the wall of the bakery. In front of him, the lifeless body of the kid. Carter, still in his heightened mode, was kneeling in front of the body while loading a new magazine into the gun. From this angle Gino could see the cracked head. It opened up like a walnut, a dry, sharp sound. No blood, no fluids, no organs. A husk, like Westerfield before him.

Emma knelt on the ground and was speaking at his head's level. He did not know what to say, really. This was an enigma for him as for anyone else. He only had a hypothesis.

"I wish I could answer all your questions, Emma, but I'll be honest with you. I do not know. What I do know is that we have to get into the Well to get all the answers we seek. And trust me, I'm the one who is most interested in them."

"What are we going to say?" she asked, still worried about the consequences of reporting to higher management more than anything else.

"What everyone else witnessed. Your colleagues here and Laura saw it. So, we can't be considered crazy, right?"

Emma stood up again and was joined by Carter, who was waiting for an explanation too.

"Look, people. I'm not sure why this village came back to our world. I can only assume breaking the esoteric triangle through the destruction of the Chichester and Hasting sigils worked. The two planes are separating from each other. We will probably see more towns reappearing."

"Without the people?"

"I'm not sure. I suspect the only survivors will be like that kid. So, just a husk, a vessel for these demons."

"Why that kid? Why was he the only one?"

"I can't answer your question. Maybe young humans are better vessels for these entities. Westerfield came back as a kid as well."

"Do I have to tell Abbot to watch out for more towns coming back and to kill children at first sight?" Emma asked sarcastically.

"Talking of the devil." A deep voice resonated behind them.

Enter Abbot. Chin up, belly out, his belt barely visible. A police hat to hide the incipient baldness. He was followed by two high-ranking officers. They moved forward like one single wedge that split the crowd. Everyone heard Gino whispering, "Oh, shit," including him. Abbot replied with a wry smile, followed by a laugh that seemed genuine.

At least he has some sense of humour, Gino thought, standing up and brushing the dirt from his clothes.

"So, what do we have here?" he asked with an imperative tone.

"Sir…" said Emma, before being interrupted by Abbot himself, a hand and one index finger up.

"I saw it. It was just a rhetorical question. I saw it all."

Abbot's and Gino's gazes locked for a few seconds, then it was Abbot who softened his stance.

"What do you need from us?" he asked abruptly.

Gino's reaction was pure surprise and he made no effort to hide it. Did Abbot really say those words? Was he really offering the RPI agents – or as he called them last time, *occult-boffins* – help? Did Emma's sweettalk really work, then? That was a sudden and unexpected change of attitude from an authoritative man like Abbot.

Gino wasted no time and asked for respirators, climbing ropes and harnesses, an excavator with a reel. The descent into the Well needed to be organised in a very detailed way. He knew what to expect in the cave and what were the most important tools to use. Abbot agreed to all of it, and asked the two officers to immediately meet his requests. He did not even ask what all that equipment was for. He looked very accommodating and almost cheerful, although this word should not be taken to indicate that typical state of happiness and light-heartedness that characterise every one of us from time to time, but rather an absence of Abbot's distinctive ever-present bleakness.

Gino sought Emma's eyes and found them smiling. She really did it. They walked back to the police cars, hoping not to have to wait too long for the tools and the excavator. They passed all the shops and the post office and only from this perspective did Gino see something that caught his attention. It was a plaque on the wall of the house with a symbol in it. A symbol he knew very well. A snake eating its own tail and forming a circle. Inside the circle were the interlaced black and white triangles, one pointing up and one down to form an exagram. Inside the exagram, the Egyptian Tau or Ankh, the T-shaped cross with a circle on top. Then the swastika and the OM word on top.

The emblem of the Theosophical Society.

How come there was a Theosophical Society section in such a small village?

What were the chances of finding such a section in a recently disappeared and reappeared town in the middle of Sussex?

"Do you know anything about that?" Gino asked Laura.

"Oh, the wizards?" she said with a sarcastic tone.

Gino didn't pay attention to her mocking the Society's accolades. She felt slightly worried when his eyes met hers and he pressed on.

"They are new. A couple. They moved in a couple of years ago and took the place of a previous charity. I've met them a couple of times at the café, but I never exchanged any words with them."

"Where were they living?"

"Church Road. An old Victorian house. I can't remember the number, but once you see it there is no doubt who it belongs to."

The occultist's home

The house would have fit pretty well in a Gothic story. It was a Victorian two-storey brick house with a lot of wooden elements, such as the Gothic turrets domed by greenish galvanised steel roofs, the entrance porch and the three bay windows that protruded onto the street. The second storey was clad in blackened wood planks and a huge ivy climbed the entire surface of the house up until the roof where its shoots bent to follow an almost broken brass gutter whose end was dangling just on top of the entrance porch. The small front garden was unkempt and the only plant still standing high was an old cherry tree with skeletal branches that resembled the fingers of a dead man. Curtains were drawn, dust covered the porch floor, and the metal gate to the garden was broken.

It looked abandoned and devoid of any life, and yet Gino and Carter were surprised to see the door fully locked, unlike the doors of the other houses. That prompted Carter to get his gun out of his holster and heightened his police instincts. Carter took the lead and moved sideways to search for a secondary entrance at the back of the house. Gino followed, with his eyes fixed on the closed windows they were passing by their heads. Two abandoned wheely bins were standing in the narrow corridor between the house and the other house's fence. The rear garden allowed them to understand where the house was built. It was very close to the church, hence its position on the highest grounds of the town. The back of the house was facing the burial ground of the church, so the owners could have a clear line of sight just by standing in their bedroom. Gino thought that that could not be a coincidence. Also, the rear garden was devoid of plant life and neglected for years. The door to the garden was locked too, but Carter knew that it was easier to knock it down than the main front door.

He rammed it down with a single kick, then pointed the gun inside the corridor, swung the straight arms into the kitchen, then the lounge. Gino followed him into every room until he entered the lounge. It was a spacious environment. Someone had knocked down a wall and merged two rooms together. The south and north facing windows were boarded, but blades of lights could pass through. It was clear that someone didn't want this room and its contents to be seen from the road outside. An oval table, a couch and several chairs were the only objects that you could consider as normal furniture in the room.

Everything else belonged to a world he knew very well, tools and objects he was attuned to, bound to, even. The space was filled with candles, pentacles drawn on the floor, grimoires, scrolls and parchments, ritual knives, altars, esoteric emblems and sigils, tarots, Ouija boards, alchemic bottles and alembics, crystals, etc. Gino recognised many objects and texts were linked to Ancient Egypt and Mesopotamia. For example, there were stone and clay statuettes of the gods Anubis and Thoth that seemed original; knee-high stacks of clay tablets carved with cuneiform writing; a huge and partially damaged stone tablet with hieroglyphs that was standing on the floor, leaning against the wall. Other pieces were lying on the floor, almost like someone was trying to stitch them together.

It felt like a museum, but with the sole difference that the objects were not displayed but rather disorderly accumulated. Almost like someone had hoarded the most bizarre collection in their home over the years.

What caught Gino's attention were the several parchments hanging on the wall. It was a collection of ancient maps, sigils, drawings, all noted in different languages and writings: from Latin to Ancient Greek, from Egyptian hieroglyphs to Sumerian cuneiform. One map depicted the Ancient Egypt and the Middle East overlaid by a triangle – an esoteric triangle! – whose three points were Alexandria, Babylon and Aksum. Another map showed the Messina experiment with the triangle connecting Messina, Rome and Cagliari. The third map, the Greenwich triangle, with Greenwich itself, Chichester and Hastings.

Gino was in a state of true shock. They had just entered the house of someone who was very familiar with the esoteric triangles that were opened in the past, and who had access to information that only an RPI employee of higher rank could have. The fact that this house belonged to a person affiliated with the Theosophical Society who had recently moved into the very same town that vanished and reappeared was not a mere coincidence. The implications were vast, and finding this person could help in solving the puzzle.

Gino was so immersed in his thoughts that he did not hear Carter calling him from the corridor. He had to be pulled back by Carter to realise that.

"I went upstairs and there is no one. The house is safe. But you'd better come upstairs to see what I found."

They both climbed the stairs and found themselves in a room, one single room that was created by knocking down all the walls to merge three different rooms. In it there was another collection, this time of photos, some framed on the wall, others spread on the floor. It was clear that there was a clean divide between the framed ones on the walls and those on the floor. The ones on the floor depicted objects, most of which were the ritualistic tools from the room below. Gino recognised some of the rituals that the occultist performed. It was mostly summoning, but also protection and astral travel. This person knew them all.

Then Gino stepped on an album that was lying on the floor. Its leather cover had a sigil that resembled the one Westerfield had. Inside there was a collection of peculiar photos, none of which belonged to the ritualistic tools or the people series that were spread across the room. It was unique, and probably the most important single piece of evidence in that room, and yet it was the most inscrutable of them all. The photos were in black and white and depicted what Gino could only describe as landscapes. There was a wide black field, or perhaps a sea/lake surface, that touched the horizon and therefore the sky. One of the photos was indeed divided into two halves: the black surface at the bottom and a milky cloudy sky at the top. Another one depicted a mountain or an island floating at the very edge of the horizon, so that most of its outline stayed in the top half of the photo. Some other photos replicated the same subjects, but were often ruined by overexposure or random flashes of lights that ran like threads across the photo. It was like someone had tried to take several photos until only a couple were of good quality. And yet, the photographer had decided to keep the bad ones and place them in the album. He could not understand what it was and why it was associated with Westerfield's sigil.

Carter pointed his hand, still holding the gun, to a series of very dark photos. Gino took one of them and watched it carefully. A nineteenth-century sepia photograph of a man sitting on a chair. He wasn't looking at the camera but at an empty point in the room to his right. It looked pretty normal and typical of those years, if it wasn't for the unearthly pale shape floating behind him. Same for the other photos of that group. People from the last century with whitish shapes floating behind them. Spirit photography. Gino looked at Carter and saw in him the same worry he had. They had entered the home of a person that had been in contact with the same demonic entities they had been trying to hunt down for the last few days.

He then moved his attention to the hanging framed ones. The majority were in black and white or sepia and from the nineteenth century. Gentlemen and ladies wearing Victorian-era clothes and hats. There was something that reminded him of the photos that were hanging in the RPI canteen, something familiar. Indeed, they were all occultists and spiritualists from different secret societies: the Theosophical Society, the Order of the Golden Dawn, the Stella Matutina, the Alpha et Omega, the Ordo Templi Orientis, etc. It was clear that there was a connection that linked all of them, but Gino could not quite understand what.

"Carter, look at these photos. Can you see a thread I cannot see?"

"That they all look like the nineteenth-century equivalent of today's RPI employees?"

Gino ignored his sarcasm and focused his attention more and more on the photos.

"There is something..." he said holding his chin with one hand.

"Hang on," Carter said, moving to another wall. "Look at this other group of photos. This man is posing with Madame Blavatsky, Yeats, Crowley, Dion Fortune. These are the heavy-weights of the nineteenth-century occult scene, right? And he is the same person who is standing here in these other vintage photos. And here, and here, and there! He is everywhere, but with different clothes depending on the historical period. How is that possible if Blavatsky is from the 1850s and Crowley from the 1930s? I mean, he should have aged considerably and... Gino? Are you okay? Gino?"

Carter realised that Gino had been in a sort of trance during his analysis of the photos. He was looking at the photos of Aleisteir Crowley and Lady Blavatsky. In both of them, the mysterious man was wearing a bowler hat and holding a walking stick with an ivory handle.

"It's him. He has always been behind all of it. He witnessed it all and this is his home," Gino said in a barely audible whisper.

And while holding another photo that showed the mysterious man with yet another person in front of a tall obelisk, with an unmistakably Italian urban landscape, he said: "He is the man I saw in the cave and he knew my father."

***

"You know, you can always say no. Descending into that well will be dangerous," Gino said, holding the framed photos in a stack as if they were playing cards.

"Gino, it's my job. If you ask me to come with you, I will."

"I'm not asking as an RPI Gran Maestro. I'm asking as a friend. I cannot..." he stuttered and corrected himself, "...I won't force you or report you for insubordination."

"We are in this together, we just have to finish the job."

"But to me it's personal. To you... it's just a job."

Carter did not answer that. How could he have answered it? There were so many factors involved, one of which was his sense of duty, the potential shame if he didn't follow him, and the realisation that stopping these things from passing through our plane would save more lives in our world, including Lizzy's and Jamie's. He wanted to call Lizzy so much now, but he suspected there was no line in the town. He stood up and went down to the kitchen, where he saw the phone. He picked it up. No line, obviously. How could the town's telephone cables have survived the connection with our world when it vanished into the thin air? He hung up the phone and saw a phonebook with several numbers carefully written in a beautiful and almost vintage calligraphy on multiple pages. Tens of numbers both in the UK and with foreign country codes, many of which were +47. Norway.

"It seems like our man was also behind the Black Metal scene," Carter said throwing the phonebook onto Gino's lap.

Gino had a quick browse and confirmed what Carter had said. Lines and lines, pages and pages of names and phone numbers. Most of them must have been occultists, others Black Metal musicians from Norway and other countries. This was an incredibly important piece of evidence. He thought of giving it to Emma later on, before their descent into the Well.

"James Shackleton," Carter said.

"What?"

"His name is James Shackleton. Look at the first page."

It was true. The first page had that name and the address where they were right now.

He tried to remember if that name reminded him of someone. He dug into his childhood memories, when his father was younger and could have entertained a relationship with other occultists. The problem was that Amilcare Marcotti was one of the leading figures in the field at that time, so he'd met hundreds of them. He tried to focus on the photo that he was holding in his hand now. It was Rome in the background. And that was the Aksum obelisk that the Fascist regime brought to Italy as a war trophy after the defeat of the Ethiopians. His father must have been forty-two in that photo, a few months before Italy surrendered and Sicily was invaded by the Allied forces. A few months before he was taken as a prisoner of war and sent to a British prisoners' camp together with his wife and son.

Although he had fond memories of his short childhood in Italy, most of them revolved around his grandparents and the cobbled streets of the little medieval town he grew up in. He was too young to pay attention to his father's friends and colleagues.

However, there was something that told him he met that man with the hat during his time in Italy. He just had to dig deeper and deeper. He knew there was a way to perform auscultation in the same way as he did with that policeman on his hospital bed. This autoauscultation was a way to reach one's deeper memories, a sort of autohypnosis. He knew it could be done but he knew it was potentially dangerous. He didn't want to lose himself inside his head, although it sounded like the most contradictory thing in this world. But now he had that photo in front of him and he was in the very home of the person he wanted to remember. Both things would be extremely helpful in his quest to dig into his memories.

He focused on the photo: Rome in the summer, the excruciating heat of the midday deserted roads, the celebratory parades of the soldiers coming back from the front-lines in a vain attempt to show that Italy was, despite all the bad news coming from El Alamein and Ethiopia, still winning; his house at the top of the low hill next to the cathedral and the remains of the Renaissance city walls; his mum calling him for lunch and him saying goodbye to his friends still playing in the street; the smell of the hot bread and the carbonara; his father in the lounge, a pipe in his hand, sitting on an armchair next to his hundreds of books lined up on the shelves, talking to a stranger; his mum pulling him away to the kitchen and telling him, "Do not disturb your father"; after lunch, peeking from the door, trying to eavesdrop what the two men were saying: Thoth, Ra, Aksum, all new words to him; his father letting his guest leaving and then holding the door, saying, "Thanks for passing by, Meren-Ptah"; the man donning a black bowler hat just before exiting, looking at Gino and saying with a great smile, "Goodbye, little one. I'm sure you will do great things like your father. And I'm sure I will see you again in the future."

"Meren-Ptah," Carter heard from a visibly shocked Gino, who looked like a memory had suddenly resurfaced from the depths of his mind.

"What?" Carter asked.

"This man we are after, Shackleton. This is just the name that he uses to blend in during our age. His real name is Meren-Ptah. An ancient Egyptian from four thousand years ago."

"This is insane."

"And yet, it explains everything. He is a theurgist, a sorcerer. Instead of channelling the inner forces to perform magic, a theurgist would use the magic coming from spirits and demons. I suspect he is not only behind Black Metal's rise but also behind the nineteenth-century's occult resurgence. He might be one of the founders of the secret societies we saw popping up between Britain and the US. Even Mathers, the founder of the Order of the Golden Dawn, spoke of an unknown master who had instructed him to found what would later become the first temple of the Order of the Golden Dawn."

Gino's words were stopped when the lock of the front door clicked. Someone had got in. Carter pointed the gun at the bottom of the stairs. They heard someone rummaging inside drawers and then walking from one room to the other, in what seemed like an agitated fashion. Then, the noise stopped. Four quick steps and the sound of the rear door creaking. Gino threw his head back, and closing his eyes, he thought, "We forgot the door was open!"

There was no time to waste. The intruder – who could have been the owner of the house, actually – had understood that someone broke in. Carter sprinted down the stairs and Gino followed him a few steps behind. Gino had to stop suddenly in his descent and he almost crashed into Carter's back. Carter stood like a caryatid in the middle of the staircase and held Gino's weight. There was a man at the bottom of the stairs, standing still with his bald head up, looking at the barrel of the gun pointed at him. His hands were down, all fingers spread, like he was caught in a very embarrassing situation and didn't know how to justify himself. His torso and head were partially illuminated by the light coming into the corridor from outside. A diagonal line of light cut his body from shoulder to hip. Although the lighting conditions were poor and the situation was hectic, Gino had no doubt that the person in front of them was the man with the hat and the walking stick. James Shackleton, the man behind all that was happening.

In those few seconds, which seemed like ages, both parties were locked in surprise, their brains trying to compute their own and the others' next move. It was Shackleton who decided to unlock the situation and dashed sideways with a speed and agility that surprised both Gino and Carter. Gino pushed the stunned Carter down the stairs, risking making him tumble down. Shackleton did not rush out of the house as expected but took refuge in the lounge, locking the door behind him.

Gino threw himself at the door with all his weight, but it was a vain act. He banged his fists on the wood and shouted:

"We know who you are, Shackleton! You are Meren-Ptah! We know it was you behind all of this! There is no way you can escape this!" he began. "I want to know! Where is my father!! Where is Amilcare Marcotti!"

Carter pushed him away from the door and kicked it just below the handle. Nothing. It did not bust or crack. He tried to knock it down with his shoulder, to no avail. He looked through the keyhole and closed his eyes. His face showed disappointment. When Gino looked through the keyhole, he understood what happened. It was all dark. Shackleton had probably moved a cupboard to block the door. The windows were boarded, so unless he had a hammer with a pulling claw, he was imprisoned inside.

Why did he take refuge inside that room when there were easier ways of escape already opened, like the two main doors? Why did he come back home now? And what was he trying to find downstairs? These were the questions that stormed Gino's mind.

While Carter put his ear to the door in the hope of listening to any sound that might come from the lounge, Gino went on a tour of the ground floor in search of any clue to what Shackleton was trying to find. The kitchen drawers were open, some cutlery had been displaced and now lay on the counter. He moved to the entrance where a short and very thin table stood next to the door and below a mirror. Its drawer was open as well. Inside he could see several candlesticks and matchboxes. One of which was opened, letting several matches overflow into the bottom of the drawer.

An incantation! Gino thought.

"He is starting an incantation in that room! We have to stop him before it's too late!"

He could already smell the sulphur of the matches and the smell of frankincense coming from below the door. Carter pushed him away from the door again and ran outside, into the garden. He came back with a spade.

"Let me work on this," he said before bashing it on the door.

The wood cracked open, and after several blows gave in completely. The hole was now big enough for them to get their heads in. They could see the back of the cupboard. They both inserted their hands in and pushed with all their might until it flipped over inside the room with a crashing sound. Carter reached the lock with his arm through the hole, and they were finally in.

Although they thought they knew what to expect, it seemed they were not prepared to see what it was in front of their eyes. The cupboard's left side was an inch away from Shackleton's body. A body that was lying on the floor within a frantically drawn pentacle. At first, they thought they had killed him, but it was clear that the cupboard had missed him by a hair's width. Carter drew his gun and pointed it at him, nevertheless. Gino ignored his warnings and threw himself on the floor, brushed the lit candles away with a single slide of his open hand, and checked Shackleton's neck.

"He is still alive," he said with a sigh of relief.

The man's skin felt shrivelled up, like it had lost all water. His face was ragged and carved by age, and he looked in his seventies. However, there was something that made his wrinkles and furrows much older. Ancient, perhaps, was the right word. Indeed, if Gino thought of all the vintage photos from upstairs, in which he looked exactly like he was today... Gino shivered, realising who they had in front of their eyes. Meren-Ptah, the sorcerer. Now that he looked at him closely, he could see some Mediterranean features, not modern though. More like the ones he saw at the British Museum in the Egyptian section. A crazy theory but it would explain the Thoth triangle's map and the exotic and ancient tools that were present in that room.

Meren-Ptah. A Methuselah of eldritch origins. And now he had no doubt who he really was in the Tarot spread. His challenge, his nemesis. The sly, corrupt old man who he had to fight to reach the peace and harmony of the Two of Cups. It wasn't Sadir the necromancer, neither Westerfield, the Mystagogue. Meren-Ptah, the ancient sorcerer, was the King of Pentacles.

"What happened?" Carter asked, lowering the gun.

Gino stood up and looked at the Thoth triangle's map hanging on the wall.

"He is gone. Astrally gone."

"Damn, we missed it by a few minutes."

"Not necessarily. I think I know where he went. But first I need to call Emma."

PART III

Through the Well

Intermezzo III

From the Diary of Amilcare Marcotti
Aksum, Africa Orientale Italiana, 29 March 1941

The Church of Our Lady Mary of Zion is two roads across from the inn we are staying. I can see its dome and the fence that surrounds it. Two Coptic priests are guarding its entrance 24/7. It looks very simple and anonymous. If I hadn't known it was holding the Ark of the Covenant, I probably wouldn't even noticed it.

We arrived in Aksum yesterday, two days after the failed ambush. Aksum is a small village with little importance, if it wasn't for the church and its contents and the tens of obelisks that litter the countryside. These obelisks were transported to Ancient Egypt through the clever use of rolling logs until they reached the Nile, where they could be easily transported on barges. A titanic undertaking for that time. The obelisk that is now standing proud and tall in Rome comes from here.

Tamiru recovered from his wound in the head, also thanks to my bandages and care. The ascari kept their distance from us and offered no help. I had to explain to him how we got through the Tigrynians' gang safe and alive. Well, apart from his wound. He knows I'm a séance – he was told at the embassy when he was hired – but it is one thing to hear that someone claims to be talking with the dead, another to see that same person summoning spirits through use of the dark arts. Incredibly, he is not shocked and he is not scared of me. He understands that I was forced to do what I've done to save our lives and he is very grateful for it. That makes my life much easier, given what I'm about to perform tonight. He will be the one who will help me.

He also commented on the ascari that are now staying in the stables with the animals. It's right below our room, I can smell the animals' stench when I open the small window. And I can hear them talking loudly. Probably still talking about me and about what they saw in the highlands. They are visibly scared of me. They saw a side of me that few have seen, and I can't blame them.

The inn, if we can call it that, is a simple two-storey hut made of hay and mud bricks. It was made a few years back to host some Italian soldiers that were stationed here. When it is not hosting Italian travellers, it's the house of the local blacksmith's family. The locals were very curious to see our small convoy approaching the town from the north. Our first encounter was a goat shepherd on the outskirts, then rumours of our arrival spread thanks to tens of children running back and forth from house to house. Tamiru had to explain to several people why I was there and why I was escorted by three ascari. The local chief, who was given some administrative powers by the Italians, welcomed us into his house and offered us coffee. In good Italian, he said that the Italians left a few weeks ago, when they heard of the British troops taking Addis Ababa. There are only some civilians left here and there. A Catholic priest and two nuns, an old war veteran who now owns a garage and a few others. He was surprised to hear that I had crossed all the way to Aksum just to see the Ark of the Covenant, which he told me could not be seen by anyone but the priest guardian. I'd heard of this before my journey, but I thought that by being polite and by bringing some gifts, I might be given an exception. The chief says there is no way I can get in. The priest has a rifle too, and he will use it if necessary. He was twice as disappointed when he found out that I wasn't disheartened by his words. He doesn't know I had a plan B.

Aksum, Africa Orientale Italiana, 29 March 1941, around midnight

I've prepared the room. I've asked for enough candles to last until early morning. I moved the furniture – not that there was much – in such a way that I can have enough space in the centre. I drew the pentacle on the floor with the chalk. Then, I opened the empty diary and took several pencils.

Tamiru knows what I'm about to do tonight and he is still sceptical of my powers. If he only saw what I performed earlier in the highlands. He has no idea how I can achieve it, and most importantly why I'm doing it. I told him a few things during our journey, but he didn't fully get it. Perhaps on our journey back to Asmara he will have a better understanding of the terrific prodigy he is going to experience tonight.

Before I start, I give strict instructions to him not to disturb me under any circumstances, save for the inn burning or someone pointing a gun at me. The door must always stay locked. He has to observe only, and if needed help me with the writing, if I drop the pencil or if my hands cannot find the diary. Any twitching of my body or voice coming out of my mouth must be ignored. I really hope he follows my instructions to the letter.

The whole town is sleeping apart from some dogs barking at the full moon. From my window I can barely see the dome of the church with the lunar light. I cannot see any guardian priest or the door of the church. But it doesn't matter because I do not need to see for what I'm going to do tonight.

I start my incantation and focus my mind on the astral realm. It takes longer than expected, probably because of the troubled days during the journey and because of a new environment. I can feel Tamiru's presence in the room, his breath and the occasional swallowing of saliva in his throat. I can hear the most subtle of sounds in the room and in the whole inn. The creaking of the wooden floor, the draught passing below the door, the mouse on the roof, the warm breath of the donkeys in the stable, the snoring of the ascari lying on the hay.

Then, it happens so quickly I can't even tell when the right moment of detachment was. I see myself sitting in the lotus position inside the pentacle, holding the pencil, the candles that illuminate the empty pages of the book. Then, a few metres away, a bit bored, Tamiru who has no clue of what just happened. He is looking at the candle flames burning slowly. It's time for me to focus my attention on the very objective of my mission. I turn and float out of the window. From the top of the roofs, I can see the town asleep. The moon shines on the far away obelisks that shine with a silver tone. The dome of the church is in front of me now and it calls me in. No one is around, apart from a dog that it seems to bark at my astral body. Did it really see me? They say animals can see the astral realm, but I guess we will never know.

The wooden doors of the church are simple and with rough decorations. I pass through them easily. I immediately find myself inside a small forecourt with two accesses on both sides. I move to the left until I find a brick wall. At its base, a human figure is sleeping on a mat. It's the Coptic priest, still dressed in his ceremonial clothes. An old rifle is leaning against the wall next to him. I go inside the church proper and a bigger space opens up to me. The walls are decorated with scenes taken from the gospels and from the Coptic tradition. All the figures are black, even Christ and the Virgin Mary. They look very simple, like a child has drawn them. Very colourful and full of symbolism. I recognise most of the scenes, including St George who kills the dragon. There are several Coptic crosses, both made of wood and of cheap tin. Two thuribles are suspended to the ceiling via a chain. If only I could smell odours in this form, I would smell the frankincense, the intense smell of the leather and of ancient stones.

I was told the moonlight would shine inside the church on this night, and so it was. From a small, high meshed window a beam of light descends on the church pavement and wall.

Although the moonlight is not that important – I'm sure I can find what I need without it – having Thoth, the moon god, guiding me through these ancient stones seems like a good omen. The light is touching a wooden panel at the very end of the church. I get closer to have a look. I know – *I feel it!* – what I'm looking for is behind it. I float around it and see an ancient wooden chest, painted with several Gospel and Old Testament scenes. By the look of it, it's several centuries old. The Ark of the Covenant! Although I'm not here for this, I can't help but wonder what it looks like. I trespass the wooden planks and find... nothing. The chest is empty. They protect and revere an empty box. What a disappointment. I would have expected at least a replica, or any other artefact to be honest. Instead, just nothing.

While I'm still inside the empty chest, I feel a chill. Something which should be impossible during astral travel. Could my body in the inn room be in danger? Why did I feel an earthly phenomenon that only the senses of my body could detect?

I immediately get out of the chest and have a look around. I fly back to the centre of the church and see nothing suspicious. The priest is still sleeping, snoring like before. The moonlight is still shining on the wooden panel. I cannot explain what happened, but I can't stay too long in this form. I move back behind the panel and I analyse the area. I can sense the sigil in here, but I cannot see it. I focus my attention as much as I can, like a pointing hound trying to detect its prey in the bushes.

It's on my feet? How is that possible?

It's under my feet! I immediately move down, below the pavement, and after several layers of stone I find a crypt. The stones here are clearly older. Ancient blocks recycled from an earlier Egyptian temple. I can see hieroglyphs here and there; some are whole, some are partial where the stone was cut. The empty space is quite small, two metres by two. No visible entrance. Probably untouched for the past two thousand years. It seems incredible that they left this space empty and did not fill it up with stones or debris. Perhaps they knew what was inside and did not want to interfere.

And then I can see it, glowing like the beacon of a lighthouse. The sigil I have been seeking for for so long. I did not expect it to be like this. All the guessed shapes I saw in ancient texts and grimoires were wrong. Now, I have to transcribe it, and to do so I need to perform what in spiritualism we commonly call automatic writing. But instead of writing a message received by a supernatural entity, I will need to simply copy what my astral body sees. I pause and focus all my energies for the task ahead. It's not an easy task, because while I'm away from my body I have to control it remotely, but if I lose too much of my concentration, I can lose the tether and get lost outside of my body.

I can feel my arm moving very slowly. The hand is still holding the pencil and is on top of the empty page of my diary. I start to write the convoluted symbol, trying to be as precise as possible. A wrong angle or distance between lines and the sigil won't work. I can only imagine the shock in Tamiru's eyes now that I'm about to write the sigil on paper. He is probably looking at a man in trance and with his eyes shut, but still able to move his hand and write. He might try to talk to me, although I won't be able to hear him.

I'm doing all of this, when at some point I feel that chill again. Tamiru might have seen my hand stop, and he might have thought that I had finished my sigil, but I'm still three quarters through. What is it? Is this through my astral body or my earthly body? I decide to continue drawing and leave my thoughts to later. But it's when I finally finish that I hear a whisper. Inside the crypt. I turn to look around, but I don't see anyone or anything. Only the ancient blocks of stone, silent as they have been for thousands of years. Then, the chill again, all over me, and I finally see something appearing between me and the stone wall. At first it reveals itself as a halo, like a warm breath on a cold night. But then it becomes a distinct figure. A human figure.

And then comes the realisation that there is someone else with me in this crypt. A crypt that was sealed two thousand years ago!

I immediately jump up to the ground level, then I project myself towards the door of the church, through the dry and thorny bushes, ignoring the barking dog, ignoring the streets, and I pass through houses, courtyards, furniture, sleeping people and donkeys without looking back a single time, until I get back to my earthly body.

Tamiru is surprised to see my eyes and my mouth opening almost like I've just experienced a drowning accident. He jumps back and mumbles something. I look at the diary and my heart is relieved to see the sigil perfectly drawn. I stand up and I lean out of the window trying to figure out if I can see the church in the dark of the night.

Tamiru asks me what happened and why I look so shocked. I don't know where to start. Shall I start with the astral travelling? Or the trespassing of the church? Or the emptiness of the chest that was supposed to contain the Ark that is not? Or with the ancient crypt that kept the sigil for two thousand years? Or perhaps I should just tell him about the eerie, eldritch feeling I felt when a stranger with a hat and a walking stick appeared to me in the sealed crypt and smiled.

The descent

Gino supervised the transporting of Shackleton's body to the police van. Two policemen secured him to the stretcher with straps, after a doctor injected him with a sedative. It took Emma quite a lot to explain to the doctor that Shackleton would not be transported to a hospital, and that the straps were required for his safety due to the possibility of major seizures. In the end it was Abbot's authority that made him give up.

"You know what to do now," Gino said to Emma while giving back a big, squared cellular telephone.

Gino had never had the chance to use one of them before that day. It felt weird not to have a wire attached to the handset. During the call to the RPI, he kept staying close to the bulky receiver inside the car, thinking that the call would hang up if he was too distant from it.

"Yes. I'll follow your instructions to the letter," Emma said, setting the cell phone back on the car receiver.

"Don't worry, Marcotti." A deep voice made Gino's head turn immediately. "I'll make sure it will be done. I'll oversee it all," said a serious-looking Abbot.

Abbot's change of heart was a true mystery to Gino. That authoritarian man who until the day before would have happily seen them gone – together with the whole RPI – was now collaborating, merrily approving any of their requests. How was that possible? Gino was sure it wasn't because of Emma's sweet comments. Of course, she helped a lot in hiding all the dirty details from him, but that wouldn't have been enough. Perhaps it was the scene he saw on Hartesbridge High Street, when an otherwise normal kid revealed himself as a blood-sucking demonic entity, that changed him.

The digger was already working on the church's graveyard, overseen by many policemen. Among them, Carter was watching with a worried look. Gino saw him, and he went to his spot next to him. It was time to go down. And Carter knew it. He knew it better than anyone else.

"Who did you call on the cellular telephone? I've never seen you holding one of them before," Carter said without looking at him.

"Yes, you are right. They are not that bad," Gino replied, chuckling a bit. "I was with the RPI. I'll explain later, though."

Carter pointed at the burial vault that the digger was going to work on. It was a Victorian-style squared vault, not taller than two metres and containing at most two coffins or caskets. Two classical columns framed an entrance sealed by a bronze door decorated with Egyptian motifs. It was the only such structure in the whole graveyard, and possibly in the region. Not difficult to spot where the sorcerer Meren-Ptah was hiding. The columns were holding a thin architrave with carved letters saying: J. SHACKLETON.

"So, here is where he was hiding," Carter said.

"No. Here is where he was accessing the other plane," Gino corrected him and almost if the driver of the digger had heard him, the long boom protruded out and the massive black bucket ripped the green brass roof from the vault.

Then it was the turn of the brick walls and the columns. There went the bronze door, as well. Gino felt a knot in his throat, thinking of such an exquisite architectural piece being destroyed like that. He pulled Carter back, way back by several metres.

"We'd better stay away from it. I don't want to end up like the storks last time."

Bricks, columns and door were gone, and from the debris a single casket appeared, all covered in dust and fragmented bricks. It fell onto the stone floor and the lid cracked open. It was empty. Gino's guess was that it was the place where Meren-Ptah used to leave his earthly body to rest, while his astral one was travelling through the Well.

Yes, the Well. *Where was it?* Gino thought.

He gave a signal to the excavator's driver to pierce through the stone floor. The bucket went down like a punch, and nothing happened. Then, its teeth grabbed one of the slabs and pried it open. Immediately a fluorescent glow darted up.

"It's there! As I expected it to be."

Gino finished his words and signalled for the driver to open it more. Most of the slabs were pried open, and the whole rim of the Well was visible. Shortly after, a bell-shaped wall of air appeared out of nowhere. The anti-cosmic field. Gino gave instructions to the driver to move back and look away from it. They all kept a ten-metre distance from it. Everyone remembered what happened to the storks and didn't want to have the same experience.

"It's time Gino," Carter said, walking towards the police van where Emma and Abbot were waiting.

On the way, Carter said, "I have a question. When Abbot asked you what we needed, you said respirators. What do we need them for?"

"It's a different plane of existence. We don't know what the atmospheric conditions are going to be. It's just a precaution," Gino replied. And then, after a pause, "Still happy to come down the Well?"

Carter did not reply but he nodded in silence.

After a few minutes they were all suited up and ready to go. A light helmeted airleak-proof suit with a small respirator that was supposed to last for a couple of hours maximum. A Kevlar-type vest with a sigil carefully drawn and glued by Gino (this time they didn't want to burn any more chest hairs). It was the same sigil that Garibaldi drew on the blackboard and – Gino reassured Carter several times – it would not only protect them from the ripping of their flesh in another plane but also from the time difference with Earth. They didn't want to stay there for seven years with the passing of each five earthly minutes. But that was not all: a rucksack each with some climbing tools; harnesses and carabiners; two powerful torches with extra batteries; Carter's gun clearly visible now in a chest holster, although everyone knew it would be close to useless against their foes. All in all, they felt like astronauts or deep-sea divers ready for a scientific mission.

Carter couldn't help thinking about *The Dead Mountaineer*. They were wearing the same tools as Crowley on that peak, and it was time for both of them to take a decision. A fork in life. Would their doppelgangers stay here and let the world die, while they were getting into the Well? Carter doubted his sanity when the mere thought of a doppelganger splitting from his body triggered an unexpected sexual pleasure from his loins.

Gino and Carter clamped the carabiners to the reel that would be their only lifeline to our world. The other end was attached to the boom of the digger a few metres away. Emma gave both a hug, and the gesture felt a bit clumsy with all their gear. They waved their goodbyes and the Well sucked them all in one single powerful draw.

***

Gino's heart was pumping while the reel was unspooling them towards the abyss below. Carter was just a few metres below him, clamped to another carabiner. Once the Well had sucked them in, the green fluorescent glow of the rim was gone, and so was the afternoon sky. It was just pitch black, cut only by the blades of the light from their torches. Darkness was so complete that there was no up and down.

The silence inside the space they were descending was truly astounding. He swore he heard his heart pounding at some point. So, what was *that* space? Or was it just emptiness? The Well did not have walls, only a rim visible from the outside. The anti-cosmic field was having different effects on their sensorial system, now that they were on the other side. If there were no walls, was it all hollow around them? It seemed like it, because their torches could not reach any wall, either natural or artificial. It felt like they were floating in space, although there were no stars blinking at them and the temperature was lukewarm, actually a bit hot, thought Gino. And that wasn't something he'd expected; in fact, quite the opposite.

He didn't tell Carter, but he had never been sure they would survive the descent into the Well. And how could he have ever known? After all, what he was doing was trusting an old dog that spoke to him and drew a sigil. To his knowledge, no one from our world had ever crossed to the other plane of existence in human form. That's why Meren-Ptah used to traverse it using his astral body instead. Needless to say, he was glad it did work. He had gambled with his and Carter's life, and he felt utterly guilty. But now, the other challenge was what to do against Meren-Ptah and his minions. He had several cantrips that could help him but, in all honesty, he had no idea whether they would work in a different plane of existence.

Apart from their electric torches, the only other source of light was the sigils on their chests, which this time weren't burning through their clothes and skin. Their dim white glow was a sign that without them they could have been already dead, perhaps torn apart by the other plane's laws of physics.

Carter said something and his voice sounded like thunder after so much silence.

"What?" Gino asked, looking down at his feet.

He could see Carter's head bobbing around and his torch pointing down.

"I can see something now. It's like a grey, rocky surface," Carter replied, pedaling with his boots like he was trying to touch it.

Gino knew Carter landed on the rocky surface when the reel became floppy beneath his feet. He made sure he didn't land on Carter's head and leaned towards his right as much as possible. In less than a minute they were both standing on top of a three-metre round slab of what they assumed was rock. They inspected the surface closely and it seemed like a volcanic type of rock, with thousands of tiny pores like pumice. Gino laid on his belly and peered down from the edge, and the torch revealed more rock underneath for many metres below. It was a tall, cyclopic column.

"It's the pillar!" Gino said, getting to his feet. "We have reached the cave that I visited during my astral journeys!"

They followed the light beam down until the pillar disappeared, sucked away by the darkness. In a way, the sight of matter after so much empty space made them feel even more anxious. Emptiness can be reassuring, a giant pillar of rock that vanishes in the darkness plays a different trick on your mind.

In the meantime, the reel continued to unspool downwards, and they felt its weight growing more and more on their belts. They decided to continue their descent alongside the rocky pillar. It meant it became more difficult to manage their fall, due to their bodies bumping on the rocky surface every now and then. Gino tried to stabilise himself by grabbing some of the crevices that he encountered here and there with his gloved fingers. Carter was doing the same but with better success. They dropped for several metres, possibly fifty, but it was difficult to say. The light beams of their torches could maybe penetrate up to thirty metres into the darkness. So, the cave's bottom was always thirty metres away from their light blades.

They reached the bottom of the cave a few minutes later. Gino looked at his watch. It had taken them twenty minutes to descend. It would take them probably twice as long to climb, so they only had an hour of air in their respirators. They would have to be quick. Gino took the lead once they'd detached themselves from the reel. They left the rucksack there at the base of the pillar, together with an activated red glowing stick. They had several of those and they were planning on dropping them at regular intervals if they had to move away from the pillars.

Carter recognised the cave although he had never seen it. Gino's description a few days earlier had made an impression on him. The uneven rocky floor, the fluorescent crystals, the cold and the humidity, the small critters scuttling around that reminded him of the sand fleas running on the beach from his childhood in Cornwall. It was hard to imagine that Matt's astral body had lived in there for seven long years.

Carter drew the gun from its holster and followed Gino, who was moving carefully along the uneven floor. The rock was so jagged and sharp, obsidian in its shard-like texture, that it could have ripped their boots or suits very easily. The implications of that thought were not lost in their minds. One mistake and the air from their suits would be gone. They trod very carefully and their torches were pointed down most of the time. That meant they might be surprised by any encounter, but what was the alternative?

After several metres, they reached the wall of the cavern. There, nestled in the recesses of the rocks, hundreds of crystals were glowing to a very regular rhythm. Gino switched his torch off, followed soon after by Carter. Once their eyes got used to the dark, they realised that the light coming from those crystals was sufficient for minimal vision. Gino reached out to one of them and felt a spark of energy flowing to his fingers. It wasn't electricity, nor any other sort of energy that humans were used to, like magnetic or thermic. He recognised it as a *qi*, the vital force of beings. Upon closer examination, he quickly realised that the crystals were pulsing in unison. Gino started to suspect that the cave had very little to do with the natural formation of a cavity through geological forces, but more with a *purpose*. It wasn't a cave but a chamber. In a way that was even more disturbing than thinking of it as a mere random natural place. If there was a purpose, there was a mind behind it.

"Is this the Oz we were looking for, then?" Carter asked.

"Not sure. I'm more afraid of the Wizard, though," Gino said in a whisper.

He moved around the cave patting the rock in search for something.

"Here it is," he said quietly, pointing at the low entrance of the tunnel he'd seen during one of his astral travels.

Carter placed a hand on his shoulder to stop him. He went forward and inspected it with the full power of his torch. Gino signalled to him that there was no need for him to lead.

"I go first," Carter insisted, removing the safety from the gun.

"*Lasciate ogni speranza, o voi che entrate.*"

Carter turned with a puzzled face that clearly read: "Why are you speaking in Italian now?"

"It's the beginning of Dante's *Inferno*. Never mind."

As they left the cave, they made their way down the dank corridor.

A cold and distant sun

The corridor had a squared cut that left no doubt about its artificial nature. The walls were smooth and so was the floor, and yet it felt like it wasn't made by machines. Gino thought of the difference between a human-made building and a bee-made hive. Both were artificially made, but could the latter be considered architecture? He had the impression it was made by sentient beings more than by bee-like animals. They proceeded cautiously as the corridor made several ninety-degree turns, obstructing their view right in front of them. Carter was leading with his torch and gun pointed forward, and Gino had to trust his colleague's sight and judgement, given that the width of the corridor did not allow two people next to each other. Every now and then he threw his head and torch back just in case someone or something might attack them from behind. In one of these moments, the red glow of the stick he dropped behind illuminated a part of the floor that was unusually uneven. He stopped Carter and kneeled down to investigate.

There was something that interrupted the smooth surface of the floor. He cleared away the dirt to reveal inscriptions that, in a perfect line, crossed the full width of the tunnel.

"What's that?" Carter asked, shining his torch on it as well.

"I cannot tell. Writing of some sort? Or simple decoration?"

"Where are we?" Carter asked with a concerned voice.

Gino did not know how to answer that question. He did not expect demonic entities to be able to build or even write – if what he was looking at was even a form of writing. He pulled a sheet of paper from a notebook he had in his rucksack, and with the help of a pencil he started to carbon copy the reliefs. He wished he had a camera with him and more time, but both were impossible to obtain. He then stood up and slowly hinted at continuing their advance into the corridor.

When they began to walk again, Gino found himself in the mood to talk about something that had bugged him since Josepha's card reading.

"I think it's time for you to know about Abbot," he said.

"What about him?"

"I think he is the Hermit card."

Carter stopped and turned, his face puzzled.

"I have no idea what you are talking about."

"When Josepha read my cards and I experienced my visitations, one of the cards was The Hermit. It's an old, bearded man holding a lamp. Card nine of the major arcana. It signifies many things, among which are personal transformation and – now I can see it – treason. He retreats from the world to a place that will eventually change him to such an extent that he becomes someone else. It's a rebirth. Someone will betray us. I have pondered for many days who that would be, and I could not see it until today when

259

Abbot came across as the most innocent lamb. Didn't you find it curious that he used to be so rude to us and then suddenly all this help?"

"I thought Emma managed to..."

"Do you think you can change the character of a man such as Abbot in one day?"

"I don't know, but it felt sincere."

"This is exactly what makes it even more suspicious. It was a play, all theatre. You don't change your attitude from one day to another like this, unless you are planning it as a lie."

"So, you think he is one of them? By 'them' I don't even know what I'm referring to."

"He might be possessed by one of those demons, yes. Perhaps he has been approached by some musicians from the Black Metal scene. Or even by Meren-Ptah himself. Who knows."

"And how is he going to betray us?"

"That I don't know. Perhaps he will mislead us in our investigations. Or he just got us trapped."

Carter stared at Gino for a few tense moments.

"What do you mean?"

"Because, if he is one of them, there isn't a better opportunity to get rid of us than this: facilitate our descent into the Well and then let us not come back out from it."

After he said that, Carter, visibly angry, started to walk again at a faster pace. Gino followed him silently, realising that perhaps he should have kept it to himself. He had just killed Carter's morale.

"Those maps we saw downstairs. What were they?" Carter asked at one point, trying to defuse his anger with a different subject.

"Previous attempts at making esoteric triangles," Gino replied, happy for the sudden change of subject. "You know the Messina one, in the Mediterranean. My father did not come up with that out of the blue. It was based on ancient knowledge passed down through several generations of occultists and thought to be lost forever in the Middle Ages. One day, in the library of the Vatican, he found an ancient text that told of a massive esoteric triangle, called the Thoth's triangle, between Alexandria in Egypt, Aksum in current Ethiopia and Babylon in current Iraq. The idea behind it was to communicate with the realm of the dead. To summon all previous pharaohs and ancestors. Little did they know that instead of summoning the dead, they summoned demons from another plane of existence. The chronicles talk of pestilence, death, drought, but in reality it was the opening of the gateway that let these entities in our world."

"But then, it means that your father knew he was going to trigger the same thing."

"Yes, but he was sure he could control the demon hordes using the same sigil that Ankhtifi, an Egyptian priest of Ra, used at the time. We know it worked because the Egyptians won two battles against the Nubians and the Babylonians using such entities."

"Mussolini wanted to do the same."

"Exactly. And my father's knowledge could have changed the outcome of the war. Unfortunately for them, the Allies landed in Sicily days after the opening of the gateway and they broke the Messina sigil, followed by the Cagliari one, before any summoning could happen. A couple of Sicilian towns disappeared, though, but at the time it was thought the Allies bombed them or used a special weapon to pulverise them. Crazy, huh?"

"And then Churchill wanted that power too, for Great Britain."

Gino nodded in silence, hoping Carter would not continue with that conversation. He always felt uncomfortable speaking about his father's past. Especially that elephant in the room. The fact that his father was a fascist. Yes, he'd switched side after the war, like all Italians did, but there was no doubt he believed in what Mussolini wanted to achieve and he actively collaborated with the government. Years later, his mum would say that the Fascist Party was only a means to an end for his father. He wanted to open the gateway and Rome allowed him to do it. But it could have happened with London, Washington or Moscow.

"Maybe", Gino used to say with a shrug, not knowing exactly what his father really thought of the war. His premature death gave Gino the benefit of the doubt. In a way, Gino thanked that accident, because it avoided a confrontation between an adult Gino and an old father.

Now there was a dim light at the end of the main corridor, this time unlike any they had seen before. As they approached it, they realised the light coming from the crystals gave way to a milkier, nebulous background light. It was clear there was a bigger source of light coming from above that was filtered by a thick fog.

Their guesses were proven right when the corridor ended abruptly to reveal a vast landscape that could only be described as outdoors, if it wasn't for the claustrophobic feeling that the thick and low masses of grey clouds and white fog transmitted to them. The space immediately in front of them was covered in water. Or that was their first impression, which quickly changed when they realised that the liquid that sprawled for miles and miles to the horizon was not the familiar waters of the Earth, but more akin to mercury or melted lead. It was a placid grey sea or an immense lake almost devoid of motion. In general, the whole scene looked artificially static, like a painted background in a theatre.

The mouth of the corridor where they were standing was directly connected to a long causeway, which cut it into two halves made of what it seemed like a single slab of stone (obsidian? slate?) or possibly polished concrete. It was indeed artificial, and it had been built to lie just an inch above the sea level. Meaning that if it weren't for the different reflection of the used material, they would have seen a seamless liquid surface from their feet to the horizon.

The causeway was a straight line that reached the faraway horizon until it found a black towering peak. Possibly an island of cyclopic size that occupied a fourth of their horizon. Atop the rocky formation were dozens of spires. Calling them towers wouldn't have done them justice, as they were defiant of the gravity that affects normal towers on Earth. They spiralled up with sharp ninety-degree turns like the antlers of a giant stag. The island's silhouette was outlined by that milky light that was illuminating the whole scene. It was like a low, dim sun that was setting beyond the island.

The sky was incredibly low and overcast with lead-coloured clouds that didn't move. It was indeed a static scene, with no wind, no moving sun, and calm waters that made them doubt it was an actual outdoor setting at all.

"Gino, I've got a feeling we are not in Kansas anymore," Carter said without a trace of irony.

Gino recognised that scene. He'd seen glimpses of it in Shackleton's home, inside the photo album with the anti-cosmic sigil, spread among several vintage black-and-white photos. That peak crowned by the spires that made it look like a rolled hedgehog. The pale white sun that never sets beyond it. The vast liquid metal sea that reached the straight line of the horizon, interrupted solely by the immense island. Who took those photos? How did they bring them back? That meant they were not the first and only humans to have crossed between the two planes and come back. Shackleton/Meren-Ptah? And yet he chose to use his astral body to cross them. And how did he manage to do it? In order to take a photo, it would have needed the oxygen for the chemicals to react. Did it mean that...

"Carter, did you bring your cigarettes with you?" Gino asked out of the blue.

Carter opened his mouth in surprise. How could he ask such a question before such an alien landscape? Had he lost his mind? He looked at him like he was talking to a crazy person. And yet Gino was waiting for an answer.

"How could you think of –"

"Just answer me."

"Yes, here in my pocket, but I wasn't going to smoke any in here. I swear. Just the habit of having them in my pockets."

"Give me the pack."

Carter reached inside one of the external pockets of the suit and produced a white and red pack. Gino took it, discarded the cigarettes, and grabbed the lighter. He lit it and the flame reflected on his helmet. Gino gave the lighter back and unlocked the helmet from the collar of the suit. Carter dashed forward with the palm of his hand open, in a vain attempt to reach the helmet before it was too late.

"What are you doing?" he yelled at Gino, visibly terrified.

Once Gino had taken, he breathed in as much as he could with his eyes firmly shut. When he exhaled, he did it with a big smile.

"It's breathable. Take it off too. We will save valuable oxygen that we might need during the climb."

Carter stayed in that awkward position – his torso leaning forward and his hands extended – for a few more seconds. He couldn't believe what had happened. He watched Gino removing the respirator too and placing it inside the entrance of the corridor. That was madness. How could he do such a reckless thing?

"We will collect them when we come back," Gino said, helping him removing his helmet.

Carter held his breath for a few seconds after the helmet was gone, then he let some air in through his nostrils. The air was fine, just fine. Very fresh and neutral, not even a different smell. Somehow his mind linked that infernal world to sulphur, something that had been imprinted since childhood. Still, he wasn't sure that was the right thing to do. What about other gasses, pathogens, fungi? Well, too late.

They felt much lighter now and less worried about the time ticking away. They decided to cross the causeway. The surface where they were walking was solid stone, cut and polished in one single block that spanned a mile or more. How was that possible? Gino tried to find signs of fractures or joining lines, but failed.

Once they were halfway through, they turned their heads back. The tunnel that they emerged from was bored inside a massive towering structure that pierced the low clouds like a giant finger. It was quite evident now that their descent into the Well was actually a crossing through that tower's height. Now there was no doubt in Gino's mind that the cave was an artificial structure, and that the crystal had some sort of unexplainable function. They looked at each other without saying a word. What was there to say? They were in an alien world with laws of physics which were probably very different from those on Earth. They could only observe in awe.

"The Tower," Gino said in a whisper.

It was exactly what the Tarot had predicted. They crossed it through its height in this upside-down world, exactly like he saw in his vision.

THE TOWER.

The Tower meant destruction, true, but destruction brings new beginnings. It was a rite of passage in which they had to kill themselves in order to find this place. It was a sacrifice they decided to make of themselves, risking their very lives. The Well was a fork in space and time, and either they – or their doppelgangers – traversed it.

They hurried up a little. Now that they were halfway through, they felt an impelling drive to reach the island peak as soon as possible. They knew all their questions will be answered there. They knew Meren-Ptah was hiding in there.

Carter stared constantly at the immobile waters as if waiting for something to float up. And yet during all their crossing not a single wave or bubble reached the surface. Neither of them attempted to touch the lead sea, – as they had started to call it. The sun did not move from its position behind the island peak, neither did it set. That was disconcerting to their natural senses, as if they were witnessing the winter sun at the North Pole, with the sole difference that the latter at least moved across the horizon rather than staying still like a cosmic lamppost.

The crossing took them a good portion of half an hour, and the closer they were to their goal, the more they could see the details of the alien rock formation. It was indeed a mountain made of solid and jagged rock that was interspersed by artificially made structures, the closest of which was a giant stairway that led up to a plateau or terrace of huge proportions. Beyond that and higher, almost on top of the peak, a series of structures that resembled what in human terms can only be described as a city. Rectangular blocks built on the steep rocks with holes that could have been windows, and the tall spiralling structures that they saw from a distance were now clearly artificially made and organic to the city. The architecture of the city did not resemble anything linked to humans, but rather was closer to the animal world, like a beehive.

The realisation of what they were approaching did not slow their pace; quite the opposite, it sped it up. They finally reached the clean line of the shadow cast by the peak on the causeway. Where you would have expected a difference in humidity and moss presence after that line, there was none. Temperature didn't change either, suggesting the source of heat in that outdoor environment did not come from the pale white sun. A curious rhythmic sound started to echo from above the ramp of stairs. It was incredibly regular, interspersed at five-second intervals. It seemed like a hammering but there was no metal involved.

After a few hundred metres they reached their destination. The ramp of stairs that linked the causeway to the plateau was irregular and almost random in size and proportion. One step was low, another high, another one was protruding, another concave. They had to select the right steps and move sideways to find the best path up. There was no logic or if there was, it was totally inscrutable to them. They were both driven by curiosity to find out what or who was making that lumbering sound. The further they ascended, the louder that sound grew. And that would have been obvious if it wasn't for the fact that the sound was also changing pitch. It was now similar to wet clothes being thrown on the floor. Were the echo and the peculiar architecture playing with their hearing?

Carter was the first to peek at the terraced surface. Whatever he expected to see, it was not a factory chain of huge proportions with dozens of figures carefully pulling soft, long objects and letting them pass through tanks of liquid and conveyor belts. There was a huge amount of fog or steam that concealed most of the details, but there was no doubt those creatures were quite dissimilar to the parasites inside Westerfield and the lost kid in Hartesbridge. Gino joined him, peering from the safety of the last giant step that covered them almost entirely except for the top of their heads. Indeed, he had to stand on his toe in order to see what Carter could easily see by standing normally.

And then the sound. That regular splatting sound of wet clothes or towels hitting the floor. It was coming from the end of the conveyor belt. At the very end of the factory chain the objects were thrown away without any care on top of a large mound. Through the short gap in the fog, they could recognise pink, grey and brown shapes with four appendages and a wobbly rounded tip. The realisation of what they were witnessing hit them almost simultaneously. Both shaken and with their mouths agape, they slid down and hid behind the final step that divided them from that pure horror. Was there anything more horrifying than watching your own kind being butchered and treated like animal meat? Was there anything more revolting than witnessing the demise of hundreds of men and women and children?

Gino had to breathe in and raise his chin to stop the puke from going beyond his throat. Those poor people who disappeared with their towns. All of them. They were just harvesting them to make them into empty husks and wear them. Gino felt Carter's warm hand on his knee in an attempt to support each other. It felt reassuring, and it woke him up from the creeping loss of sanity that he knew was coming. They had to move forward. There was no other way around that circus of horrors. He reluctantly decided to face it again and raised his head. The process was still ongoing, unperturbed, each demon focused on a particular stage of the chain. These were minor entities, possibly D-class in the Yuruniev scale. Minions without any particular skill apart from total obedience to higher archdemons. They looked humanoid apart from the absence of noses, ears and hair. Their claws were sharp but short, their large mouths tightly packed with needle teeth, no tail. They wore no clothes and their skin was pale grey. Carter joined the watch and slowly scanned every single detail of the process, until his head locked in one particular direction. A figure was moving among the working demons. It was white in appearance, almost fluorescing with its own light. It wasn't like all the others and it was moving very fast *across* the machinery. Yes, Carter didn't imagine that at all. He blinked to check his sight but there was no doubt that the humanoid shape emanating a dim white light and floating in the air was going *through* objects.

Carter stopped and crouched, leaning towards the rocky wall of the step. Gino was pulled down by Carter's hand and made himself as small as possible behind his wide frame. They stayed like this for more than a minute, their breathing becoming more regular, second by second. The figure in front of them was a human, there was no doubt, but it was floating and ignoring the matter.

"Gino, what am I looking at? Is this what I think it is?"

"No, Carter. It's not a ghost, strictly speaking. But it's something close. It's how I would look if I'd projected my astral body."

"But why are we seeing it?"

"That's a mystery for me, too. Perhaps in this plane astral bodies are visible."

Gino peered again and whispered, "Meren-Ptah!". They'd finally found him. He was there, floating around that plateau like it was his home, master of his surroundings. He was inspecting each stage of the process, checking each demon, and in order to do so he was floating from spot to spot, sometimes going through the machinery and even the demons that were ignoring him, possibly unaware of his presence. It was very clear now that Meren-Ptah was no stranger here and that he was one of the minds, if not *the* mind, behind this horrific slaughtering. After this repetitive chore, he directed his attention to the heap of empty corpses, emptied of fluids and organs. He started touching them one by one on the back between the shoulders, and each time a flash of light was shot. Gino knew what was happening but couldn't believe he was seeing it before his very own eyes. He was marking each corpse with an anti-cosmic sigil, the same as Westerfield had on his body. He was preparing them for the parasitic entities to wear them. He was marking one per minute, meaning that in an hour he could more or less prepare sixty of them. Multiply that for several hours per day, he was setting up an army. They had to stop him before it was too late. But how? He doubted his powers would work as well here. The very fact that they could see the astral bodies was a sign that the laws of magic here were different.

Carter did not join him and stayed on his knees, so Gino thought he would check on him. It must have been a crude test for his sanity, given that he had been exposed to so many supernatural events and creatures in the span of a couple of hours. He was indeed still crouched, but instead of being paralysed by fear and panic, he was intent on watching the causeway. His eyes fixed on a faraway point. Gino looked back and saw the same white dot crossing the land bridge at high speed.

"It's another astral body?" Carter asked in a trembling voice.

"Yes, it looks like it."

"What do we do? This won't do anything, right?" Carter said, waving the gun in the air.

"No, but keep it handy in case those demons approach us from behind. I believe our weapons can wound them in here."

"And what about that thing approaching?"

"Let me handle this."

Gino drew a white chalk circle that contained both Carter and himself. Then, he sat in a lotus position and closed his eyes. He mumbled for several seconds while the figure continued to dash along the last leg of the causeway. It was now at the base of the ramp of the stairs, which didn't slow its pace. It simply floated to a higher level each time it encountered a step. It would reach them in a few seconds. Carter started to panic and stood up. He stepped back and found the cold wall of the last step with his shoulders. He stopped, knowing that he shouldn't have stepped out of the drawn circle. He looked at Gino, thinking to wake him up from his concentrated trance, but he was anticipated by Gino's eyes which opened like camera shutters.

"I can't believe it," he heard him saying.

Then he saw him standing up and exiting the circle he'd just drawn to jump down to the lower step.

Carter did not know what to do, and pointed the gun at the approaching figure, although he knew it was going to be useless against *that*.

The astral body was that of a man in his sixties, with sideburns and a moustache that had last been fashionable in the 1970s. His face was haggard and was perched on a slim frame. His black moustache was dotted with grey spots and his hairline was receding. Carter had the realisation that if it weren't for the moustache and the vintage clothes that man could have been Gino in a few years.

Gino had now reached the floating figure and only a few inches were dividing them, and yet there was no intention from either of them to close that gap and touch each other. Gino was on his knees, sobbing, slow tears carving his tired face like late spring streams. Although the floating figure's expression bore the pain of solitude and distress, he was exactly as he remembered him on that day he died. Even with the same clothes, which did not surprise him given that the astral image was simply a mirror of the earthly body from which it had detached.

"I wish I could cry like you, my son," Amilcare Marcotti said in a whisper.

"Babbo," Gino said in Italian, and then switching to English, "How is this possible? I thought I'd lost you."

"You did lose me. At least, my earthly body. Somehow, in the infinitesimal moments between touching the sigil and my death by the lightning bolt, my astral body detached and was drawn away into this plane of existence. And I've been wandering as a

THE HANGED MAN.

restless soul like this for centuries. But how can you be alive and so young?"

"Time flies differently for astral bodies here. Your centuries are mere days for us on Earth."

"So, Debora..."

"I'm sorry, Dad. Mum passed away five years after you. It's only me now. And you..."

"I'm lost in between realms, neither alive nor dead. I'm just a reflection, a mirror cast in time."

"But there must be a way to rejoin you with your mortal body. If only we could revert –"

"Trust me. I'm condemned to wander in this plane forever, but I'm glad I managed to see you in the flesh and still alive. Your presence here is just a glimpse in my centuries-long astral life. A white luminous dot surrounded by the pitch black of the immensities of the cosmos. And what a magnificent dot you are, my son."

Gino did not know what to say. His father had been alive and yet dead for what he perceived as hundreds of years. These minutes with him were just hiccups in time for him, like some temporary background static when you tune the radio.

"What is this place?" he asked.

"It's not just another plane of existence, as you might think. It's not above or below or even beyond ours. It's just parallel, and now, unfortunately, contiguous. It's the very place from which our most inner fears come. It's the repository of human myths, religions and superstition that you and I have dedicated so many years of our lives to study. Every time there was a crossing between these worlds, we thought they must be gods, demons, spirits. Instead, it was them."

"You mean there is no afterlife? That the gods are–"

Amilcare raised a hand and stopped him.

"I can't answer these questions. My knowledge is limited to this plane, not beyond. These creatures sometimes leak into our reality, and some of us leak in their reality like I'm doing now. This much I know."

Until then, Carter had been a mere spectator of that rather unusual family reunion. He decided to get closer to the two. Amilcare looked at him with calm eyes for the first time and saw him lowering his arm.

"He is my colleague, Carter Williams. We both work at the RPI now."

"Why are you both here?"

276

"Towns have started disappearing in Sussex, in the middle of the esoteric triangle you built. We have also uncovered a group of these demons that crossed our reality using human corpses as vessels, and they disguise themselves as musicians of a new rock subgenre called Black Metal. We know who is behind this, and you know him too. He is behind us there, harvesting human bodies and preparing them for the demons."

Amilcare nodded in silence.

"Meren-Ptah. I've seen him wandering these lands too many times and I knew he was up to no good since we met on Earth in 1933. He – going under the name James Shackleton – was the one who introduced me to Thoth's esoteric triangle and the possibility of replicating it again in Italy. He gave me all the knowledge and materials needed to find the Aksum's anti-cosmic sigil. He introduced me to the wife of a Fascist Party official who was very fond of the occult and thought she had powers herself. She then introduced me to the highest ranks of the Fascist Party, and I explained how the magic I was hoping to resuscitate could reverse the fortunes of the war. They believed me and financed my travel to Ethiopia, where I got to know the true design of the anti-cosmic sigil necessary to open another esoteric triangle, this time in Italy. I fell to it like an idiot. But I was so young and eager to prove that I was the greatest occultist of my time. It is clear now that he used me for his mischievous plans. He was behind the creation of the first esoteric triangle in Egypt, and when the Gateway was opened hordes of demons poured out in our world, devastating the land of the Nile River. If it hadn't been for an equally powerful sorcerer such as Ankhtifi... Gino, it wasn't Ankhtifi who took control of the demons and led Egypt into war against the Nubians and the Babylonians. It was him, Meren-Ptah. Ankhtifi stopped him by breaking the sigils in Alexandria and Babylon and casting him away to this plane. He then managed to return in the nineteenth century, summoned by an occultist of a British secret society, and found me, his new tool for his master plan. After the opening of the Messina triangle and the invasion of Sicily in 1943, he understood that the Axis were about to lose and he turned his attention to the British. He had many allies in England, some of which whispered in Churchill's ears and convinced him to employ me in the RPI to build the third triangle. And here we are. He is a sorcerer of great powers and he is older than the pyramids. He tricked time."

"Talking about time," Carter said, pointing up at the plateau.

Amilcare swung his head left and right very slowly.

"There is nothing you and I can do to stop him. Or to stop what he is about to summon. A war is coming."

"I think I know a way. I just need more time. But what is he about to summon?"

"These humans he has been harvesting from our world are just the troops, cannon fodder with little to no weight in the war he is about to wage against our world. There are creatures and powers way beyond our comprehension, and I'm afraid even beyond his ability to control. He doesn't understand he is awakening something that will devour us all. Something that has no master."

Gino's face went blank. If what his father said was true, Meren-Ptah was summoning more than he could ever handle.

"Gino, I think our little friend over there is running out of corpses to mark, so it's better if we do something now. But what do we do?"

Gino jumped up the two steps that separated him from Carter and watched the scene again. It was true. There were very few remaining, and this was their last chance to stop him before he would float away somewhere else.

"The demons. If they attack me, you shoot them. I'm pretty sure they can be killed by your gun in here. My father and I will deal with him."

Amilcare floated up to their level and frowned.

"There is nothing we can do to stop him," he repeated in a grave voice.

"Trust me, Dad. I got a card up my sleeve. You just need to distract him as much as you can."

As above, so below

Carter watched Gino preparing the conjuring. He'd seen him do that so many times in the past that he could have done it himself if it weren't for his lack of ability to access the "factor X", a legendary place in everyone's brain or soul (depending on whether you were more science- or spiritual-leaning) that could enable you to use the occult arts. "You see, Carter," Gino told him once, "every single human in this world has these latent abilities, but our rational brains are so dominant that only a few will get access to them." It was all about the access, and the ritual did not bring any meaning or magic at all, it was simply a tool. Like the Buddhist's mantra *om*. It was for that reason that Carter used to move aside and keep quiet when Gino started one. Like this time, when Gino drew the typical circle with his ritual chalk on the floor of the rocky terrace and sat inside in a lotus position.

Carter took a defensive stance inside that circle, kneeling with one leg and ready to shoot any incoming demon with his gun. The astral body of Gino's father floated away from the scene, with Carter unaware of what his contribution would be in that final fight. A fight that started earlier than he thought when the sound of the incantation reached Meren-Ptah's ears. He immediately stopped marking the sigil on one of the corpses and turned his head left and right, trying to identify the source of the humming. He hovered on top of the machines and the demons' heads, like a hound sniffing for his prey.

When he saw Gino at the top of the stairs, he recoiled. His eyes popped out of their sockets. He couldn't believe his eyes, literally.

"You! How did you...?" the mad-eyed Meren-Ptah shouted at the top of his lungs.

He then floated towards them, completely ignoring Carter. He made sure his body would be kept at a safe distance and certainly far away from the white circle that Gino drew. Gino was extremely calm and was keeping on chanting with his eyes closed.

"It's over, Meren-Ptah. We know of your plan," Carter said, staying put inside the circle.

"Ha, ha, ha, ha! What are you going to do about it? You are just mortals playing with cantrips," Meren-Ptah said, pushing the invisible protective field that Gino had summoned around the perimeter of the circle. Blue and violet sparkles engulfed his astral hands and he had to retract them.

He cannot cross it, Carter thought, *and he cannot attack us with his magic as long as we are inside the field.*

"Besides, it's too late. This is just the last batch. I've sent thousands of them to Earth already. Your presence here is useless. You risked your life for nothing. And the only way out from here is through the tower. Your chalk lines will not protect you forever."

Having pronounced these words, ignoring their presence altogether, he turned his body towards the pile of corpses again. Then, his body jolted like he had been struck by lightning. He spoke several syllables in an unknown language and these interacted with the air they traversed warping it. Ripples expanded across the space before him and hit the factory chain, including the demons still working in it. These woke from their catatonic state and turned towards Gino and Carter.

The first group of demons, those closer to them, left their positions at the factory chain and started to gallop towards them, lurching with their claws drawn and their mouths wide open. The latter were an extraordinary sight of terror, for they spread from ear to ear, or at least where the ears were supposed to be in a human. It was a split in the face more than an opening, and this revealed a great deal more teeth than before. It was a bristled forest of tiny, sharp and densely packed fangs.

Carter had to look away from those mouths and started to shoot at their chests. He hit three of them, straight into their protruding sternum. Two fell on the ground; one continued for a few metres, then collapsed.

"It works, then!" he yelled, despite knowing that Gino was concentrating too hard to hear him.

He shot five more bullets and three landed on their targets. But more were coming and they were not afraid of the rounds. If anything, they were more galvanised. They started to screech and that made Carter shiver so much that he seriously thought of running away and crossing the causeway back to the cave in the tower. He focused on his task and shot more rounds. They all dropped dead a few metres away from the white circle.

The first wave was gone and that gave Carter pause, but now more syllables were exiting Meren-Ptah's mouth, and so more demons were summoned and started to charge.

"He is calling more of them! Gino, where is your father!" Carter yelled before shooting again.

"Stay put!" Gino shouted, still keeping his eyes closed.

Carter hit most of his enemies with a pelting of bullets, but he quickly understood that this game could not last for too long. The first magazine was almost gone. He had another one, the last one, but what if there were more demons coming? He could not hold the line like this forever. Besides, although his aim was incredibly good some shots didn't hit their targets and so there was a bunch of demons that were still charging towards him. There was no way he could stop all of them before they reached him. Indeed, one of them dodged his last bullet and leaped several metres in the air, and it would have slashed his throat if it wasn't for the field of magic that Gino created inside the white circle. The demon was stopped mid-air, unable to move a single muscle, and that gave Carter the time to get the gun's barrel to his forehead and shoot its brains (or whatever equivalent to the brain they had) out. The body dropped to his feet with a splatting sound, staining his shoes with dark fluids. Carter recoiled in disgust and was scolded by Gino for stepping out of the circle, even though his eyes were still shut. Carter jumped back in, and with a kick moved the carcass that was occupying half the circled area. Then he continued to shoot, starting with the new, and last, magazine.

And when he thought he was going to get overwhelmed by the third charge, a bright light shone behind the heap of corpses. Meren-Ptah was struck by a powerful burst that made him fly back for several metres. He, caught by surprise, let his link with the demons drop and focused his attention on his new enemy. Amilcare Marcotti rose on top of the mountain and continued to hit him with gusts of energy.

Carter noticed the demons had slowed down considerably now that their master had been distracted. This gave him time to hit them one by one before they reached the circle.

"Your father! He is fighting him!" Carter yelled, dropping to his knee to recover from the fatigue and the burst of adrenaline.

"It's not over. You can't kill an astral body. You can only distract it," Gino said.

"So, what do we do then? What is all this for?"

"We wait."

"For what?"

"For my card up my sleeve."

Gino opened his eyes, got to his feet, and pulled up his sleeve. Carter watched the curious movement. No card. Only a watch.

"It's almost time."

Carter didn't have the strength to ask more questions and only waited for something to happen. But a minute passed, and nothing happened. The two bright floating figures were hitting each other with powerful bursts of what Carter could only describe

284

as energy, although he knew there was a better technical term in the dictionary of the occult. They were both floating up, twenty metres higher than the terraced plateau they were on now. And the more the time passed, the more they were rising up, until they were at the same level as the first stones of the city perched on the rocky slope of the mountain. Demons started to appear at the many windows, curious to see the unexpected fight that was unrolling in their neighbourhood. Some had membranous wings and they leapt off the buildings to get a closer look at the fight, probably the first time two astral bodies had managed to cross into their world at the same time.

Gino was nervous and was often looking at his watch. He swore in English and Italian and in other languages that did not require many vowels. Carter understood that something was not going as planned for them, and yet he had no courage to ask what it was about.

A brighter than normal burst of light erupted from Meren-Ptah's body and the air rippled so much that it hit the winged creatures, spreading them across the sky. Some hit the buildings and fell down, crashing to the ground. But that did not stop those still flying to circle back again around the two combatants. And more took off from their perches on the spiralling towers to join the audience. If it weren't such a dangerous moment for Gino and Carter they would have considered it a true spectacle. What an amazing sight that was: an alien world covered with lead water that spanned the horizon, a towering mountain island with a perched megalithic city inhabited by demonic winged creatures, two powerful occultists in an air fight.

But something changed. A grumbling came from beneath their feet and shook the stones so much that they rattled. A cacophony of shrills, howls and screeches flared up from the cyclopean city. All the demons scattered around at once, some back inside the buildings, some up the towers, some down from the roofs where they were watching their version of the match of the century. It was like a colony of cockroaches surprised by the sudden turning-on of a light at night in a dark alley. It was a retreat, a very disorganised retreat. The only ones that knew where to go for safety were the winged demons that stopped encircling Amilcare and Meren-Ptah and flew as a single flock across the sea of lead. Carter followed their trajectory and saw them heading to the massive tower across the causeway from which they had emerged an hour or so ago.

As this happened, Meren-Ptah's astral body grew brighter and brighter until it was engulfed in a blinding beacon of pure white light.

"What's happening?" Carter shouted, holding Gino's arm.

"I think we are about to witness what my father was so scared about. Something that has no master."

The tremors continued until the whole mountain shook. Towers swung like canes in the wind, entire buildings collapsed, together with many of their demonic residents. The mountain was crumbling before their very eyes and they were just at its feet. A bigger seismic wave propagated from the mountain to where they were standing and they lost their balance, rolling to the lower steps. When they got on their feet again, the light had changed. A massive pinnacle of rocks had collapsed from the top of the mountain, disintegrating into thousands of smaller pieces as it fell along the western side. Its crumbles hit the sea of lead and produced wide ripples on its surface which moved across it for hundreds of metres, but without the wave effect that you would see during a tsunami on Earth. A blade of white light was now piercing through the mountain and hitting the highest towers of the city. An enormous object coming from inside the mountain cut that light across and then perched itself on the rim of the rocky crest that remained of the peak. The object had fingers, and at the very end of them claws that spanned several metres. They could easily have fitted inside one of the spiralling towers and still pierce through the roof because there was not enough space.

"Jesus. What's that... that thing?" Carter said slowly and with a calm that surprised even himself.

"Something you don't want to mess with," Gino replied in awe.

Another gargantuan arm appeared and knocked down another huge portion of the mountain. This time the hand grabbed part of the city, crumbling tens of buildings in between its huge fingers. It looked like the hand of a child destroying a sandcastle they had just built. As it failed to find a solid footing there, it swung back and forth, knocking down more buildings and towers in the process. Whatever it was inside the mountain that had been woken, it was trying to stand up, and in order to do so it was grabbing at anything, the mountain or the city.

For the first time in his life, Gino doubted his sanity. He had seen a lot in his life, struck deals with spirits, communicated with the dead, manipulated reality in order to fight his enemies. This was different, though. He had been trained to react in one way or the other before the supernatural, in the same way a scientist does before the natural. Spirits, magic, the dead follow certain rules as much as the electrons and protons in the atoms. This world, this alien plane of existence they had entered, had played intensely with their perceptions. Seas shouldn't behave like that, the sun shouldn't stay still for hours on end, demons should not dress with human skins. And mountains shouldn't hide things so vast they could barely contain them. This was impacting his inner-most fears, bypassing the most rational part of his brain. It was a primeval reaction, the fight-or-flight rule that no animal can suppress.

While all of this was happening, Meren-Ptah's intense light had faded away and his figure was now plummeting to the ground. Something had happened to him. Amilcare followed and reached Gino and Carter on their level. His face was scarred by fatigue and what looked like pain. Could an astral body really experience pain?

"Gino, I did my best, but he is too powerful for me. We failed," Amilcare said in a defeated tone.

"Don't worry, Father. He won't be a problem for us any longer. Look," Gino said with a satisfied smirk.

Meren-Ptah's astral body plunged to the ground, as if a puppeteer had suddenly cut the strings. He lay still for several seconds, then it twitched as if in the middle of a seizure. The movements of his arms and legs were uncontrollable. He started to scream a sound so high-pitched that should not have come out of a man's mouth. It wasn't human, nor of that plane. It was a voice coming from the deepest crevices of time. When his body shifted sideways towards the tower and across the causeway, it happened so quickly that to their eyes it seemed like a comet dashing across the summer sky.

"Twenty-one minutes later than expected," Gino said, looking at his watch.

"How...?" Amilcare started asking.

Gino stopped him almost immediately and replied, "We have secured his earthly body at the RPI and I've asked a necromancer to summon him back to his body. And it worked. A bit later than expected, but it worked."

"Clever," Amilcare said, just before another seismic event cracked the mountain open. "But that does not change the real danger Earth is going to face."

Amilcare flew up to have a better look at the gargantuan arms that were still getting a grip on the rocks.

"The Well is open, and *that thing* will use it to get across."

And the moment he said that, the stairs where Gino and Carter were standing started to crack open and huge gaps appeared, revealing terrifying empty spaces below.

"We have to retreat back to the Well!" Carter said, jumping down a step.

Gino hesitated. He looked at his watch once again for no reason, just out of habit. His plan had not entirely worked. Meren-Ptah had managed to send thousands of demons disguised as humans, and had summoned *that* thing. Carter was right. They had to leave now. What if the causeway cracked and did not allow them to cross the sea of lead? What if that thing that had been awakened attacked them before they could even reach the Well?

"*Babbo*, how do we kill that thing?"

"You can't, but you can close the gateway so it will be sucked into this plane again."

"How? By removing the sigil at Greenwich? I have no way of demolishing the RPI building."

"That won't be necessary. If they have followed the original plan I designed, a shaft should have been left open in the foundations of the building. This shaft leads straight to the sigil. Josepha knows how to access it. Find her!"

"What about you?"

"Don't worry about me. This is but a glimpse into my eternal life here. But a beautiful one. I'm happy to have seen you again, Gino. Now go, the world is more important than me."

Gino wanted to stay longer, he wanted to talk to him for hours or days on end. He wanted to know everything about a father who had been so absent in his childhood. He wanted to know why he had made those choices in his life. Why he had neglected his son for his career to the point of barely seeing him on a daily basis. A father that was a stranger. A stranger who, with his absences, impacted his life so much. In fact, hadn't he followed the same path as that stranger? Didn't he continue to try to achieve that stranger's dreams? And later became a stranger to his mother in the process? What about his happiness? What about his normal life, with a family? What if he hadn't been such a stranger to him? Would have he been as happy as Carter? That stranger killed his life, and yet, like a dog to its human master, he remained loyal to that stranger's dreams and now he just wanted to hug him and cry on his lap. He wanted to do all of that, but now that luminescent figure with his gaze lost towards the abysses of time was hovering away, a speckle of dust and yet immortal like a god.

He turned to Carter, who was still waiting impatiently. They ran and jumped from one step to the next, risking tumbling down at every trembling and crack. They reached the causeway with a long, desperate leap, grateful they had managed to leave behind the shaking island. They heard more rocks crashing on the terraced plateau and on the sea, but they did not look back. Soon, the ripples on the sea reached the causeway but did not submerge it. Luckily the behaviour of that liquid was not like the water of Earth. An otherworldly sound, like a deep roar from an unearthly behemoth, thundered behind them. It impacted their chests and stopped their breath for a few seconds. Gino felt his lungs deflate although his ribcage was still dilated. It was like that growl sucked the air out of their lungs. They had to stop to breathe in again, their chests heaving like a furnace's bellows. They barely looked at each other. They still had a few hundred metres that separated them from the cave entrance. And they didn't intend to stop now. Once the air filled up their lungs again, they dashed off faster than before. The adrenaline was running wild in their veins; however, they knew it wouldn't last for too long, so they pushed as hard as they could.

As they approached the entrance of the cave, a sudden burst of light projected their shadows several metres in front of them. Instinctively, Gino turned in spite of himself and saw a tall silhouette towering on the horizon, higher than the island mountain. A globe of light was beaconing in the sky next to it, and it was so blinding that he had to turn his head. In two long running strides, Gino covered the distance to the tunnel and reached Carter, who was already inside.

"Grazie babbo," he whispered, leaning his back against the damp surface of the rock.

***

They reached the chamber in a few minutes, following the trail of red sticks they had left behind, not even realising the distance they had crossed. They grabbed the torches they had left at the entrance, but they left the suits and the respirators. Whatever risks they might encounter at the higher altitudes on the pillar, they were certainly lower than what was following them. If what Amilcare had said was correct, it would try to cross into our world through that same well they were going to climb now. So, they had to hurry. The chamber they had left two hours ago looked very different now. A mist was clinging to the floor, a thin veil that was barely disturbed by their quick steps. A chill froze their lungs and made their skin clammy. The crystals' glow was nowhere to be seen. Just crystals nestled on the cold rock. Something had made them stop glowing, and Gino had a suspicion that it was somehow linked to Meren-Ptah's disappearance. Not only that, but the pillar itself looked shorter. Or was the inky darkness that acted like a ceiling much lower now? They couldn't quite figure this out. It was time to climb back to their world.

The ascent

"This is not the England we left two hours ago."

Those words cut through Gino's mind like a knife. It felt like a stab in the back. During the ascension he had felt so optimistic. They'd managed to defeat Meren-Ptah, escape alive from that nameless entity, against all the odds they'd survived on an alien plane, and they even climbed up the massive pillar despite his fear of heights. And now that they saw the light at the end of the tunnel – quite literally! – those ominous words came out of the blue.

What did they even mean? What had happened to the England they knew? Why did his words bring such a gloomy tone?

He could not wait to get to the surface like Carter had. He could see his legs still dangling from the rim of the Well. The pillar was moving slowly now. Only a few metres separated him from the light. He saw Carter's hand reaching his face. He grabbed it and Carter did all the heavy lifting for him. He was now out of the Well.

When his eyes began to adapt to the dim light of the dawn, he slowly realised what Carter meant. For miles and miles on end the countryside around Hartesbridge was scorched. A lead-grey sky covered the landscape, bringing it close to the sky in the same way they had experienced on the other plane. Its sight was oppressive, almost like a low ceiling in a stuffy room. They had a sense of claustrophobia even though they were in the open. High columns of black smoke smothered the village. Some houses and shops were gone in flame, some were just rubble. Hartesbridge was no more. The few remaining trees were skeletal fingers pointing to the sky, the few bushes looked like giant blackened mushrooms. The excavator that held their reel was a carcass that had miraculously survived against all the odds. It was leaning on its side, its long arm bent and crashed into shattered headstones.

No one could be seen for miles and miles, and the silence was deafening. Not even birds chirped, nor wind blew through the dead branches.

"Look," Carter said, pointing at Gino's sigil.

It was fading away, and in a few seconds both sigils died out completely. They removed their Kevlar vests and dropped them in the graveyard. They walked on towards the High Street and found no signs of people or police. From that high vantage point, they could see where the police vans and cars used to be parked. It was empty.

"What happened? Where is everyone?" Carter asked, visibly worried.

"Meren-Ptah was right. We are too late. His troops have already started the invasion," a worried Gino said running down the High Street.

He stopped at the key-cutting shop, miraculously still standing. He checked the watches and clocks behind the shop window, and then his Casio watch.

"Two days!" he shouted to a perplexed Carter, who had reached him in the meantime. "We have been there for two earthly days."

"I thought you said the time difference wasn't going to be an issue."

"I thought the sigil would have protected us from the asynchronicity, but it didn't. It means that –"

"That we are very late," Carter finished his sentence.

All of a sudden, the ground behind them shook and the pillar appeared on the surface. Instinctively they moved away from it and kept their distance, and that saved them from a sure death, given that the ground around the Well cracked open in one single opening. A scar along the ground that started to run faster and faster until it reached the main road. They ran away along the High Street, hoping to find someone or some way to escape, like a car. The crack was following the road behind them but at a slower speed than their pace. Carter slowed down and looked behind.

"It's swelling."

"What?" Gino asked, stopping as well.

"The soil is going up. Look!"

The soil around the Well, and with it all the headstones and stone crosses, was going up and down like bubbling cheese in the oven. It felt like something big was bulging up and trying to pierce through from the bottom of the Earth.

"We'd better run," Gino said, turning on his heels and projecting himself down the road, past the pub, the charities and the bank, past the many burning houses and cars, past the whole village until he reached the outskirts where they had left their car.

The Ford Escort was still there, parked on the side of the road next to an oak. Gino unzipped and removed his suit in a few seconds. Then he threw it away into the bushes and waited for Carter to come. He saw him rushing down the road and signalled to him for the keys. Carter checked all his pockets while still running, and for a moment he panicked thinking that he might have left them in the rucksack. Carter did not realise what was happening with Gino. Yes, of course his eyes just saw this small white figure, all suited up, who was running towards him at full speed, but it was the background that caught most of his attention. The silent and empty village suddenly became the centre of a major explosion that involved tons of soil, stones and bricks being ejected up into the sky, followed by a column of dust and smoke that smothered the landscape. The bang was so loud and continued for so many seconds that he didn't hear Carter shouting to him to take cover inside the car. Carter had to pull him by the shirt.

When the car's tyres screeched on the tarmac, several bricks and chunks of turf had already reached the roof and smashed the back window of the car. It was a miracle they survived without a scratch, and without the car being covered in rubble. Carter drove at full speed down country lanes, passing farms, cottages and mooing cows that were smashing their heads on fences and thick hedges, trying to escape as fast as possible from the dark shape that erupted miles back. Gino turned his head and tried to discern what was happening behind them from the ever-changing landscape. Oak trees lined the road and partially shielded his view. The sky was darker above Hartesbridge, a column of dust and smoke covered it, but apart from that he was pretty sure nothing was following them.

He turned his attention to the front of the car. Carter was driving like mad, risking accidents with lampposts, cattle or farm fences at every turn. Gino placed a hand on his to signal that it was fine now. That they were far enough away from Hartesbridge.

"What was that?" Carter asked in a falsetto voice that contrasted wildly with his hulking physique.

"I'm not sure. That crack, that enormous wound that opened up, can only be the nameless thing that was awakened by Meren-Ptah."

And the words of the Venerable Mother echoed immediately in Gino's mind: *Our world is truly paper-thin.* She knew more than she had liked to show. How had that thing crossed to our world without a sigil? Meren-Ptah must have marked it with one before they defeated him. He must have worked on this moment for decades, if not centuries. This was a carefully thought-out plan, and now he can't even see it rolling in. They must destroy the sigil before that thing ran amok on the Earth.

They drove for miles and miles. Up ahead the trees thinned, replaced by fields and fields of farmed land.

"Aren't you going to say the line?" Gino asked in a raucous voice at some point.

"Which line?"

"'There is no place like home,' and then you click your heels three times?"

"Funny, very funny. Maybe I didn't say it because I don't have silver slippers."

They both laughed and that helped cut the tension. Carter took his hand off the gear stick and opened the window. Fresh air stormed in and ruffled their hair. Gino leaned his head out of the window and closed his eyes for a few minutes, trying to regain his energy.

"Can you tell me what happened down there?" Carter asked with a tone that requested an honest answer.

Gino got up from his slumber and looked at him. He immediately understood what he meant.

"Sadir summoned him back to his body," he replied. "I've asked Emma and Abbot to take Meren-Ptah's body to the RPI, and I gave clear instructions to Sadir over the phone. Probably illegal under British law, but... we are still alive, right?"

"I thought you didn't like each other."

"Well, we still don't, in general. But I changed my mind about his skills. I think he's clever and he was the only one able to perform this task."

"Why didn't you tell me?"

"I thought it could have worried you too much. Me being anxious for it was fair enough."

"Right. But by doing so, you are always keeping me in the dark. I need to know. I might not be an occultist like you, I might understand just one per cent of it, but I *deserve* to know what's going on."

And then, in an unexpected twist Gino admitted it with a calm voice.

"You are right. What else would you like to know?"

Carter, taken by surprise, hesitated for a minute, then he asked,

"What are we going to do when we arrive in Greenwich?"

"Well, it's a long story, but I guess we have plenty of time before we even reach the M25. So, the Thoth's esoteric triangle between Aksum, Alexandria and Babylon ended in 2,000 B.C. Of all the sigils that made the triangle, only one survived, the one inside the church in Aksum. Then, my father activated another triangle, the Messina one. Of all the sigils that made *that* triangle only one survived, the one on the Ethiopian obelisk in Rome. It's our turn now: we removed the sigils in Chichester and Hastings, but we kept the one in Greenwich. By doing so we created another triangle, a massive triangle, between Aksum, Rome and Greenwich."

Gino paused, waiting for his reaction.

"Bloody hell. That's why all the events and the towns' disappearances didn't stop, and actually accelerated so quickly after we removed the two sigils."

"Exactly."

"So, it wasn't your father…"

"It was us. The RPI did it with their dismissal order for Chichester and Hastings in the late 1980s. Unknowingly, we created the biggest esoteric triangle ever created and we attracted the two planes. This in turn had given the possibility to those entities to cross into our plane, and to our towns to cross into their plane. We are both leaking through each other's cosmoses."

"Fascinating and scary. So, now we have to break the sigil in Greenwich?"

"Exactly. With the hope that this would stop the leaking and that thing."

They were driving on a wider two-lane country road now, approaching a small village whose name they missed on a sign. They decided not to stop to ask for directions. They wanted to arrive in Greenwich as fast as they could. And even if they wanted to, the village was empty. Not a single person or car. They were driving north, that was for sure. They needed to find a junction with the M25. Gino rummaged inside the glove compartment and found a roadmap. He studied it, and concluded they were just fifty miles from the M25.

"What's our plan?" Carter asked and then after a second, "Do we have a plan, right?"

"Yes, we do. In fact, you can now turn right at that garden centre."

"What?"

"There. See that *Blue Bell's Gardens* sign? Get in."

The car stopped abruptly at the shut wooden gates of the garden centre. It was very early in the morning and no employee was inside.

"Ram it."

"What? Are you crazy?"

"I said ram it now. Or I'll do it."

Carter didn't want to argue, so he reversed for a few metres, then he hit the accelerator and went through the flimsy gate. Gino catapulted himself out, ran towards a rack full of spades and other tools, and grabbed a pickaxe. Then, he threw it in the boot and told Carter to continue towards London.

"Are you going to tell me what that is for?"

Gino smiled without looking at him and said:

"The sigil isn't going to break itself."

Zombies and all that

London welcomed them with high columns of smoke on the horizon, ambulance and fire brigade sirens in every direction and a roadblock guarded by the police that prevented them from getting to the RPI building. Several yellow TRAFFIC DIVERSION signs indicated an alternative route, away from Greenwich. They stopped and Gino addressed the policemen, saying that they were RPI employees that needed to get back to Greenwich as soon as possible. The answer was negative and details were scarce. They were told a group of terrorists had attacked London City and the army had been called in to neutralise them. Carter proposed mentioning Abbot but Gino stopped him. If Abbot was what Gino thought he would be, they would be losing their advantage. Abbot must not suspect they were coming or that they knew.

They drove away following the proposed directions, and saw several more police cars blocking access to Greenwich. There was no way other than to proceed on foot, hoping they wouldn't be stopped. They parked the car on a minor road and their first thought was: how would you walk around with a pickaxe during a major security emergency without looking suspicious?

Gino thought there was no way they could make it with so many police around. Then, Carter had an idea. He took the pickaxe and removed the head from the wooden handle. Then he put the iron head in a rucksack he found in the boot of the car.

"Yeah, and the handle?" Gino asked.

"Well, I don't know. Just pretend you're an old man with a walking stick."

"It won't work."

"These is no other way I can think of."

"Okay. Thanks for saying that I should only *pretend* to be an old man. I appreciate the courtesy."

They walked through empty streets, seldom crossed by distrustful pedestrians. Along one stretch of road someone had set several tyres on fire, the smouldering smoke filling the road. Teenagers were yelling from the windows of some old flats nearby. It wasn't easy to understand whether those yells were directed at them, but, in doubt, they decided to leave the area and take a different route, until they found the Tube signs on a major road. They were getting close to Greenwich Tube Station, which was in the vicinity of the RPI building.

However, they had to control their excitement when the shouts of many people started to echo around the empty streets. What followed were sounds of clanging and battering against all sorts of surfaces, from shops' shutters to glass and rubble. They saw some human figures running like shadows in front of their field of view – which, at this point was simply the end of the lane road several metres away – but nothing more. Difficult to say whether it was those demons attacking people or simply looters taking advantage of the situation. Something was going on in the main road, and they would be best to stay away.

They trotted across the small lanes to avoid the mob on the main road. They knew it would take longer, but it would be safer. These narrow lanes have been visited by their nine-to-five selves during their lunchtime breaks, and they were not afraid of getting lost. They slowed down at the entrance of a lane which they knew would open up to a wider main road. They heard no mob this time, no fracas. Only the sound of a metal object being dragged along the cobbled pavement. They stopped altogether, eyes peeled and ears focused. Ahead the way was clear, so they could not identify that sound.

The black poodle scuttled faster with its tail between the legs when it saw the two humans. Its eyes were two vitreous stones that hid fear and mistrust. Something had happened to its owner, and it hadn't been good. It had that look that said it would take more than a day to gain trust in other humans again. Gino heaved a sigh of relief when he saw the dog, the leash still attached to its collar, jangling on the pavement. It immediately made him think about Garibaldi, though. Josepha used to take care of him in his absence. She had the key to his office and the dog trusted her. He thought about them, and wondered if they were safe and still in the RPI. His thoughts then switched to Carter. There must be a whirlpool of anxiety, stress, anger and pessimism inside his head now. He was probably thinking about Lizzy and Jaime all the time. Were they safe? Where were they? Earlier, he'd seen him grab the handset of a public phone only to realise there was no line. If only they had that cellular phone the police used in their cars.

They finally walked into the open space of a main road. Roads were empty, shops shut; only a faraway police car was driving away from them with its sirens on. Some people were leaning from their windows, looking at them like they were crazy. An old lady shook her head in disapproval. Whatever had happened in the past two days, it must have been terrifying. A cab drove passed them and startled them, as they thought it was the police. Then, a voice called to them from a dark alley. Carter stepped in front of Gino and held his gun, but kept it under his jacket.

A figure crept forward from the shadows. The man could barely walk in a straight line. His hair was ragged. His hand propped him up against the brick wall and the other one held a plastic bag. He advanced kicking cans of beer and empty kebab boxes.

"Any change, mate?" the old man said.

Immediately, Carter and Gino relaxed. It was just a homeless guy. He was the first person, civilian at least, who they'd met since entering the city.

"Here," Gino said, handing him some pennies he found in his pocket.

"Thanks, mate," the man said with a fake smile.

"What happened here? Why is the city empty and the police everywhere?"

The old man face changed from the smile to puzzlement. His brows furrowed and his jaw protruded.

"What? Did you sleep under a rock for the past few days?"

"Why, yes. Quite literally," Gino said, dismissing his sarcastic tone. "Could you tell us what happened?"

The man looked at them in disbelief, probably thinking they were crazier than he was. He craned his neck left and right, suspecting something, perhaps a trick set up by the police or a prank from the TV. But the two men did look oblivious and very convincing indeed. Perhaps they were tourists.

"The zombies attacked London. That's what. They swarmed like insects and attacked anyone on the bloody street. They set buildings on fire all over the city."

"Zombies?"

"Yah, barely dressed, they use their teeth and nails to attack you. And all of that."

Gino and Carter exchanged a worrisome look. It seemed like Meren-Ptah's army had not only crossed successfully to their world, infesting London, but it was now even attacking people. And that was only the infantry; now the heavy artillery was coming, too.

Another siren was approaching. They threw themselves into the alley and hid behind the bins with the old man. The siren's sound grew louder and louder until they saw the blue lights flashing all over the street. It happened to be the fire brigade truck.

When the flickering of the lights was gone, they moved out and said their goodbyes to the still puzzled man. He looked at them in silence. Then, he threw an empty bottle of gin to them, missing them by a hair's width.

"Stay away from them! They will eat your guts! I saw it!" he shouted, waving the plastic bag he had always with him. "And that gun won't help you, mate."

They ran away. Better leave that man alone, or else he could attract unwanted attention to them – or worse, the police – with his shouts. Carter closed his jacket, surprised that the man had seen or guessed about the gun. They moved towards Greenwich Park, focusing their attention on the Royal Observatory. On their left, the banks of the Thames, and further away Canary Wharf and Tower Bridge. The RPI building was very close now. They just had to turn the last corner and... they froze in place.

"You've got to be kidding me," Carter hissed through his teeth.

The Royal Paranormal Institute was a six-storey neo-Victorian building. Its façade was austere and simple, with tall columns framing the entrance and the two main wings. Windows on the first two floors stood open, and from at least two of them black smoke was coming out very slowly. A walled garden separated it from the main street. The big letters, *RPI*, which used to hang on the wall next to the wrought-iron gate, were nowhere to be seen. Only a paler shade of grey left on the wall suggested they had been hanging there for half a century. The majestic gates were torn off and laid on the ground. Where the cars of the employees used to be parked, only smoking carcasses. The only exception was a white van standing immaculate in front of the entrance of the building. On its roof two men were sitting guarding the premises. Two others were patrolling the outer perimeter of the garden, although there could have been more, hidden by the wall. It wasn't their presence that shocked them – in a way, they expected some sort of confrontation with the enemy – but rather their look. For they were not "normal" folks like the people who had disappeared in Hartesbridge, but Black Metallers. With corpse-paint on their faces, long dark hair, leather jackets with studs, bullet belts and long-nailed maces.

Gino and Carter backed up to the corner they had just come from. Luckily, they did not see them appearing, given how far they were from the building.

It was Carter who started to speak, "Of all the enemies we could confront, it's our main nemesis that is between us and the RPI."

"It's fate, Carter. It's called closing the circle. We were supposed to finish our job with what started it. Meren-Ptah sent them to the RPI for this specific purpose: to confront us."

"What do we do?"

"How many bullets do you still have?"

"I've got half a magazine left and I managed to find another one in the car. Not many bullets for a group of enemies that are expecting us castled in."

Gino took the pickaxe head from the rucksack and fixed it onto the wooden handle.

"We have defeated worse foes down there, and we must destroy the sigil before it's too late," he said, walking out into the open.

"Are you crazy? Wait a second." Carter whispered without exposing himself.

"I'll be the bait, like last time. You do your part," Gino said drawing a circle on the tarmac with his chalk.

As soon as he finished, he yelled at them. The men immediately turned their heads and, with visible grins, started to charge towards him.

The time has come for bitter things

"Bloody marvellous," Carter hissed holding his gun out before leaving Gino alone.

Three men started to sprint while the fourth one, a beefy two-metre-tall bloke, stood a few metres away with the axe well balanced on his shoulder. The first man who entered the magic circle got struck by a powerful anti-cosmic field that made his body levitate a metre from the ground. If it weren't for the gravity of the situation, it would have looked like a comedy sketch. A man, ridiculously dressed and with clownish make-up on, floating in the air trying to swing his mace left and right. A sharp hit from Gino's hand on his forehead triggered a spark that immediately stunned him. His body flickered and his face splayed open, revealing the demon inside.

Gino got back into position and focused his chanting once again, knowing full well that the anti-cosmic field had weakened now. Would the other men know that? The answer arrived very soon, when the other two slowed down and avoided entering the circle. They clearly understood they could be fried like their mate. They started to walk around it, grinning like mad dogs. One tried to swing the nailed bat, only to find that the field was still up.

Soon they will find out they can enter it, especially if they are doing it together, thought Gino, worried about Carter not showing up. *Where is he?*

Gino put all his mental energies towards the fortification of the field, but the first man who'd been trapped and annihilated had taken a toll on them. He decided to hold the pickaxe, and that decision probably became one of the best he made in his life, because one of the men decided to cross the field. He was barely stopped by it, acting very surprised. Probably too surprised, because he didn't see the pickaxe coming straight to his left thigh. The pointed head almost crossed the entire leg from part to part and stunned him. Then Gino touched his head, and after a loud click his skull cracked. But it wasn't over, for the man's body continued to swing the bat against his attacker, and the second man jumped inside the circle. This time there was not a tickle to be felt. Gino's situation was dire. He managed to duck the bat of the now blind and brainless man, but not the nailed mace that pounced down on his shoulder from the second man. The pain rose sharply when the mace was pulled out of his flesh, and it made him kneel on the ground. His magic could not save him, after all; it was over.

The shotgun resonated loudly in the street, but Gino only heard the sound of the blast hitting the man's chest.

Carter!

Several other shots were fired afterwards, and Gino heard all of them but didn't know where they landed. He opened his eyes and saw the two bodies lying on the ground within the white circle. Both of them had fatal wounds but no blood came out from them. The demons inside the human husks turned to ashes once exposed to the Earth's atmosphere, their protective sigils broken.

On the other hand, Gino's shoulder was bleeding profusely and any movement transmitted an excruciating pain to his brain. He held onto the pickaxe handle to stand up; he wiggled it with his still functioning right hand to remove it from the corpse's thigh, and when that failed, he used a foot to hold the thigh in place. Once done, he wanted to greet Carter and thank him for having saved his life, but he wasn't to be seen. And neither was the big beefy man.

He walked, a hand holding his shoulder wound and the other dragging the pickaxe, towards the RPI's brick wall, looking left and right, but he could not see them. Then, he heard a clanging sound coming from a secondary road. He followed it until he saw an axe-wielding giant man trying to kill a crawling Carter, who had dodged too many hits to be lucky another time. Gino was too far away to intervene, so he decided to yell to distract him.

The axe stopped mid-air and the man turned immediately to him. His corpse paint resembling a skull was melting under a sheen of sweat. His long black mane covered half his back, hiding most of the band's logo on his leather jacket. His mouth showed rows of white teeth that contrasted with his black lips. He was truly ghoulish, a beast in berserk mode. He reminded Gino of the wolves' description from Westerfield.

He started to walk towards Gino without any particular hurry, probably knowing that he was wounded and wouldn't stand a chance against his axe. Each pace was a clanging of metal studs and stomping of leather boots. Gino had no idea what to do, and he instinctively stepped backwards until his back found the brick wall.

Another bullet saved his life. Actually, three bullets, given that the giant axe-wielding beast did not give in with the first one. His body thumped to the ground, and Gino could hit him easily with the pickaxe.

"Thanks," he said, breathing in as much air as possible.

Carter walked towards him, holding the gun and checking with his foot whether the demon inside the corpse was gone.

"Why did it take you so long?" Gino asked puzzled. "I thought you had my back."

"Apparently others had my back, too," Carter said, pointing at the two dead bodies a few metres away. "I walked around these houses so I could take them by surprise, but I found these two. Once I'd liquidated them and shot the ones that attacked you, that beast came from nowhere and attacked me. I dropped my gun, and if it weren't for you I would be sliced in half by now. Thanks."

"Well, thank you for saving my life earlier on, too," Gino said clearly in pain from the shoulder wound.

"How is your wound?"

"At least one nail went through my flesh, and I fear it touched the bone and nerves. But I will survive. We should go now."

Still shocked by recent events, they walked slowly towards the RPI entrance, wary of any sound or movement in the gardens. The van parked in front of the RPI doors happened to be the same police van where Gino had helped with Meren-Ptah's body transportation. Two more police cars lay damaged on their sides with no sign of any occupants.

"Abbot is here. He tried to sabotage everything, but he doesn't know we are here," Gino whispered to Carter.

The RPI's main doors were opened. The guards were missing in the foyer and their booth was ravaged, with sheets of paper and other stationery spread all over the desk and the floor. Carter inspected a couple of rooms and the canteen, while Gino guarded the stairs. He came back shaking his head left and right. No sign of anyone in the canteen and kitchens. They decided to walk upstairs to inspect the other floors. Sadir's office was on the top floor, whereas Josepha was in the basement. Gino thought that checking on Sadir should have priority over Josepha, given that Meren-Ptah could still be at large thanks to Abbot.

They passed the Temple hall door on the second floor, and something attracted Gino's attention. He felt an irresistible draw to check it. He signalled to Carter that he was venturing inside it. The double doors were ajar, and a suspiciously humid draught was hitting his face through the gap. There were no windows in the Temple hall, Gino's rational part of his mind communicated to the emotional one. If that wasn't enough to scare him, a far away rattling was coming from beyond the doors.

He walked in, visibly limping and barely suppressing a scream from the agonising pain that sprung out at every step. Carter followed him, and at some point, held his arm up. Apart from the meagre furniture that made up the Chief Magus's office – namely the mahogany desk and chairs and a short cabinet – the hall was empty. And dark. Carter reached out to the light switch, but it didn't work. Not surprising given that the whole city had become a war-torn battlefield.

Although devoid of objects, the room was filled with a stench that Gino couldn't place. It wasn't the Venerable Mother's old granny musky odour, and yet he could sense a little of that too. Neither the extinguished candles. It was something else. Their eyes took a while to adapt, but when they did, they could see beyond the barely illuminated desk. Some nightmarish unnamed thing shrouded in dimness squirmed and made a noise.

Their hearts shifted to fourth gear. They both stopped breathing and slowly raised their weapons. It seemed that the thing hadn't seen them or heard them yet. They parted ways, left and right, with carefully placed steps that were, however, betrayed by a plopping sound. In fact, the dais was covered in thick blood and they could trace its origin from under the desk. There, mutilated and violated, was a corpse. It was the Venerable Mother. That thing was working on top of her, but it was difficult to understand what was going on. It made several sounds, but none could be linked to a body profanation. Quite the opposite; it was not the sound of organic matter being slashed, but of inorganic objects being shifted.

It is digging! Gino realised.

At the periphery of his vision there was now a dark shape, and neither Carter nor he was prepared for what happened next. The first girl pounced on Carter and dropped him with a fist. She came from the mezzanine, where she had been hiding all the time. The second girl – what they had referred to as the *thing* up until now – left her business under the desk and jumped towards Gino, missing him by hair's width. This gave Gino the time to swing the pickaxe around, but to no avail. With a high-pitched scream, the woman charged him and threw him over the dais. For a moment Gino's lungs had to work twice as hard, as his chest got compressed on the floor.

It was a desperate moment. He was down, at the mercy of a feminine figure he could not recognise save for the long hair and high stiletto heels – which in a moment of hilarious inner consideration, he found very inappropriate for that type of wrestling. It was so dark he could barely see the silhouette of his attacker; He lost the pickaxe somewhere. He lost Carter's whereabouts.

The only hope he had was that his attacker had no weapon. But even that hope vanished when he saw a quick glimpse of light flashing on a metal surface. There was a weapon – a long knife, to be more precise – that was shining in her hand. The young woman was inching towards him brandishing it with the only aim of using it on him. In an attempt of finding the lost courage, he did what was unexpected to him and to the woman. He skidded forward and headbutted her. This managed to accomplish two things: the knife did not pierce his skull, which was a good start; and she fell back, banging her head on the dais.

This gave him the chance to crawl on all fours and get under the desk. From there he could see the body of the woman lying on the floor, and the pickaxe's metal head shining in the light from the open doors. It was too far away and too close to her. He had to think about something else.

From the corner of his eye, he finally noticed Carter wrestling for his life against the second woman. She was as strong as the first one, or even stronger, given Carter's bigger body. She was trying to bite him on his neck, but Carter's elbow was in the way. Gino felt the urge to help him, but he was worried about his attacker, who was now... Yes, where was she?

His wrist was grabbed in a cold grasp, and almost instantaneously some sort of energy jolted through him until it reached his head. In a single flash, he saw the Magician card that Josepha showed him. A tall man draped in a red robe, holding a stick in the air with one hand and pointing to the ground with the other. His face wore a calm but resolute expression. You could have judged his motivation as malignant, and you would not have been wrong. His eyes were orbs of fire, his hands' tendons were popping, so much was the concentration required to summon the bolt. And yet he was drawn to him like you would be to someone familiar, so well-known and trusted.

It was a mirror. He was looking at himself, jolting a powerful lightning bolt summoned from high above and delivered there below to destroy.

THE MAGICIAN.

When he woke from this reverie, the room was alight with the flames engulfing the clothes of the woman who had attacked him. She dropped lifeless onto the dais seconds later. Carter removed the lifeless body of the second woman from his chest. Her hair was still burning from the bolt that had cracked her skull open. Carter's expression – with a dropped jaw and popped-out eyes – said it all: these were the goth girls who were smoking in Westerfield's office in the record shop basement.

The lights turned on suddenly, as something had been keeping the Temple in the dark until then. A skeleton of a hand was still grabbing Gino's wrist. The Venerable Mother's last gift to him and the RPI. The desk was cracked open and blackened in its fracture. What was the meaning of that? What did she do with him? How did she know about the Magician card? How did she possess him to evoke the lightning?

They both tried to put themselves back together and took care of their wounds. Carter had two bloody holes in his neck like he'd been bitten by a vampire.

Gino gently freed himself from the Chief Magus's clasped hand. He placed her hand on top of her belly, closed her eyes, and cleaned some blood from her chin. Next to her body, several tiles had been removed. They could clearly see the nails trying to dig into the concrete below.

"What's under there?" Carter asked, triggering buried memories in Gino's mind from the last time he had met with the Chief Magus.

Gino stood, grabbed the pickaxe and walked slowly towards the doors.

"You don't want to know. I don't want to know, either. Not now at least. We are lucky we stopped her. Let's move on and find Sadir."

A beginning

The last floor was empty. No one was sitting in their office or walking in the corridors. Gino had never seen the RPI so empty and devoid of activity, not even on the occasional Sunday when he used to come to work for a couple of hours.

They found Sadir in his office. He was sitting in an armchair, long streaks of blood caking his head. He barely acknowledged their presence with a simple nod. His hands were gripping the chair's arms like he had been experiencing the quaking of a storm on a sailing boat. Meren-Ptah was lying unconscious on the floor. Taped mouth, taped ankles and wrists. His hands were joined together over his crotch. The arms were squeezed to his torso by more tape which ran all around the body. They had secured him well, in case he became dangerous once made whole with his astral body.

His face was craggy and unpleasantly lined, as if from a long lifetime of disagreeable expressions. The King of Pentacles was now dethroned.

"What happened?" Gino asked, getting closer to Sadir and inspecting his head.

"We were attacked," Sadir whispered with a neutral tone, like someone fed up of repeating the same story over and over again.

Carter found the dead body of Abbot behind the bashed-open door, sitting with his back leaning against the wall, his dangling bloody head kept in place only by his wide chin on his chest. He was still holding a pistol in his lifeless hand. His hat was sitting upside down next to his leg. He looked like a beggar asking for money in the street.

"I knew he was going to stop you. I'm sorry I couldn't figure this out earlier," Gino said with a sigh.

"Stop?" Sadir asked, breaking his neutral stance with a puzzled face.

"Was he alone when he attacked you? How did you kill him?" Gino asked with an insistent tone.

"What? Abbot did not attack me at all. And I wasn't the one who killed him."

"I don't understand."

"Abbot saved me, and possibly saved all of us. Indeed, we were so close to seeing Meren-Ptah free again. Abbot shot the bastard when he found me unconscious on the floor."

Gino looked perplexed, and his gaze shifted from Abbot to Sadir and vice versa several times.

"So, who did Abbot save you from?"

"A woman. His colleague."

Gino turned and looked at a shocked Carter.

"Emma," Carter said in a barely audible whisper.

"Yes, she came in two days ago with a bunch of other colleagues," he said, looking at their incredulous faces. "I've been guarding his body for the past forty-eight hours, waiting for your return. Then, she killed them one by one with a gun. When I heard the shots, I barricaded myself in the office, but she managed to ram it down with a strength that I thought impossible in a human, let alone a woman of

THE HERMIT.

her size. She jumped on him and the last thing I remember was a pain in my head. She probably thought I was dead because she did not finish me, neither did she restrain me while she tried to free what I think we can now call her master. Abbot arrived just in time and shot her several times, but she managed to dodge the final deadly one and killed him there on the spot. I was awakened before he intervened, so she didn't see me casting a protective spell on the room and Meren-Ptah. When I activated it, she was thrown away by the magical field and cast away from the room. Since then, she has been trying to enter, but has failed every single time. She is still around. You should be careful."

That was an unexpected development that threw Gino's mind into panic. They had been tricked by Emma all this time? Was she possessed by the demon since the beginning, or did it happen when they were in the Well? He suspected the former, given that her body had to be repurposed by Meren-Ptah, and that could not have happened after they descended into the Well. If that was the case, all the help she had given them would be put into perspective. She helped them gain their trust, and when they were gone, she struck and did her master's bidding, but failed thanks to Abbot. Poor Abbot, thought Gino. He felt so ashamed to have doubted him and to have considered him The Hermit card. How could he have missed it? How could he have not seen it in Emma?

Carter woke him from his thoughts.

"Look!" he said, pointing through the window at a far away column of black clouds that was advancing through London.

The colossal shape towered over any London building and was wading through the city like a rice-picker in a paddy field. The occasional skyscraper was a reed to pass by with a lazy wave of a hand.

"It's coming," Gino said with a desperate tone.

"What is it coming?" Sadir asked.

"There, in the other plane, Meren-Ptah awakened something that should have stayed asleep. Something that broke through a crack in between our worlds and is now making its way here."

Almost immediately after he finished his sentence, screaming broke out from the stairs. It seemed like many people were running up in agitation. At the same time, Carter saw a group of people raiding the garden of the RPI.

"Yes, they are here," Sadir said. "The whole of London had been invaded by these hordes. They seem possessed."

"They are, and so is Emma. These were the people that disappeared together with the Sussex towns. It's a long story, I'll explain later," Gino said running towards the stairs.

Carter reached him and took out his gun. He then pointed at the lift door and shouted, "The sigil!"

Gino hesitated for a moment, then reached out to the lift button.

"Right, I'll find Josepha."

He got into the lift car and pressed -4. He hoped the lift still worked and with each floor it passed he emitted a sigh of relief. At some point – second or first floor? – he thought he saw people running up the stairs and heard the *bang-bang* of a faraway gun.

The lift door opened after a metallic ding. It was dark, save for a couple of light bulbs hanging in the silent main corridor. He walked at a slow pace, skirting the wall, paying attention to the smallest sound he was making on the uneven and creaking wooden floor. All the doors to the offices were shut, no sign or sound of anyone around. For a moment he doubted Josepha was even in the building and he feared a trap from Emma, when he heard a raucous growling coming from the end of the corridor. A shape was advancing, covered by the darkness, a clicking of claws on the floor at each movement of the four limbs. Gino stopped breathing and held the pickaxe with both hands, and that sent excruciating pain to his wounded shoulder. He regretted coming to the basement alone.

The beast was hardly visible in the dim light. A fuzzy line suggested fur, an intermittent shining suggested fangs. The growl grew in intensity and now Gino could hear the flapping of the tongue against the frothy lips, and even the saliva dripping onto the floor. Was it a wolf? Or another human turned demon crawling on all fours? Or a combination of the two, a demon inside a wolf? After all, those villages could have contained animals too, right? Dogs of all breeds. Even a small zoo?

Then, a familiar voice broke the tension and the growling stopped.

"Garibaldi. Who is there?" it asked.

Gino relaxed and dropped the pickaxe.

"Garibaldi, can't you recognise your old man?" he said, and the dog ran the length that separated them in long strides.

The dog licked his hands and jumped as high as he could to welcome him. Gino patted his head but avoided lifting him up due to his wounded shoulder. Josepha walked towards him with a grave expression on her face. He didn't expect an equally joyful welcome from her but at least a smile. She did not say anything, standing a few metres away from him.

"Josepha, I came here for –" Gino started.

"I know. I know already. I'm not a premonition expert for nothing. The cards told me." And she finished her words with a long sigh.

After reaching into a pocket of her shirt, she held out a rusted key in front of Gino.

"This. I have been keeping this for almost thirty years, not knowing when this moment would come. When your father gave it to me, I knew you would come to search for it, but until this day a fog was hiding the when and the how."

"Why didn't you tell me?"

"Because it would have changed the premonition. All the chain of events that you went through led to this moment, Gino. You had to go through that ordeal. I'm sorry. Now, go and destroy that sigil."

She showed him an otherwise anonymous door at the end of the corridor. She opened it and a deep, dark shaft revealed itself. A gelid and musty draught raised from its depths and hit Gino's face. It reminded him of the chamber at the end of the Well, and this association made him retract. It had metal bars cemented on one side to work as a ladder. The bottom could not be seen, or its height guessed, given that there was no light.

"You will need this," Josepha said, holding a torch.

Gino shone the light and let out a sigh of relief when he saw that the bottom wasn't that deep, probably five metres or so. He dropped the pickaxe and the clanging sound resonated loudly throughout the whole floor.

"Okay, I'm going," he said, stepping on the first metal bar, the torch in his mouth.

The ladder was humid and caked with rust and his hands became clammy and red. During the descent, instead of focusing on the immediate task at hand, his mind flew to Josepha. Her face wore a mask of mourning. Something was wrong. Something did not add up.

What else did she see with her cards? Gino thought.

Once down, he could not immediately see the sigil. He checked the concrete floor, then the walls, but he

326

could not see it. For a moment, he thought the workers had covered it with concrete, not understanding how important his father's instruction had been. Then, he kneeled and checked with his hands and realised the surface wasn't smooth at all. In the centre he could recognise the many convoluted lines of the sigil, but it was covered in a crust of dirt and mould. His nails were able to remove it, and after a few minutes the whole sigil was now visible. Thanks to the light, its gold lines shone for the first time in more than thirty years.

He paused, because he thought he'd heard a thump up above in the corridor, but he immediately dismissed it as just Garibaldi or Josepha moving around in between rooms. Thinking about Josepha, he found it odd that she had disappeared all of a sudden once he got into the shaft. You would think she would stick around to see how he was doing, and whether he found the sigil or not.

A faraway rumble shook the ground and reminded him of the menacing entity that was approaching the city. He had to act quickly. He adjusted his grip and held the pickaxe high, ready to strike, when he heard Garibaldi whining. He looked up and heard a clattering sound and a final thump. He refrained from shouting Josepha's or Garibaldi's names, and he switched the light off. He heard the dog whining more and more and then his claws on the floor clicking away. Feet walked along the corridor, a hand closed a door, the same hand probably opened another one. A nose sniffed the air like a bull releasing all its tension after a rodeo. He wasn't alone. He squeezed himself as low as he could and controlled his breathing, but it wasn't enough.

It was impossible to shake the sense that something was looking out at him. He looked up. A shape of a head with draping hair appeared at the top of the shaft. It was a dreadful sight, but not as terrifying as what happened next. The body dropped down through the shaft like a rock, knocking him to the floor. A five-metre drop that would have incapacitated any human after the landing, and yet Gino felt the other's fury through fists pounding on his head and kicks cutting his chest. There was nothing he could do to stop it, other than protect his head and torso with his arms. The beating continued and grew in intensity, with grunting and squealing sounds that made him think he was facing a wild boar instead of a human. Then, it all stopped with a thump, and the typical heaviness of a dead body leaning on him.

"Second time I saved you today, mate," Carter's cavernous voice said.

Gino could see a dark silhouette standing against the dim light coming from the corridor, holding the pickaxe. He immediately searched for the torch, which he found on the floor, still intact. When he turned it on, he could not believe his eyes. Emma's body was lying on the floor, the arms grotesquely and unnaturally bent beneath her dead body, a huge hole in her head showed the trembling body of a demon.

Gino felt an immense sadness ebbing up into his mind. She had been used by these demons like a tool. Like a human would use a hammer for the simple goal of pushing a nail into the wall. She had been stripped of her brain and soul, to such a degree that this body in front of him was not Emma any more than a footprint was a foot. She was the Hermit card. The lonely hermit that withdraws from society to achieve personal transformation and comes back changed. When did the possession happen? Was it before or after their beer at the pub on that rainy day in London? Was he talking to the real Emma, or to the demon that took hold of her body on that day? He would never know.

"I'll let you finish your job," Carter said leaving him with the corpse and the pickaxe at the bottom of the shaft.

***

When the pickaxe struck the golden sigil and a fountain of violet sparks showered his shoes, Gino had a vision. In hindsight it felt more like a déjà vu. Of his father in that same position, being struck by the lightning that eventually killed him. That blow of metal against metal bridged those two moments kept apart by thirty years. Father and son, the latter just the temporal projection of the former, in the same spot in front of the same sigil. One created it, one destroyed it. Two different things, and yet to Gino they felt like the same moment, for there was no difference between creation and destruction, and fate bound the two persons together. The circle was now closed.

He had finally found the meaning of the Two of Cups. It wasn't Emma and him, joining their souls and bodies in a harmonious bond that would have brought peace and tranquillity to his life. Emma was the Hermit, he was the Magician. There could be no bond between the two. The two people holding the cups were not lovers, but opposites working together on a task they could not have achieved by themselves. Female and male, conscious and subconscious, black and white, ying and yang, father and son. A duality that follows the arrow of time. Like a river, always flowing but always the same.

He was flying now. He could see the body of his father lying on the floor next to Emma's, the pickaxe still in his hands. He could see it from above, like a spectator watching a film through the hovering camera. The bodies became smaller and smaller until the dark swallowed them. Now he could see the corridor. Two figures kneeling and helping a motionless body with a colourful familiar skirt. He recognised Carter and Sadir. What where they doing there? They should not have been there thirty years ago. And why was Emma's body next to his in the shaft?

Gino could not think straight. It was all foggy and confusing now. Especially due to that annoying barking. What was Garibaldi doing there? And why was he barking at him? Didn't he recognise him? He tried to say something, but his mouth was sewn. His hands frozen. He was just a pair of eyes and a mind floating away. Higher and higher now, so high that he went through the ceiling and up to the roof. The last thing he saw was Sadir trying to calm Garibaldi and looking at Gino flying away. Sadir saw him and he understood.

London appeared and now Gino could see the Thames, its sinusoidal banks cutting through Canary Wharf and then squeezing in between London Bridge's pylons. Big Ben towering over the Houses of Parliament and thousands of houses and parks until the horizon. From the south he could see a looming black storm of dust and clouds that was devouring the landscape. Then, a sharp reddish line rippled through the city – like the clean line generated by a stone in a placid lake. The ripple expanded from the RPI, originating exactly from the sigil he just broke. It travelled through houses and parks, churches and streets, hitting everything and everyone in its journey. Now, from his vantage point close to the lowest clouds, he could see the ripple interacting with some people but not others. The anti-cosmic wave field killed the demon-bearing ones immediately and spared all the others. He made it. He had managed to break the esoteric triangle once and for all, and anyone who didn't belong to their plane of existence was being annihilated. It was just a matter of time until the ripple would hit the impending nameless thing that was marching from the south. But Gino had no chance to see it as he fell to the ground at a shocking speed, through the roof, the ceiling and the whole height of the shaft, until he hit the floor. The last thing he saw was Sadir holding the head of his lifeless body like a mother would with her dead child.

**

Gino woke up in a dimly lit room. Someone had placed him on a sofa. A blanket covered him from neck to toes. A low coffee table had a glass of water standing on it. A Ouija board hung on the opposite wall. He could see the red spine of his favourite book, *The Dead Mountaineer*, standing out from the bookshelf. It was all familiar and all in place.

When Garibaldi saw him awake and started wagging his tail the smoking figure who was sitting at his desk put out the cigarette in the ashtray and smiled.

"Welcome home, Gino," Carter said.

Appendixes

Discography

Part I - The Vanishings:
- John Carpenter style retro synth mix
- Nirvana – Smell like Teen Spirit
- Ace of Base – Living in Danger
- Oasis - Supersonic

Part II - Hideous Wolves:
- Darkthrone – Transilvanian Hunger
- Burzum – Hvis Lyset Tar Oss
- Immortal – Pure Holocaust
- Dissection – Storm of the Light's Bane
- Bathory – Under the Sign of the Black Mark

Part III – Through the Well:
- Burzum – Fallen
- The Thing's soundtrack – Ennio Morricone

An occult chronology of the late 1800/early 1900

1875: Madame Helena Petrovna Blatasky founded the Theosophical Society in New York.

1882: The Society for Psychical Research is founded in London with the aim to study psychic and paranormal events and abilities.

1887: William Robert Woodman, William Wynn Westcott and Samuel Liddell Mathers founded the First Temple of The Hermetic Order of the Golden Dawn in London.

1890: William Butler Yeats joined the Hermetic Order of the Golden Dawn.

1894: The Hermetic Brotherhood of Luxor is founded in England by Max Theon.

1895: Carl Kellner founded the Ordo Templi Orientis (OTO) in Germany.

1897: Ordo Aurum Solis is founded by George Stanton and Charles Kingold in England.

1898: Aleister Crowley joined the Hermetic Order of the Golden Dawn.

1902: Aleister Crowley attempted to climb K2.

1903: Robert Felkin founded the Stella Matutina in London.

1907: Aleister Crowley founded the Astrum Argentum.

1924: Dion Fortune founded the Fraternity of the Inner Light in London.

An occult chronology of the early 1990s

1990-1994: the second wave of Black Metal starts in Norway and includes bands such as Mayhem, Burzum, Darkthrone, Immortal, Emperor, Enslaved, Satyricon, Gorgoroth.

1990: Twin Peaks premiered in April in the US.

1991: Øystein Aarseth, better known as Euronymous, founder of the Norwegian band Mayhem, opens the record shop Helvete in Oslo, de facto starting what it would be later called the Black Metal Inner Circle.

1991: Per Yngve Ohlin, also known as Dead and vocalist of the Norwegian band Mayhem, commits suicide.

1992: Twin Peaks' prequel *Fire walk with me* is released in cinemas in August.

1992: Bård "Faust" Eithun, drummer of the band Emperor, kills a gay man in Lillehammer, Norway.

1992: Varg Vikernes, aka Count Grishnackh, releases the first Burzum album, Burzum.

1992-1996 Burning of more than 50 Norwegian churches attributed to Black Metal musicians or fans.

1993: Øystein Aarseth, better known as Euronymous, founder of the Norwegian band Mayhem, is killed by Varg Vikernes, founder of the Norwegian band Burzum.

1993: The X-Files premiered in September in the US.

1994: The Crow is released in cinemas.

1994: Brandon Lee is killed in the set of The Crow.

1994: The singer and leader of Nirvana Kurt Cobain killed himself in April.

1994: Varg Vikernes is sentenced to 21 years for the murder of Euronymous and the arson of three churches.

Acknowledgments

I'm enormously grateful to those who read parts or all the book at various stages and had words of encouragement: Adam Jolly, Gary Sutton, Giles Darling, Susan Ferguson.

A heartfelt thanks to my editor, Dan Coxon, who had the patience to go through the many typos and grammar mistakes of the final manuscript (the remaining errors are entirely my responsibility).

I'm also grateful to Brad Kelly, who during an unforgettable Tarot reading on Zoom, showed me the Two of Cups in the future position. It was destiny, my friend.

Finally, I owe a lot to my wife who never complained about the many hours (1500 hours to be precise) I passed in front of my laptop.

And I would like to thank in advance whoever would consider leaving a review on **Amazon** and/or **Goodreads.** Self-published authors like me rely on word of mouth and reviews on these sites to be known and to ultimately sell, so even a short sentence or a star makes a huge difference to us. Thanks.

Printed in Great Britain
by Amazon

39531790R00199